MENACING SHADOWS

One shadow remained; a long black shape lying along the floor motionless and stretching as far as the table's edge. It came nearer, touched the hearth-rug and merged into the shade that suddenly filled the kitchen again.

Lydia and I stood up in a single movement and faced the door. A man stood there watching us: a tall man wearing a slouch hat and a black cloak turned back over his right shoulder. One end of a long red comforter dangled from his neck like a narrow blade. . . . I saw the man at first as an embodiment of darkness.

He took off his hat. His hair, like his unkempt beard, was the color of wet sand.

"Have I the honor—"

He looked around as if to make sure there was no one else present, then looked Lydia up and down, taking in her sleeves, her muslin apron and elaborately dressed hair—

"—of addressing the mistress of the house?"

Look for these other Anna Gilbert novels
available from Dell:

Flowers for Lilian

A Walk in the Wood

THE Leavetaking

ANNA GILBERT

A DELL BOOK

Published by
Dell Publishing
a division of
Bantam Doubleday Dell Publishing Group, Inc.
666 Fifth Avenue
New York, New York 10103

ISBN: 0-440-20790-8

Reprinted by arrangement with the author

Printed in the United States of America

Published simultaneously in Canada

November 1990

10 9 8 7 6 5 4 3 2 1

OPM

1

I found them the other day while turning out a drawer: two or three pieces of lilac-coloured dress material kept for patchwork and never used. The colour has faded but otherwise the fabric is as good as new and so it should be: we paid nearly four shillings a yard for it. Even so Lydia insisted on buying an extra eighteen inches.

"You may not grow much taller," she said, "but surely you won't always be so thin. We may have to let out the bodice later on. In any case, if I were you, Isobel, I would wear the dress *freely* every afternoon and *enjoy* it. You have your black and white gingham for mornings."

Smoothing the crumpled cloth, I heard Lydia's voice so clearly that she might have been at my side again. Her voice, I recollect, was always clear and not only in quality. In all her diverse moods Lydia was, to say the least, articulate.

The sensible thing would have been to throw the useless pieces away. But it was too late. They had already revived the old sad longing for Emberside as it used to be and enough of the old bitterness to make me wonder if these were all that remained of our life there: a handful of faded fragments and clinging to them obstinately, a few dry spikes of rosemary.

The dress itself vanished long ago. Time has carried it away with the summer afternoon when I first wore it, a year and a day after mother's death. Coming out of mourning was like stepping from a darkened room into bright day; stepping, moreover, with a new dignity. The skirt was the longest I had ever worn. Its purple folds just grazed the bricks as I sailed down the garden path to the summer-house and sank gracefully upon the seat.

No hint of disaster clouded the hour. The clouds came later. In those days Emberside was not the shadowed place it has become. Haunted? It is not a word to use lightly. The house was certainly not haunted then. Its long past had left no sombre legacy to

disturb a later generation. Not yet. At my feet lay a bridal scat-
tering of petals from the pink thorn. Orange blossom scented the
air. I might have been—and for a while pretended that I was—a
guest at a wedding. Instead I found myself witness to a parting.
On the other side of the sweetbriar hedge Lydia and Charles
Stack were saying goodbye.

"I've asked you a score of times, Lydia. I won't ever ask you
again."

Absorbed in my new elegance, I thrilled nevertheless to the
beautiful sadness of their leavetaking, noting at the same time
how the cuffs of lilac barège flattered my skin. Black bombazine
had blanched my hands and wrists to waxen whiteness but now
they had taken on the warm bloom of a peach. Sunlight through
the trellis cross-barred my half-pagoda sleeves with gold.

The summer-house had been mother's idea. "Somewhere for
Isobel to do her lessons in warm weather," was what she envis-
aged. They cunningly kept me out of the garden for a few days
and I first saw it, complete, on the morning of my fourteenth
birthday. In the angle between the pink thorn and the sweetbriar
it had risen magically like the pleasure-dome of Kubla Khan.
Father designed it. "Nothing too grand, Eugene," mother had
warned, as she told me afterwards, knowing his large ideas; and
he had to be content with wooden walls, red roof tiles and a white
arch with an ornamented bargeboard. It was Robert Wayland
who had thought of painting the inside of the roof a Mediterra-
nean blue. He had done it himself. Taking it for granted that they
all wanted me to be happy, I was as happy in it as they could
have wished. From time to time a sense of decency obliged me to
carry out an exercise book and copy down a few extracts. More
often I was idle there or read for pleasure.

On my lap lay *The Curse of Claverdon* open at the first page.
Presently I would plunge into its mysterious depths but not quite
yet. I was content for a while to do nothing, half lost in languor-
ous dreams of a future filled with such flower-scented days as
this.

It was, I suppose, a high peak of happiness; and from a peak
one can only come down.

"I can't hang about here any longer," Charles said. "It's a bit
of luck, this offer from the Ottawa River Timber Company. Nobody but a fool would let it go."

"No, no, Charlie. Of course you must take it." The pitch of

Lydia's voice was higher than usual. She was trying to be cheerful. "You'll make your fortune and come back rich."

"What is there to come back for? Unless . . . If only I had your promise, Lydia, there's nothing I couldn't do. It wouldn't be right to ask you to go out with me. You're used to a delicate style of living here. A timber station would be too rough-and-tumble for you. But I won't deny that I've gone on hoping right up to the last minute. When my eye lighted on this piece in the *Daily Telegraph* about the mail steamer"—there came the rustle of newspaper—" 'Special accommodation for married couples', I thought . . . Never mind. But when I'm settled, you could come out to me."

"It's no use, Charlie. I can't."

There was no question of eavesdropping. They would neither of them have minded my listening or paid much attention if I joined them. For years—I was four when Lydia came to live at Emberside—I had hovered in the background while they talked: an infant chaperone, loved, protected and ignored. My notions of romance had been formed at second hand and at an early age. Once in the sunny pasture above the lime quarry Lydia made me a cowslip ball in the vain hope of getting rid of me perhaps. Grasping it, my senses ravished by the heady scent and silken feel of the flowers, I grasped at the same time the proposition that Charles loved Lydia and that when people loved each other, they married.

Sure enough, when we were picnicking by the river one day, Charles boldly pushed out the birchbark boat he had made me (in an equally hopeless attempt to distract my attention, no doubt) and said, "Marry me, Lydia."

"We're too young," Lydia replied, quite rightly, as she still wore her hair loose on her shoulders at the time.

"Look, it's drowning," I screamed as the boat turned widdershins and sank.

"Can't you love me, Lydia?" Charles said, turning his back on the wreck and taking her hand.

I had no difficulty at all in loving him. He brought me gingerbread men from Netherlaw market and ribbons for my hair, took me to see the first lambs and showed me how to make flowers from the white pith inside rush stems.

"You've a way with children," Lydia said once when he lifted me up to look at a thrush's nest. "You should marry and settle down."

"Any time you say." Squinting sideways, I saw the eager look in his eyes under their curling lashes. Lydia laughed and shook her head. "There's no call to tease me like that," Charles said. "You'll be sorry some day."

But she wasn't teasing. He should have known that she would never marry him. By this time I knew it. Quite early on I had found it necessary to revise the simple rule whereby people who loved each other married. In the case of Charles and Lydia something had gone wrong, though I could not at first identify the trouble or make out who it was that stood between them so that early as it was, Charles had come too late. The nature of the obstacle defined itself so gradually that once acknowledged, it roused no surprise; but it remained unspoken, too strange and mysterious to be mentioned.

"Then that's the end of it," Charles said on the other side of the sweetbriar.

The words, sounding as they did the very depths of sorrow, were so momentous that for a second I failed to take them in; but I felt the change in Charlie's voice. The pleading note had gone. Many a time I had heard it, seen his face darken with disappointment and watched him walk angrily away; but he had always come back. For months he had talked of going to Canada but could never quite bring himself to go. Was he really going at last?

A shivering sense of crisis brought me anxiously to the edge of my seat. I forgot that the situation was romantic and beautiful and felt only the pain of it.

His next remark after an unhappy pause was more prosaic. "I'll be leaving for Liverpool next Saturday and sailing on the Monday morning."

"You'll come and say goodbye before you go?"

"No. I'm off now to see Grandmother Lucerne at Hagthorpe. I'll go straight from there to Netherlaw railway station. This is the last time you'll see me at Emberside or anywhere else for that matter."

"I wish you hadn't come to love me so much." Lydia sounded distressed. "If I've encouraged you, I'm sorry. But even if I felt as you want me to feel, how could I leave them here? What would happen to Isobel now that Prue Bailey's gone?"

"There's no reason why Prue Bailey's marriage should stand in the way of yours, is there? They could find someone else. You've your own life to lead. Oh, I know you've been like one of the family."

"I am one of the family. Isobel's mother and mine were full cousins."

"That isn't so close. Besides, you're a dependant here. It's not like your own home."

I knew so well what Lydia's answer would be that I could have made it for her with just the right degree of injured pride.

"I'm not a pauper. My Aunt Welbecome has a nice little property in Martlebury and it's sure to come to me. I could go to her any time I like as you know very well."

"I should know. You've told me often enough."

"I stay here from choice, not because I have to. I was glad to come, Charlie, and they were glad to take me in. They were both so much younger than poor Aunt Welbecome. At fifteen I didn't want to go to a house of old servants and one old lady. Cousin Flora treated me like her own younger sister and now that she's gone, that's how I feel towards Isobel."

"If it was only that, I'd throw up the idea of going to Canada. Mrs Wayland would let me have Hackets' farm. She's pleased with the way I've managed it. The house is standing empty."

"That old wreck!"

"There isn't a prettier situation in all Limmergill. If we were to live there, you could keep an eye on Isobel. She could be with us all the time." Charlie waited. There was no reply. "But it isn't just Isobel. I know that."

The despair in his voice warned me that we had come at last to the heart of the matter. Clutching *The Curse of Claverdon* in a grip that left its pages crumpled for good, I waited, trembling, for him to uncover the mysterious hidden truth, long known, never spoken.

"You've set your heart on him. There never was a chance for me."

"I can't help it, Charlie dear. You're the best friend I have and it'll wring my heart to let you go but you know how it is. When Cousin Flora was alive I was happy enough just to worship him from a distance; and I would have gone on like that. There's no need to tell you that I never had a wrong thought or any wish to come between them. But now . . ."

"He's a scholar"—Charlie made it sound like an insult—"but

a good enough man, I dare say, with the ways of a gentleman such as I haven't got. But he's too old for you. It would never do. And he doesn't treat you as if he had any thought of loving you."

"How could he? It's too soon. There's plenty of time."

"You're just waiting then? How long will it be? You're a good fourteen years younger than him, but you're getting on . . ."

"I'm four and twenty." Lydia sounded quite naturally indignant. "Oh, don't let's quarrel, Charlie. You'll find someone else and she'll make you a better wife than I ever could."

She would stay with us then, always. There would always be the three of us. It was father she loved and some day when he had recovered from mother's death, they would marry. Mother would approve if she knew. I looked up into the sky for confirmation and a memory came to me of mother clapping her hands and smiling from the sofa as the music stopped. In her day there had been evening parties at Emberside and carpet dances. She had laughed and applauded as the polka came to an end and Lydia in a white dress with blue bows, her curls still bobbing, vanished into the conservatory. But the partner she had vanished with was Charlie.

The picture faded and with it every sensation but grief at his going.

"I'll be on my way then." They had got up. "If you should happen to change your mind"—he was trying to make a joke of it now that there was no hope—"I'll be leaving Netherlaw at half past eleven next Saturday night . . ."

Their voices died away as they went into the house. I ran up the garden and through the stable yard to join them at the front gate.

"Charlie! I heard what you said. I was in the summer-house. You haven't said goodbye to me."

"I was coming to look for you."

"Don't go. Not so far away. Not yet. Please."

"You mustn't cry, Isobel, my little dear, or I won't be able to go cheerfully."

"Will you write to me?"

"You know me. I'm not one for pen and ink. But I'll do my best. At any rate I'll send my address when I'm settled and you'll maybe write and tell me the news. Young Robert has promised to write."

We stood awkwardly enduring the last moments when there

was nothing left to say. The house lay half in sun, half in shadow, drowsing in the scent of roses which reached in at the open windows and clung about the porch as if they would never let go. How could anyone bear to leave Emberside?

"The sooner you find somebody in the place of Prue Bailey the better," Charlie said. "It isn't fit for the two of you to be on your own so much. You shouldn't leave all the doors open when Mr Penrose is away from home, Lydia. Anyone walking this way might be tempted to walk right in."

" We're safe enough with Sambo to look after us," I said.

"And I haven't said goodbye to him. You're a good friend, old boy, but not a ha'porth of use as a watch dog, are you?" The old dog whined and laid his head affectionately on Charlie's boot. "I'm sorry not to have seen Mr Penrose before I go."

He kissed my cheek and held out his hand to Lydia.

"I wish you well, my dear." Her grey eyes were brilliant as they always were when she was feeling deeply. "I'll miss you," In her impulsive way she threw her arms around his neck and kissed him.

He left us abruptly and took the path that cut diagonally through the cornfield, wading knee-deep in green waves of wheat as if the ocean had already come between us. Lydia and I watched like castaways until he had disappeared over the rise. Across the fields Petways' cock crowed a farewell.

Then I saw Robert Wayland leaning on the wall on the Limmergill side of the lane with his head bowed over the moss-covered stones.

"He's upset," I whispered, "because Charlie's going away."

"Let him be," Lydia said before I could call to him; and presently he brushed his sleeve across his eyes, turned his back and disappeared among the trees.

The cock crowed again, a shrill challenge to the empty afternoon. The weird flourish of sound wavered and died, leaving behind something of its primitive mystery. The familiar scene became less friendly. Clouds were moving in from the west. They brought a shift of emphasis, a hint of deeper change. Lydia and I seemed all at once conspicuous, exposed to the wide sky and whatever might come out of it.

2

"We'll manage very well," Lydia said.

I watched her from the kitchen window-seat as she pulled on her lawn sleeves in an airy, casual manner as if the domestic competence they imposed could be taken for granted.

"Manage without Charlie, you mean?"

We had recovered a little from the sad scene at the gate. Lydia hummed a tune as she tied the broad bands of her apron. It seemed to me that she had recovered almost too quickly until I recollected that, unsubdued, she would have been not just humming, but warbling in her thin, sweet, unpredictable soprano. Lydia was the only person I ever knew who actually warbled, chiefly at the piano where she also 'vamped' (as she put it) an accompaniment effective to my unpractised ear and, I suspect, to no other.

"Poor Charlie! No. I meant that we can manage without Prue." Prue's marriage to a woodman as pious as herself on an estate seven miles away was rather a relief. As Lydia said, with Prue in the house, every day was Judgment Day.

Lydia had indeed the air of being able to manage very well; not, of course, by taking Prue's place as cook-housemaid. The sleeves alone established her superior station; not to mention her grey poplin dress and knots of rose-coloured ribbon. She had stayed loyally in half mourning to keep me company, except for the ribbons.

"The trimming simply makes a dress," she had often told me and her velvet bows were lavish enough to make nonsense of her mourning. She was wearing one as part of the complicated structure of her back curls. But even if she had been swathed in black from head to foot, her vivacity would have been undimmed. It radiated like an electric force from the hearth-rug where she stood; a confident happiness which her final refusal of Charlie's offer had released; as if now that her secret hope had been acknowledged, a step had been taken towards fulfilling it.

"In fact we'll do better without her. Prue had a heavy hand with pastry. Mr Penrose has said so a dozen times."

She smiled as she spoke his name and we both looked at the table: at the pie: at the pastry rose adorning it.

"Prue certainly couldn't have made that." I got up to have another look and to count the interfolding petals of the rose. There were actually seven. "It's the best you have ever done. Father will say so, I'm sure."

"He'll be ready for a meal when he comes in." Lydia adopted the restrained, practical manner of a busy housewife, that being her present role, though she was bursting with pride and poetry. "But, it won't be until six or seven o'clock. It's a shame to waste the fire."

Interpreting the signals correctly, I put on my own apron and dragged out the gridle from the cupboard under the back stairs, greased it with lard and set it on the bar. The fire was hot and red and would remain so for another ten minutes. It had been no hardship to leave the garden for the warm kitchen. The weather was changing. Gusts of wind shook the lattice and darkened the panes with the threat of rain, then died down, leaving intervals of sunshine. We had closed the windows to keep dust from the sills but the door still stood open in the country fashion.

"I believe"—Lydia flapped energetically at the batter—"that Addy could do a little more in the front of the house and upstairs if we had more help with the scrubbing. I could take on the cooking." She glanced at the pie. "Your mother always said that a lady should be capable of taking charge in her own kitchen."

I crouched by the fender, armed with a long knife, as she dropped spoonfuls of batter on to the gridle, where they expanded gently like yellow flowers. Waiting for the exact moment to insert the blade under the first scone, I paid no attention nor did Lydia, when Sambo growled and pulled his chain across the yard. The fitful wind had set the stable doors rattling. There was something vicious in the way it wiped out the rectangle of light on the kitchen floor and sank the whole room into shade. The gust passed; the squares of light sprang back; Sambo growled again. I turned my head and saw that one shadow remained; a long black shape lying along the floor motionless and stretching

as far as the table's edge. It came nearer, touched the hearth-rug
and merged into the shade that suddenly filled the kitchen again.

Lydia and I stood up in a single movement and faced the door.
A man stood there watching us: a tall man wearing a slouch hat
and a black cloak turned back over his right shoulder. One end of
a long red comforter dangled from his neck like a narrow blade.
Still dazzled by the red fire and the black gridle and faced with
the same colours in a different form, I saw the man at first as an
embodiment of darkness and heat.

"Good afternoon." His voice was bland, pleasantly modulated
and on the whole reassuring; but it was also, like his whole manner, too familiar and easy to be comfortable in a stranger. "Forgive me. I should have knocked but the picture was so—engag-
ing." He made a sweeping gesture. It encompassed Lydia and me
and a good deal of the furniture. The long movement of his arm
revealed him as a very big man and when he took a single step
forward, it brought him right into the room. "This must be Emberside Grange." He took off his hat. His hair, like his unkempt
beard, was the colour of wet sand. "Have I the honour—" He
looked round as if to make sure there was no one else present,
then looked Lydia up and down, taking in her sleeves, her muslin
apron and elaborately dressed hair "—of addressing the mistress
of the house?"

I have sometimes thought that events would have taken a different turn if he had begun with a different question. No stranger
could have been expected to know how complex an answer it
required. That Lydia saw herself as mistress of the house and
hoped some day to be what in every practical sense she already
seemed, was as undeniable as the fact that she had no claim to the
title. I must have been the only person on earth who understood
the delicacy of the problem and I waited with interest for the
reply. And yet, stranger as he was, the man had looked carefully
from Lydia to me and back again and had glanced at Lydia's
ringless left hand before he put the question, as though from the
very first he had known how to vex her and wanted to.

I was close enough to feel Lydia's slight body stiffen. She had
been holding the big bowl of batter on her hip, encircled by her
left arm. Now she set it down on the fender.

"You may tell me your business. We were not expecting visitors."

The man smiled. His head came within a inch or two of the

beam under which he stood, seeming to fill the kitchen where a
minute ago we had been alone with the wall clock, the dresser,
the bunches of sage . . . Did he know that we were alone?

The scones were burning. I made a nervous dab at one of them
and toppled it into the fire. It hissed and was gone. Lydia seized
the gridle and heaved it angrily on to the setpot.

"Who are you?" she demanded.

With a movement of his right arm so swift that it made me
jump, he threw back his cloak, felt in an inside pocket and
handed Lydia a card. We read it together.

"Simeon Graw. Portrait and landscape artist. Oils, water-col-
our and pastels. Miniatures a speciality."

It must have been his profession that made him more than
ordinarily observant. There was a kind of agility in his attitude,
alert and watchful, like an animal expecting to be pounced upon,
or more likely in his case, I felt uneasily, prepared to pounce.

"I have recently painted portraits of the young ladies at Oversay Hall. Mr Penrose was mentioned to me as a possible client,
since I happen to be in the district . . ."

He had moved as he spoke—it needed only another of his
immense strides—nearer to the oak screen which ran at right
angles to the hearth and shut it off from the doors to the scullery,
dairy and hall. Through the open hall door he could see the foot
of the stairs and a portion of the drawing room, as with a turn of
his head he could see the back stairs twisting up from the opposite corner of the kitchen.

"Would it be possible for me to speak to Mr Penrose?"

"We are expecting Mr Penrose at any moment," Lydia said.
"Do you wish to leave your card?"

Simeon Graw's eyes—they were eyes of a hot-looking brown—
moved from their inspection of the kitchen, raked the persons of
Lydia and myself and came to rest upon the pie, delicately
browned, its pastry rim roughed up by the back of a knife to the
depth of three-quarters of an inch, crowned by the peerless rose.
His lips parted. For the first time I noticed that his big hands
were thin, his cheeks a trifle hollow. My impulse was to defend
the pie.

"I had hoped—"

"You could come back," Lydia said firmly. She too had seen
the pie-ward glance, the parted lips. "When Mr Penrose has
dined."

She picked up the gridle with its ruined scones and advanced upon him so irresistibly that he gave ground and retreated to the door but in a lounging, casual fashion as if he had been going anyway.

"I'll take the liberty of calling again. If I may relieve you of the card?"

He put it carefully in his pocket as if it was the only one he had, bowed and departed. Lydia instantly shut the door and slammed the bolt across with the crack of a pistol shot.

We looked at each other, our lips thin and scandalised, then rushed through the hall to the drawing room window. Simeon Graw stood in the middle of the lane in the act of shouldering a folded easel. Beside him lay a canvas bag and propped up against it, a portfolio wrapped in waterproof cloth. These details were less interesting than the fact that he was not alone. We now laid eyes for the first time on his companion, a woman dressed in black, sitting under the hedgerow, a huge bundle at her side. She sat staring vacantly in front of her until Graw jerked his head in the direction of Saxon's Gate and walked off. Mechanically, as if he had pulled a string, she picked up her bundle and followed, just failing to catch him up or perhaps deliberately keeping a few paces behind him until they were out of sight.

"Well!" Lydia's grey eyes were at their most brilliant. "What an experience!" She pulled out her skirts to their fullest extent and twirled round like a top. "What did he remind you of?"

"He really does look like an artist, I suppose."

"Lucifer! The very image! If he'd had horns and a tail."

Lydia shrieked with laughter.

"It was clever of you to say that we expected father at any minute."

"Oh yes. Had I said, 'in an hour or two', *who knows* what might have become of us?"

Not even *The Curse of Claverdon* could have roused us to such a pitch of horror as we stood revelling in, until the need to have dinner ready when father came home sent us scuttling about our tasks.

It was always Lydia's aim to be calmly seated in the drawing room for half an hour before dinner. This was often quite difficult even in the days of Prue. Today, servantless as we were save for Addy, the kitchen maid, who came back from Saxon's Gate with a laden basket as the clock struck six, it was a triumph to have the table set, the vegetables cooking, the pie warming up and to be peacefully occupied with our needlework at half past the hour. Even so I had barely time to find the right page in *The Lady of the Lake*, which father would read to us after dinner, when the rattle of the gig in the stable yard announced his return: the highlight of Lydia's day—and mine.

"How pretty you look, my dear," father said as I took his hat. "It's been a long time, hasn't it? You need not have waited a year. Your mother wouldn't have wanted it. I've a surprise for you. Wait a minute. Lydia must hear."

He took off his ulster and we went into the drawing room.

"What do you think, girls? I've had an adventure driving home from Saxon's Gate. All at once, as the story books say, a man appeared; literally appeared from behind Will Petway's haystack. A picturesque-looking fellow. I thought at first he was some sort of bandit. It's a wonder the mare didn't bolt, as I told him. He apologised courteously enough. To cut the story short, the man's an artist."

"He came, father, while you were out. He walked right into the kitchen."

"He's anxious for work. Heaven knows how he makes a living, especially in these parts. It seems he's done a portrait or two for the Kirkdales at Oversay. Not that Edwin Kirkdale is any judge of pictures. What satisfies him won't necessarily do for me. But I'd like a watercolour of Emberside. We've only those two sketches of your mother's."

"You mean to employ him then?" Lydia said

"It would be a kindness to give him a commission. A traveling artist in the 1870s! It's a recipe for starvation when all the world and his wife want to be photographed. Besides, if he's painted those gawky girls at Oversay Hall, why shouldn't he take a likeness of my two young ladies?"

He laughed, stimulated to good spirits by a meeting unlikely enough in our quiet part of the country to be remarkable.

"Lydia and I have often talked of having a photograph taken together," I said, "at Handisides in Netherlaw."

"A photograph? You too? With a broken column and a flower pot, I suppose. Oh, I've no objection if you've set your hearts on it but a portrait would be a different matter altogether." He looked at us speculatively. "Over here with the window open to show the garden path." He pushed the sofa aside "Come, Lydia.

You sit here with Isobel beside you on the stool. Look up at her, Isobel. No, not quite right. Lydia, you look down at Isobel."

Father's claim to be a connoisseur of art rested upon a brief acquaintance with Dante Gabriel Rossetti during a season spent with relatives in London. "An interesting fellow, but unreliable," was his verdict. The friendship had not ripened. But the encounter with Simeon Graw had reminded father of his visits to Chelsea. He paced up and down, telling us of the strange rooms with their blue china and peacocks' feathers and the unusual people he had met there: all of them gentlemen apparently. He didn't mention the ladies.

Though we were flattered at the prospect of being painted, neither of us felt much enthusiasm. We would much have preferred the photograph. I had quite longed for it, not only for the thrill of the operation itself and the possibility of being displayed in Handisides' window for all Netherlaw to see, but for the journey by rail, tea at a pastry-cook's and a peep at the shops. As for Lydia, she had been remarkably silent. The little flutter caused by father's return had subsided into dismay when Graw was mentioned.

"So he's coming back," she said at last.

"Coming back! He's here. In the yard. I brought him with me: easel, portfolio and all." Lydia and I exchanged glances. It was so like him. He could never refuse a favour. "The rest of his things are at the railway station waiting to be called for."

"And Mrs Graw?" I said.

"Is there a Mrs Graw? He didn't mention her. Can you find something for him to eat, Lydia?" Shaken by our stern looks, he went on less confidently, "I thought he could sleep in the coachman's rooms for a few nights. It would be difficult for him to find lodgings now and it would mean going all the way back to Saxon's Gate." Then, as Lydia made no response, "It's not fair to spring this on you but you always rise to the occasion. Something smells good. Give him whatever you were going to give me. I dined early with Haley at the Buckingham Arms. A sandwich on a tray before going to bed will do for me and that will save the awkwardness of a meal with Graw. Addy can set him down to something in the kitchen. He looks half starved."

"Lydia made a pie for you, father," I said warningly.

"A pie! The very thing. He's a lucky man. I'll show him where to put his things and send him round to the kitchen."

"If he'd said the parlour"—Lydia was red with mortification—
"I should simply have died. And the thought of sitting to that
man for a portrait and being *looked* at by him for hours makes
me positively ill. I never expected that either of us would be
exposed to such an ordeal and seriously, Isobel, I'm almost inclined to say no."

"Oh, don't leave me alone with him, for pity's sake," I begged,
falling easily and happily into the mood of gloom and dread she
conveyed.

It fell to my lot to summon Simeon Graw to his meal. His
second entrance was a little different from the first. There was a
touch of ceremony in the way he removed his hat and stood
deferentially just inside the door while Addy brought out the pie
and cut into the crust. The desecration of the rose was more than
I could bear to watch.

"He's ate it all, miss." Addy made no attempt to break the
news gently, when twenty minutes later Graw had left the
kitchen. "And all the potatoes and greens. Cheese I didn't offer
him. He's more like a hungry wolf than a man—and a gentleman
at that, supposed to be."

"You can take his meals to the coach house in future, Addy.
We cannot do with him here." Lydia's eyes sparkled with tears
but she recovered sufficiently to add vindictively, " He's too
much of a gentleman to eat in the kitchen."

Graw may have put a different interpretation on his banish-
ment but he certainly blamed Lydia for it. The antagonism between them was there from the beginning and it grew with vio-
lent energy. Lydia never forgave him for the pie. Except in
father's presence she took no pains to hide her dislike. A state of
war existed before Graw had been with us twenty-four hours.

He must have been quick to see how snug a refuge he could
find at Emberside in the rooms which had housed old Grimshaw
in comfort until he died the year before at the age of ninety: how
easy it would be to impose on father's kindness: how easy, that is,
but for Lydia. It cannot have been long before he deliberately set
himself to undermine her influence. Some careless words of my
own may have enlightened him as to the state of Lydia's feelings
for father and shown him where to attack.

The day after he came—it was Sunday—Robert Wayland
called and came to find me in the summer-house. I told him
about the portrait. We also talked about Charlie, who had man-

aged Hackets' farm for Robert's mother; and Robert told me
about timber-felling in Ottawa, a subject on which he was rather
tediously well informed. Other aspects of Charlie's life interested
me more.

"I don't believe you know," I said, "that he proposed to Lydia
again before he left."

"I suppose she refused him again. Why on earth doesn't she
marry him? She'll be an old maid if she isn't careful. All the
same"—Robert brightened. He had been rather downcast since
Charlie had made up his mind to go—"if Charlie still wants to
marry her, he'll be sure to come back."

"Charlie Stack isn't the only man in the world," I said, quoting
Lydia. "She may have other prospects."

"Do you mean she's thinking of marrying someone else?"

There were limits, even with Robert, beyond which I must not
venture.

"If she is, it's a secret, Robert, We mustn't speak of it."

"Oh, all right," Robert said with irritating promptness, "but
Lydia doesn't know many young men, does she? You'd miss her
if she did marry. Mother says she can't think how your father
would manage without her."

"There," I said, exultant. "You've almost guessed. If all goes
well," I paused significantly, "Lydia will stay here always, always."

"You surely don't mean Mr Penrose?" Robert's astonishment
was not flattering to father. "What are you doing?"

An aroma neither of clover nor thyme, though both were in
bloom, had prompted me to get up quietly and peep over the
wall. There, in a cloud of tobacco smoke, his hat over his eyes,
lay Simeon Graw, dozing in the sun.

"He's here. The artist," I mouthed and beckoned. It gave me a
baleful pleasure to have Graw for once at a disadvantage.

"I suppose he is a genuine artist," Robert said when we had
retreated to the path.

"Hush. He'll hear. He's not really asleep. I'm perfectly certain
he'll have been listening."

With dismay I wished we had not been talking about Lydia.

"Is he such a cad then? I couldn't see his face, only the top of
his hat but he has a seedy sort of look, I should say."

"A cad. Yes. That's what he is. I'm surprised father doesn't
send him packing."

I spoke with authority, knowing that Graw was a rogue because Lydia said so.

"I don't trust him," she had already said and was to say again, often. "Swaggering about as if he had a perfect right to be here. And where is that woman? What sort of people are they, I ask you? The very thought of their—*arrangements*"—Lydia lingered over the word—"makes my flesh creep."

I persuaded myself that my flesh also crept. If Lydia hated Simeon Graw, naturally I hated him too. It was easy to do so. His appearance was not appealing.

"And as for his pipe!" Lydia sniffed delicately at her smelling bottle. "The only consolation is that it smells even more strongly than his linen. How can Mr Penrose allow it?"

On the first morning we had found the study saturated with the stale smell of tobacco. Father and Graw had sat up late, talking. Many a time I have tried to account for father's unexpected interest in Graw. It could scarcely be called liking. Nevertheless, for a time at least, he enjoyed the change of company. Somewhere in his adventurous life Graw had stumbled upon enough education to enable him to talk on almost equal terms with such a man as my father, whose knowledge of the world was slighter than he would have cared to admit. Apart from his terms at Oxford and the famous season in London he had never strayed far from Emberside or extended the circle of his acquaintance beyond professional men in Netherlaw and the local small gentry. He saw Graw as a colourful character who had picked up, among other things, a smattering of conventional attitudes; an outsider with whom it was possible, briefly, to find common ground.

Moreover, Graw's blatant masculinity may have helped to restore the balance in our mainly feminine household. For all our devotion—Lydia's and mine—father missed the companionship of his own sex. One genuine sorrow of his life was that he had no son. His disappointment haunted my childhood even though it made him all the more indulgent towards me, afflicted as I was with the incurable handicap of being a girl.

But the strongest link between the two men otherwise so unlike, was their feeling for Emberside. It soon appeared that Graw had taken to the place with a liking that went beyond a stranger's admiration for a gracious old house in a charming situation. His enthusiasm won father's heart.

At any rate, for a few days—it cannot have been more and yet the time was eventful enough to seem an age—father enjoyed the novelty of Graw's visit.

"Yes, yes," he agreed when the tobacco smoke was mentioned. "The pipe is disgusting. We must ask him to smoke it out of doors. I don't want him setting the house on fire. I'll tell him."

But it was Lydia, of course, who told him; at once and with enthusiasm; with the air, moreover, of just restraining herself from telling him a good deal more.

"Mr Penrose has no idea how much the man eats," she said. Indeed Graw's astonishing appetite soon put a strain on the larder. "I don't believe he's had a square meal for months. The Kirkdales keep a good table." Her eyes narrowed with suspicion. "It rather makes me wonder where he's been since he left Oversay or whether he was ever there at all. But there's one thing. He'll stay indefinitely if we go on feeding him like this." She cast a critical eye over the tray Addy had prepared for his luncheon, removed two slices of cold lamb, cut the loaf in two and popped the larger piece back in the bread crock. "Tell him that must suffice. We'll have to bake again as it is."

If Graw did actually growl, as Addy reported, at the slender provision made for his lunch, the growling did not penetrate to the house: certainly not to the study. There was much besides our visitor's appetite that father was unaware of. Having launched Graw upon the household, he retired to his study: a comfortable room on the ground floor where he spent most of his time. His interest in natural history had recently waned and the projected work in the manner of Gilbert White: 'The Flora, Fauna and Natural Curiosities of Saxon's Gate' had been laid aside. He was at that time absorbed, if memory serves me aright, in his 'Examination of the Classical Sources of Milton's Pastoral Scenes'. On no account must he be interrupted. The rule was so inflexible that I had come to believe the Examination to be a matter of great urgency and was worried by the length of time it was taking. I judged it to be an exhausting exercise, having once or twice peeped through the window and seen father asleep.

Other factors besides his scholarly pursuits kept him in ignorance of the skirmishes between Graw and the women of the house.

"Your father cannot bear any unpleasantness," mother, and later Lydia, had often said. "It upsets him. He is so very tenderhearted."

It had become a duty to protect him from irritation and discomfort. As a rule, Lydia was more than equal to dealing with such small disruptions as ruffled our tranquil life though the hostility she turned upon Graw was new. The dislike was mutual but as enemies they were not well matched. Lydia's sauciness disturbed Graw no more than the frisking of a kitten might discompose a wolf—for Addy's description had not so far been improved on.

Those summer days were filled with a new, unwholesome excitement. Watching every move they made, hanging upon every word they spoke, I understood in a confused way that the hatred between them was less a barrier than a bond. It united them. Each was more conscious of the other than of anyone else. The effect must have been like falling in love, but this was the dark, reverse side of the coin. Lydia, at least, generated waves of feeling that set the whole house pitching and tossing. I thrilled to the unfamiliar drama—and feared it—and knew instinctively that no good would come of it.

Graw bided his time and the severity of his attack when it came was out of all proportion to any offence Lydia could have inflicted on him. The smoke, the appetite, the half-insolent arrogance of the man were pinpricks compared with the affair of the portrait.

3

On the Monday morning after his arrival, father asked Graw to make a preliminary sketch of Lydia and me.

He himself arranged our pose in the window as before and after a good deal of discussion about light and shade, background and foreground, Graw sat down on his stool and began. I remember how he used his authority as artist to look at us and especially Lydia with the intimate, devouring attention she had foreseen and dreaded. We, as victims, felt it; and yet to father, watching from across the room, I have no doubt that Graw's manner seemed no more than sincerely workmanlike.

My own dislike of Graw was so far superficial: a habit of shuddering and exclaiming, quickly caught from Lydia. But as he sat there amid the china and chintzes of my mother's drawing room, a long-limbed man, his coarse complexion and features suggesting a grossness I could feel but not identify, I felt a pang of real dislike. Mother wouldn't have permitted it. Impossible to imagine that if she had been there on the sofa, Graw would have been there on his stool in a setting so inappropriate. The unusual experience of sitting to an artist gave me no feeling of importance. I was not deceived for a moment. The central figure was neither myself nor Lydia but Graw. He exuded a peculiar power. I turned my eyes to the garden and the tiled roof of my summerhouse, half wishing I were safe under it—and alone.

"I should prefer it, Miss Isobel, if you would turn your head this way, towards me." I looked at him. His hot brown eyes rested on Lydia. His full lips turned down at the corners with the faintest touch of malice. "Do you not think, Mr Penrose, that your daughter should look down, so." He assumed what was meant to be a look of tenderness and crooked his left arm as if cradling a helpless infant or a lost lamb. "I mean of course your elder daughter."

I glanced up quickly. Lydia had turned red as fire. I felt her heart beat faster as father said stiffly:

"You misunderstand. Miss Lorne is not my daughter."

Graw's start of surprise was as false as his suave smile of apology.

"I beg your pardon. The young ladies seemed close enough in age—and in every other way—to be sisters."

"You knew," I thought, scowling. "You know everything already."

Lydia's embarrassed resentment was scarcely greater than father's. My scowl cannot have been darker than his as he plunged his hands in his pockets and stared at Lydia as though she were to blame.

"Indeed," said the insufferable Graw, "I had misunderstood Miss Lorne's position. It was a natural conclusion when she . . . er . . ." He looked across at father and positively smirked. "I have no wish to tread on delicate ground."

"Delicate fiddlesticks," father said angrily. "Miss Lorne is a relative of my late wife."

"Ah!" It is impossible to convey in words the variety of suggestion Graw infused into the single syllable. Its effect on father was not soothing. He pulled out his watch, muttered something about getting on with his work and went out into the hall, where I heard him rattling walking sticks, too much annoyed to stay with us, too much interested to stay away.

Graw's object must have been to annoy Lydia, not father on whom he must rely for his fee. Yet he had already discovered that the quickest way to wound her was through him. Her happiness depended on his; and deliberately to disturb father on her account showed a refinement of cunning in Graw which was all the more dangerous for being the only refined thing about him.

Did he sense that for the time being he had gone too far? I was not sure how far he had in fact gone. But I was sure that our comfortable comradeship had been in some way unsettled. For the first time I found myself puzzled as to what relation Lydia was to me. Were she and father discovering their lack of relationship to each other? The strange thing was that by reminding them that there was none, Graw had somehow suggested a relationship. The only one I could foresee was so much to the advantage of all three of us that I could not account for the depression we seemed to have succumbed to. It was as if Graw had puffed into the pot-pourri-scented air a cloud of his particularly vile tobacco smoke.

Having achieved his object—I had never seen Lydia looking so self-conscious—Graw applied himself to his task, working confidently and quickly, and in ten minutes put down his pencil. Father was there at once. He had recovered his temper and was well satisfied with the sketch.

"A pleasing composition. Yes, quite pleasing. Now as to colour tones . . . I was thinking of watercolour, by the way."

Graw seemed to suppress just in time an exclamation of protest. His look of disappointment was obvious enough to make father ask:

"Don't you agree? The subject lends itself to a delicate treatment. Not sentimental, of course, but unsuitable for strong colours."

"I do agree," Graw said swiftly, "but in the right hands oils can be far more sensitive. I had intended something in the spirit of Lawrence: colourful yet soft: with a richness not possible in watercolour."

"Well, yes. You may be right."

"Oils will take a little longer." My heart sank. "But the result will be —an heirloom, shall we say, to enrich the family of Penrose for generations."

The man had an unlucky knack of wounding the sensibilities. In this case he succeeded in reminding father that there was no heir to continue the family name. Father's face clouded.

"Oils then," he said, as if he no longer cared.

Lydia had left the room without a word and with none of the flouncing and head tossing she sometimes indulged in when vexed. Curiosity led me to hang about, hoping for a look.

"Here you are, Isobel. Do you like it?"

I saw, grudgingly, why father had praised the composition. Graw had imposed on the rectangle of paper an elongated circle like a protective globe enclosing Lydia and me in a single unit: her arm supporting me, the curve of her shoulder complemented by the curve of my dress. The lines were flowing yet contained so that they gave an impression of melting tenderness and security. Inexperienced as a handful of drawing lessons had left me, I could nevertheless see in the black and white sketch the promise of a charming picture. It surprised me. Charm was the last thing I had thought Graw capable of.

But there was one important omission.

"You haven't put in our faces."

"No, no, Isobel. Mr Graw was concerned with the composition."

"The details," Graw said, "will come later."

Sittings were to begin at once. Father was impatient to have the picture finished. Perhaps he already saw the advantage of getting rid of Graw or at least of cutting short a visit to which in the first flush of enthusiasm he had seen no limit. I too was anxious to have the ordeal over. Lydia was unusually quiet. She said nothing about the first sitting except, with a quivering intense seriousness, "You do realise, he couldn't possibly be my father. He isn't old enough. No one could mistake me for his daughter."

Since she was in her room more often than usual, I recall several conversations with father in which she had no part: recall them because they were rare: I was more used to listening while father and Lydia talked.

"We shall have to find another servant in Prue's place," father said. "I must advertise; and I'll walk over to Mrs Wayland's this afternoon. She may know of someone suitable."

"Lydia can manage the cooking for a while. She's so good at it. Much better than Prue."

"Yes, yes, I dare say . . . As a matter of fact—" We had been standing by the big mirror over the mantel shelf. He leaned forward, looked earnestly at his forehead and passed his hand thoughtfully over his front hair. "The time has come, I think, to make some changes in our way of life. I haven't been in the frame of mind since your dear mother died, but time has helped. Seeing you in colours again reminds me of the need to look forward, not back." He looked again anxiously, I thought, at his reflection. "The years pass. You'll soon be grown up and I . . ."

Hope revived. Some change in our way of life? I could imagine only one kind of change; and yet the development I had in mind would scarcely be a change at all. My mother, obviously, no one could supplant; but even in mother's time Lydia had been so constantly my protectress, companion and example that the change, if she were to marry father, would be, from my point of view, no more than a change of name. She would be my stepmother. I foresaw no complications, only a strengthening of security, like hauling up the drawbridge and lowering the portcullis against any intruder on our close, three-fold companionship.

In this mood of happy anticipation I forgot Graw. Father had gone out and presently Lydia joined me. She sat down in her Berlin-worked chair so quietly and with such a doleful look that I knelt down and put my head in her lap.

"It will soon be over. He'll go away. Graw, I mean."

"I'm going to tell your father that I don't want to be painted. It isn't necessary or right. You are the daughter of the house and the portrait should be of you, alone." Naturally I protested and she said with the little air of dignity she always assumed when giving the conversation this particular turn. "Our family portraits are all at Aunt Welbecome's at Ash House. She has oil paintings of my father and mother in her dining room and silhouettes of my grandmother Lorne and her sisters in the parlour. I think I've told you"—she certainly had—"that the Lornes can trace their history back to the sixteenth century. They were prosperous wool merchants at Bradford-on-Avon. The Mays were gentlemen farmers. I like to be known as Lydia May Lorne. It's an unusual name."

I agreed, privately hoping that it would soon be changed to Lydia May Penrose.

"If ever I have a son I should like him to be called Lorne. The Lorne treasures," Lydia's tone invested them with a fabulous richness, "would have come to father if he had lived."

"And they'll all be yours some day."

I had learned the lesson thoroughly. Indeed I knew them as if they were my own: the Sheraton chairs, the Chippendale mirror, the marquetry table, the Rockingham plates and most marvellous of all, the bird cage of green and gold, containing a miniature garden with mother-of-pearl flowers and a bush on which perched a bird. One wound it up and it actually sang: better than a thrush or blackbird: more like a nightingale. Lydia had promised it to me. My gratitude for such lavish generosity could have been no more heartfelt if the bird had been hers to give.

"I really should go to Martlebury to see Aunt Welbecome. She has often asked me, as you know, and she's growing old."

There was some mystery about these invitations. I had never known Lydia receive a letter from her aunt. But I knew perfectly well that she spoke about her family from a need to reassure herself that she was no mere dependant of the Penroses. I could feel that she was hurt at having been reminded of her orphaned state. Dared I tell her what father had said? My hesitation was brief. I always told Lydia everything.

"Some change in our arrangements, he said, and that he must look to the future . . ."

How pretty Lydia looked, and how young, when the colour came to her cheeks and her eyes lit up with the brilliance that seemed to shine from within!

"I believe he's worried about growing old . . ."

We agreed that it was nonsense. He had just reached the prime of life—was handsomer than ever. Our talk was so cheering that when Graw appeared and suggested that we might sit to him then and there, Lydia went promptly to her place as if she had forgotten her recent objections.

Over this, the final portrait, Graw took his time. Since the evenings were long and light it was possible to have at least two sittings a day. It was also possible for Graw to have two or three hearty meals a day and in the intervals between painting and eating to take his ease on the edge of the field beyond the garden wall, his long limbs outstretched among the moon daisies. He did a little exploring too. More than once I saw him walk through the larch wood towards the old limestone quarry. He also made a few excursions to the Cross Keys at Saxon's Gate and came back flushed and talkative but always in time for a meal.

On Friday Robert came again. He had been given a half holiday from the school in Netherlaw where he boarded during the week. I took him into the drawing room where the easel stood in the full light of the afternoon sun. The picture was almost finished. Although in its earlier stages I must have glanced at it a dozen times a day, in a sense I too saw it for the first time, for when the morning sitting was over, I had run out joyfully into the garden. At any rate I was unprepared for what I now saw. All that I had meant to say to Robert died on my lips.

The colours were as soft and rich as Graw had promised. Shadows of deeper purple between the lilac folds of my dress: the warm tints of our faces and hands: the chestnut brown of Lydia's hair and the lighter shades of my own: they had all been faithfully observed, set down and heightened by an expert eye and hand. The picture—I naïvely put it to myself—was a real one, good enough for a gallery and far better than any oil painting in the Town Hall at Netherlaw which was the only comparison my limited experience could provide. Only . . .

My attention had been roused to such a degree of awful interest that I had forgotten Robert but presently without taking my eyes from the picture, I discovered that he too was looking at it in silent concentration. Did he see what I saw? I am sure now that he did but at the time he made only one comment:

"There's a feeling about it I don't like. Is he staying long, this fellow?"

"I don't think so." Misgivings seized me. How did I know that he would not stay long? When I glanced around, Robert had gone, but presently he popped his head round the door.

"Who's that woman by the way? Going into the coach house with Graw?"

I rushed through the kitchen to the dairy and scrambled on one of the stone shelves just in time to see the door at the top of the coachman's steps close.

"A poor-looking woman dressed in black," Robert volunteered.

"It must be Mrs Graw. Where can she have come from?"

"I believe she's been living in the old limeburner's hut. Her skirt was covered with white dust. I came round that way and there was someone there. I thought it was a tramp."

"Why ever does he let her?"

"Because he's a ruffian," Robert said, "and the sooner he's got rid of the better."

I went soberly back through the hall and carefully closed the drawing room door to shut in the picture. Father was still in his study, presumably examining the classical sources of Milton's pastoral scenes. For a second I wondered how he actually did it. It didn't occur to me to wonder why. Lydia was sewing in her room. At the garden door I hesitated, then went softly to the archway and looked through the gate bars. In the stable yard nothing stirred. Across the coachman's window the faded yellow curtains were drawn. For some reason this disturbed me. The blank panes created a mystery, a secrecy which I resented not as a withdrawal but as a further presumption on the part of Graw. Visible he was bad enough. Invisible, he was much, much worse.

A fit of restlessness made me avoid the summer-house. I leaned over the wall to breathe the free air blowing lightly down from Limmergill Fell; but the bent stems and crushed flower-heads still showed where Graw had sprawled among the daisies and

Queen Anne's lace, as the reek of his tobacco still overwhelmed their fragrance.

It was a long afternoon. The shadows of the larches on the west side of the field had come halfway across to meet me when I heard the coach house door quietly open and close. At the sound of dragging feet on the other side of the sweetbriar I drew back under the hawthorn boughs.

She must have clambered over the wall instead of coming round to the wicket for presently I saw her skirting the field, keeping close to the hedge. Her dress clung to her knees, giving her the poverty-stricken look of a woman who wore few petticoats, if any: a woman used to facing wind and rain and even going short of food. She seemed to carry with her the melancholy aura of all the rat-infested barns and haystacks where she had sheltered. Her way of walking close to the thorn-bushes with her head bent was strangely frightening. It was as if she had crept out of the earth and found the sunlight too bright for her secret purposes.

From the safety of the garden I watched her out there in the field. Larks were singing; the air was sweet with the perfume of flowering grasses. Her black figure crawling across the brightness of the day seemed an apparition from the haunted world of childhood with its monsters and bogeymen. I was far more afraid of her than of Graw. It was as if I sensed in her even then a greater power to harm than his. And yet I pitied her, knowing that Graw kept her hidden because he was ashamed of her. It had been easier to impose on father when he was on his own. She must be useful to him in some way, I concluded, and was innocent enough to think of her as a kind of porter carrying the luggage.

She walked so slowly that I thought she would never reach the other side but at last she came to the belt of larch trees and was swallowed up in their shade.

Addy was laying cutlery in the dining parlour when I went indoors. It would soon be dinner time. Lydia came running downstairs. Father came out of the study. We met in the hall.

"Let's take a look at the picture," father said.

4

And there we still were, Lydia and I, suspended in our globe where even God could no longer change us. The sun had moved from the easel. The paler, more constant light was if anything less kind. More clearly than ever I saw all that there was to dislike in the picture, though I was still far from recognising the fear that underlay my bewildered resentment: a fear of Graw's diabolical cleverness.

For as a painting it was not only appealing but sufficiently in harmony with the popular taste at that time to please any but the most unreasonable client. He had caught our likenesses. The word took on for me its true meaning: something like but not the thing itself. He had given to me a cloying sweetness; made me a guileless creature younger than my years, of curls and limpid eyes and shrinking shoulders, settled like a nursery pet in the curve of Lydia's arm. He had caught the precise cast of Lydia's features: her straight nose, rounded chin and arched eyebrows.

But he had also given to her lips a thickening so slight that it could not be called a distortion any more than the equally slight hardening of her eyes. It would have been difficult to say what he had done to turn Lydia into a bold woman in a vulgar profusion of ribbons, and past her first youth: the woman, I dare say, he would have liked her to be. Somehow he had turned her zest for life into a voluptuous greed. Worse still, by exaggerating my innocence, he had shown me as Lydia's victim: a pet lamb destined to be led astray.

"One might have thought," Robert said when we discussed it afterwards, "that Lydia was a low-down woman from a fairground carrying you off to teach you her evil ways. Except that Lydia is nothing like that and although you've been a good deal spoilt, you aren't such a ninny as Graw made you look."

At a first glance, the picture had, I believe, a colourful charm. Looking at it for any length of time, one was infected by a pecu-

liar nastiness impossible to describe. It carried into the room and
wafted throughout the house a new, unwelcome personality. On
the close, sisterly love between Lydia and me, it breathed a new,
undreamed-of taint.

I knew—as surely as Lydia did at her first dismayed glance—
that this was Graw's revenge, or part of it; and yet as she reached
out to take my hand for comfort I almost moved away as though
to avoid contact with the unsavory woman in the picture. Then I
saw how hurt and disappointed she was and put my arms round
her waist and hugged her.

"There's no need for that, Isobel," father said irritably. "You
should learn to control yourself. It's time you had done with
those babyish ways."

Lydia pushed me away and seeing the figure of Graw pass the
window, crossed the hall to the dining parlour and slammed the
door.

Graw's knock was polite but confident, his manner that of a
successful painter in the presence of a gratified client. His cheeks
and forehead between the dark sandy hair and beard were sun-
burned. Already his face had filled out a little. What I shrank
from, I suppose, was a sensual force in him so strong that by
contrast father looked almost effeminate. Though of average
height he seemed smaller and paler than usual and by no means
at ease in his own drawing room.

"Ah, Graw. I see you've practically finished."

Graw towered over him and me and the picture, and waited.

"The colours I find very pleasant. Very pleasant indeed. The
fabrics are particularly well done. But—er—the faces . . . You
don't seem to have quite caught Miss Lorne's personality."

"Or mine," I thought, glowering at the insipid nurseling in my
grown-up dress.

"An invariable comment, if I may say so, when a portrait
shows someone well known to us in a slightly different and unexpected light. The artist, I need not remind you, must be both
perceptive and impartial."

"True, true," said my father. He looked troubled and vexed.

But it wasn't true. I longed to tell them so: longed to find Lydia
and tell her. Instead I stayed, listening to their talk and watching
with a fearful fascination how Graw's confidence undermined
father's. He was unhappy not because Lydia had been misrepre-
sented but because Graw had shown him a Lydia he disliked.

Incredulously I saw that he believed in this new Lydia, a blowsy
woman already lapsing into a coarseness not unlike Graw's own.
Could he not see that she was no more our own Lydia than the
wax doll at her side was myself? Robert had seen the falseness.
Father was misled. The discovery was so unwelcome that in taking the first step towards disillusionment, I forgot Lydia and
Graw and recognised father as a man who could be deceived;
who could be wrong.

My judgment—if such a word can be used of the confused
state of mind I suffered from—was too sweeping, of course. Not
until long after did I realise that Graw had merely stressed what
father himself must already have glimpsed in Lydia and in reminding him of the flaw, had devalued the gem. Worst of all,
father respected him for what seemed his honesty.

"The ribbons," Graw was saying, "give a useful contrast to the
lilac and grey as well as adding a touch of character. Yes," he
lounged across to the other side of the room, leaving us to enjoy
them, "the ribbons have come out very well."

How he had revelled in painting them! They cascaded down
Lydia's bosom and frothed and bubbled round her neck with the
vigour of a pink waterfall.

"Why does Lydia bedeck herself in such things?" father said
angrily. "You must learn to dress simply, Isobel. Simplicity and
restraint are the essence of good taste, especially in a woman's
dress."

He had at least lowered his voice so that Graw could not hear
but the appeal to my restraint and good taste went sadly astray.
Having struggled to contain my baffled sense of injustice, in a
childish attempt to redress the balance I cried out maliciously at
the top of my voice, "I didn't know that Mrs Graw had come to
stay as well."

Father looked at me sharply, then at Graw who was for once at
a loss. He had picked up an alabaster figurine of Psyche, his
attitude so entirely that of a guest and equal that I'm convinced
father resented his presumption.

"What's this, Graw? You didn't mention that you had your
wife with you. Why was that?"

Graw carefully restored Psyche to her pedestal, to my relief: it
was hateful to see her bare shoulders caressed by his big hands.
He came forward with an apologetic shrug and the smile of a

schoolboy found out in a prank; but the glance of his hot brown eyes in my direction was not sympathetic.

"I apologise. But Mrs Graw must bear the blame, if blame there is to be. She is a woman"—he hesitated—"of unusual reserve and shyness; a misfortune which has often caused me inconvenience; and yet, after all, reserve is not the worst defect in a woman." He looked deliberately at Lydia's brazen likeness and I saw how easily he could deflect my puny attack and turn it to his own advantage. "And with all respect to Miss Penrose, Mrs Graw is not with me. She is staying—in the district."

"Robert and I both saw her," I blundered on; and I heard a vulgar shrillness in my voice which was as new as every other aspect of the unhappy scene. "She was here all the afternoon, in the coach house, with the curtains drawn."

"You may go to your room, Isobel," father said.

"As I explained," Graw put in quickly, "Mrs Graw is unusually reserved. I could not have persuaded her to stay here, even if I had presumed to try, but as you know," he actually laughed, "there are times . . ."

"Isobel!"

"Yes, father."

The victory lay with Graw. As I left them he said:

"The two young ladies are less alike in appearance than I thought at first. The similarity is in manner. It's natural, almost unavoidable for a young girl to be influenced by an older companion whom she still admires." His tone was soothing. "A few months' separation can often put things right."

I rushed up to my room and wept till dinner time when hunger brought me down again. The meal was constrained. I alone ate heartily. Before going to the study, father made a speech he had obviously been preparing. His hatred of unpleasantness made him avoid our eyes and speak with an uncomfortable stiffening of the lips.

"As the picture is finished, Mr Graw will be leaving tomorrow morning. I have given him his fee. Meanwhile, will you come to the study, Lydia? I've been wanting to have a word with you."

The formality of the invitation would once have thrilled me with the hope that he was going to make a declaration but whatever Graw's visit had achieved it had shaken me out of fantasy into a more realistic frame of mind. The interview certainly brought a change but in the wrong direction. Lydia went into the

study with a set face. In about ten minutes she came out with all
her brightness dimmed. Her cheeks had a crumpled look. Her
lips were unsteady. She took no notice of me and went upstairs.

"Whatever has happened, father?" I asked, aghast.

He stood at the foot of the stairs, looking after her.

"Lydia is being very foolish. She chooses deliberately to misunderstand me. I don't wish to discuss the matter with you, Isobel,
but as I said, we must make changes. It hadn't occurred to me
that Lydia's position here might be misconstrued now that your
mother has—left us."

"Misconstrued?" I gasped. A darting recollection of the Latin
exercises father inflicted on me increased my panic.

"The least breath of gossip could ruin Lydia's prospects of
marrying well. All I said was that we must have some older
woman here to take charge and to—er—maintain the proprieties:
someone to give you more suitable guidance. Lydia is too young
and not quite . . . I disliked the way you behaved this evening,
Isobel. You raised your voice. It was—displeasing." Then as he
no doubt saw my face begin to crumple and my lips to quiver,
"Now I've upset you too. Don't cry, darling. I can't bear it. Not
both of you."

He looked wretchedly up the stairs, went to the garden door as
if to escape, then perhaps foreseeing the possibility of meeting
Graw, seized a walking stick and went out at the front. He had
been too well protected from unpleasantness.

There was no reading from the *The Lady of the Lake* that
evening. To avoid the portrait Lydia and I sat in her room nor
did we discuss it. It had already become less important than the
quarrel in the study, which cast a shadow until bedtime—and
much longer. We talked about the older woman. I imagined an
ancient crone in black satin with an ivory-headed cane and an
ear-trumpet. Lydia saw her as a military gentleman's widow with
a habit of command and a great deal of whalebone.

"We could have more fun," I ventured when we had giggled
shakily over these rival monsters. "You wouldn't be so busy. We
could pay calls and go shopping."

"I'm sure we could get used to having some dismal old woman
here, but"—Lydia gave up the pretence of thinking of other
things—"I felt a change in your father. I hadn't realised . . . He
doesn't think of me as I imagined he did."

She spoke simply but with a quality of sad acceptance I have never forgotten. During those few minutes in the study a long cherished hope had died. I grieved for it as if there had been another death in the house without realising as yet how its passing had changed our lives. Lydia had grown older and must have unconsciously assumed that I had grown older too. Otherwise she might not have said:

"You don't know, Isobel, I can't tell you what a dangerous thing it is to love someone, knowing that your love is not returned. It's . . ."

"Like Charlie."

"Charlie?" Her manner changed. She looked thoughtful. Her eyes were wide and soft as if a new understanding had come to her. "Poor fellow!" she said wistfully. "I've been living in a dream."

The awakening must have been cruel enough to drive her to something like despair. Her forehead had a strained look I had not seen before. I cast about for some consolation and knew that there could be none. Nothing I could say would make any difference.

Our hatred of Graw brought us, surprisingly, to more cheerful ground.

"By tomorrow evening he'll have gone and we'll be just as we always were." I have since learned not to make remarks of that kind. Lydia shivered. "But I shouldn't be surprised if he was here all day. Father will hate having to tell him to go."

"Isobel." Lydia laid down the pillowcase she had been half-heartedly stitching. "Let's go to Netherlaw tomorrow and have the photograph taken. We'd be out all day and as it's Saturday, Mr Penrose may dine in Netherlaw. Then when we come back, Graw will have gone."

The suddenness of the proposal took my breath away but I soon got it back and plunged into preparations with zest, talking over the arrangements so volubly that there was no need for Lydia to say much, nor did she. Father made no objection except to insist that we dressed plainly. Indeed Lydia's best dress was unaccountably short of ribbons next morning. Perhaps there was no time to sew them on. We had to run through the fields to catch the nine o'clock train.

It was a day that shines in the memory; not with untroubled happiness: a touch of melancholy afflicted us both; a foreshadowing perhaps, which gave to all its incidents the precious quality of a time never to be repeated. We were always, I suppose, in perfect harmony, Lydia and I, but I had never thought of it before. The knowledge intensified the harmony. In everything we agreed, or so I thought. It may have been Lydia who agreed to all my daring suggestions: that we should climb to the ramparts of the castle: be rowed up a green stretch of the river: buy the chain bracelet I had kept father's New Year sovereign for.

Harassed as we had been by our recent experiences, we positively enjoyed the visit to the studio.

"You'll send the photographs soon, *soon*, won't you, Mr Handiside?"

"You shall have them by hand in a few days at the latest, Miss Isobel, and very charming you will find them, I'm sure."

He took us in three poses and promised to send the two best. Lydia insisted on buying me a frame.

"While we're here," she said, "we may as well," and she chose one of maple and gilt, simple but expensive. We felt sure father would like it. "It's no use doing things by halves," she declared with a revival of her old gusto, as she took out her purse.

But when I pointed out that she would need a frame as well, she hesitated before choosing a much cheaper one of oak for herself.

"Promise me, Isobel," she began, then paused and went on more lightly. "It will look very well in your room. You'll see it first thing in the morning and last thing at night."

"It's all been perfect," I breathed, pursuing my Eccles cake to the last crumb and to the tune of 'While in a shady grove she wandered', played on the piano and violin behind potted palms, not above the mere pastry-cook's but in the plush and gold splendour of the Castle Tea Room.

We were lucky enough to find an empty ladies' compartment and sang 'While in a shady grove' all the way back in the train and across the fields to the harsh accompaniment of a corncrake.

The poppies had lost their colour in the cool twilight. The trees by our gate smelt of balsam and nectar—and rain. It was raining gently when we went in at the front door.

Father had not yet come home. Everything was as we had left it. The portrait was still on the easel.

"Good evening, Miss Lorne."

Simeon Graw rose from the best armchair like a host welcoming a visitor.

5

From the confused recollection of that evening two or three impressions remain, clearly etched, never to be forgotten. I remember how we stood, subdued, in the hall. Then Lydia said:

"He must go, now, or he'll never go. He must be got rid of. That is something I can do for you both."

She hesitated, her hat in her hand, then jabbed into it the long pin with the amber head and went into the study. I heard her making up the fire with logs. Addy had already gone to bed. "It's time you went too," Lydia called but I pleaded to stay up longer and I must have gone into the kitchen to warm some milk because it is in the kitchen that I see the scene that followed. I had taken off my outdoor things and was sitting on the fender when Lydia came in at the back door and sat down at the other end. She had taken off her jacket and her hair was wet. She was quite breathless.

"What have you been doing?"

Before she could answer Graw appeared from behind the oak screen, lured no doubt by the clatter of saucepan and cups.

"I'm disturbing you," he said confidently.

It was then that I noticed the triumph in Lydia's manner. She got up. The wall clock struck nine and the silver chime of the drawing room clock confirmed the hour. It seemed a long time before the eighteenth stroke died away. A flurry of rain beat on the window. The wind was rising again.

"It will be a storm," I said.

"Yes." Lydia spoke with the same strange triumph. "It will be a wild wet night but that need not concern us, Isobel. We shall be warm and comfortable." She took a step or two towards Graw. Her movement struck a shower of sparks from the brass weights and pendulum of the clock and the copper pans along the wall.

"Mr Penrose has given you your fee. There's nothing to stop you from leaving at once."

"In the morning, I suppose you mean." Graw's brows had come together in a dark line.

"I mean at once. Mr Penrose was under the impression that you were leaving immediately after he saw you this morning. He won't wish to see you again."

"I presume, miss"—Graw spoke the word with a contemptuous hiss—"that I may enjoy the shelter (it can scarcely be called the comfort) of the coach house for another night."

"Not for another second," Lydia said. "You've been here too long already. You've outstayed your welcome. I've put all your things at the bottom of the steps and locked the coach house door. You'll find a room at the Cross Keys. You're not without money and you've had enough to eat," she added with venom, "to last you for a while."

They glared at each other. The fire leapt. The copper pans glittered. The whole kitchen might have been on the point of bursting into flame. Seen from the low fender Graw seemed bigger than ever; and yet this time it was not Graw who dominated the room but Lydia, alert as she was with life and energy.

I watched them as one might watch a cockfight through a whirl of flying feathers, knowing that one of the birds must die. It was more than a fancy. The moment was more than a crisis. A sense of fatality came to me: a foreboding founded on something deeper than a quarrel over a pie or a picture: as though Lydia and Graw were in danger and would destroy each other.

"I had a right to expect"—Graw seemed to force himself to speak calmly as if he knew how much more deeply he could injure her by a careful choice of words than by a blow with the poker which he might well have considered—"that Mr Penrose would have had the courtesy to see me himself. But I have no doubt that you and he are, if I may so put it in a young girl's presence, sufficiently at one for him to make use of you in this way. At first I was puzzled by your position here but now I understand. In quiet country places the conventions can sometimes be—adapted a little. But under the circumstances I am not inclined to stay. A professional man must have some regard for his reputation."

Without fully understanding or taking the measure of his odious hypocrisy, I knew that he had gone far beyond the bounds of rudeness. For a moment Lydia's lively spirit was almost quenched. A look of illness came over her like a withering of inner strength. She drew a deep breath and recovered.

"Wait a minute," she said. "There's something I want you to see before you go."

With a swish of her skirts she was round the screen and into the hall. There was just time to feel the discomfort of being alone with Graw before she was back, carrying the painting.

"I don't know where you've come from," she said, "or who you really are but I know that you're a poisonous reptile. You crawled into this house and it's time for you to crawl out of it and try your luck elsewhere. You've been paid for your work and now you can see what I'm going to do with it."

The canvas was too tough for her small hands to tear but she bent it and trampled on it and threw it into the fire, and held it there with the tongs, pressing the obnoxious thing down into the hot heart of the flames. It would not have surprised me if Graw had strangled her. He looked as if he might. Being perfectly resolved to kill him outright if he attempted it, I was not afraid, only filled with the conviction that Lydia was right in everything she had said and done. It was not biased affection that influenced me: simply a straightforward satisfaction in seeing justice carried out. When the two strangers Graw had created had melted into a purple smudge, I felt the blessed relief that must come after an exorcism. We were ourselves again.

Still holding the tongs, Lydia went to the door and flung it wide open.

"You can go now," she said superbly.

The wind blew straight in and shook the saucepan lids on their hooks. The fire roared at the canvas. Graw passed within inches of her but she did not flinch. It was a moment of high drama. Lydia, I thought with deep admiration, has won.

But as I said, they were not equally matched. Lydia was less clever and more easily hurt. Graw was going but he had not quite gone. Scorpion-like, he could sting to the very end.

"My easel," he said, almost apologetically. We neither of us spoke while he fetched it. To my surprise, when he came back, he turned to me.

"I should be much obliged if you would give a message to Mr. Penrose. First, my apologies for having outstayed my welcome. I did intend to leave earlier but it has taken me most of the day to

do what I have been wanting to do all the week. They're finished
now. Two watercolours of Emberside. You'll find them in the
drawing room. No," he drew himself up with an air of gentle-
manly pride—"there is no fee. The pictures are a gift to Mr.
Penrose: the only recompense I can make for his hospitality. I
had hoped to present them myself but . . ." He smiled ruefully,
bowed with a sort of noble regret and went out into a night full of
rain.

His performance was in its way as fine as Lydia's and because
he had the last word, it was the more effective—for a while. Just
for a minute my confidence in Lydia was shaken. The poor man
had worked all day and waited in vain for an opportunity of
seeing father. Then to be called a reptile and be turned out into
the rain! My thoughtful silence was too much for Lydia. She
dropped into a chair and burst into tears; and instantly my
doubts vanished in a gush of sympathy.

"He's a liar," I said. "If he's been wanting to do the
watercolours all the week why has he spent so much time lolling
about and smoking? He did them today as an excuse for staying
longer. He wanted more money. If you hadn't turned him away,
he'd never have gone."

Lydia nodded, gulping and sniffing away her tears.

"But your father won't understand. He'll believe Graw."

She was right. Graw had known how to win father's favour
and at the same time ensure a welcome if ever he came again.
This conviction brought me to the first moral dilemma of my
sheltered, pampered life: my first opportunity to influence events.
Confronted with a choice that seemed to me momentous, I positively trembled.

"I only did it to help Mr. Penrose and you," Lydia sobbed, and
without more delay, I decided to sin.

"I shan't tell father. I won't give him Graw's message. We'll
burn those pictures as well or"—a less drastic course occurred to
me—"we'll hide them."

"Oh no, Isobel."

Wide-eyed, we considered the possibility. I felt stiff and solemn
with resolution. But it was too late. My heroism, as it happened,
was not to be tested.

I had been aware of movements in the yard as Graw presumably collected his wet possessions. A yelp from the region of the
kennel raised my anger to boiling point.

"He's kicked Sambo," I said furiously, and listened, hoping to hear an agonised groan as Sambo retaliated but the rustle of leaves and creak of branches drowned all other sounds except . . . I opened the shutter and heard it again, Graw's voice calling.

"Listen!" He must have been at the gate where a grass track led to the old lime kilns. "What is he saying? I believe he's calling her. Mrs. Graw."

I pictured her starting obediently into life, taking up her bundle and dragging her feet through the wet grass to follow him wherever he went and I wondered with a fearful sense of darkness and mystery what bond could possibly unite them when he would not have her with him yet could not go without her.

"I shouldn't have done it." Lydia looked out over my shoulder at the bending trees. "Whatever made me behave like that? It was unchristian. Where will they go if there isn't a room at the Cross Keys?"

"What does it matter so long as they go and never, never come back? I hope we never see the Graws again as long as we live."

Especially her, I prayed, with an impression of sinister depths such as a glimpse into a bottomless well might give. Don't let her ever come again.

"I don't suppose they have a home. That's a terrible thing for a woman, not to have a home. And after all," Lydia must have been speaking the thought that had troubled her for days, "I haven't a home either. Emberside took me in just as it took in Graw and I've been here much longer. Perhaps I've outstayed my welcome too."

I had hardly drawn breath to tell her how far-fetched the comparison was when we heard the gig and a minute or two later the sound of father opening the drawing room door.

"He'll see the sketches," I said in consternation. "I believe he's lighting another lamp."

He was still in scarf and ulster when I peeped round the door.

"Come here, Isobel." His voice was excited, even awestruck. "Look at this, and this. Where's Graw? He didn't mention them."

I have had ample time since then to overcome the prejudice which kept me from exclaiming at once that the sketches were, as I still think them, exquisite: one of the house seen from the field's edge: the other of the older wing nestled in sheltering trees. The rosy tiles, the pale amber stone, the windows open to the garden, are faithfully drawn yet softened as if set at a little distance from reality. If one were to see Emberside in a dream, as many a time I have seen it, it might have the same quality, ethereal as the sunlit hour in which Graw arrested it. Loth as I am even now to admit it, Graw as an artist had re-created and given permanence to the serenity he had, as a rogue and adventurer, destroyed.

Some dim notion of the paradox confused me as I saw and felt the undisturbed beauty of my home for the first time and understood that he too must have felt it. It puzzled me that a man so flamboyant should have been capable of responding to so delicately tranquil a scene. It troubled me that I had not known how dearly I loved my home until I saw it through his eyes.

"I suppose he is still here? The easel's gone, I see. I shall want to tell him"—father's voice trembled—"how very much I like them. Strange, isn't it? One can feel his love for the place as if it has got into his heart, like mine. Where is he?"

"He's gone, father, not long ago."

Reluctantly and yet as if she couldn't stay away, Lydia had joined us.

"He'll come back, I presume. I must pay him. These are worth a good deal. Did he say what he wanted for them?"

Even if I had not taken my splendid resolution I could not for the life of me have uttered a word in Graw's favour. It was Lydia who said slowly—and it must have cost her an effort—"He meant them as a present, to repay your kindness."

"Couldn't you have persuaded him to stay until I came back? It's odd that he should go off in this weather at this time of night."

"I sent him away," Lydia said. "I took his things out of the coach house and locked the door."

"You took a great deal upon yourself," father said bitterly.

"He may not quite have gone," I put in quickly, in the hope of diverting his anger. It was worse than that: a cold fury such as I had never seen before. "He was waiting for Mrs. Graw."

"Good heavens! I'd forgotten her. Wherever has she been all this time? She must have been staying in one of the cottages, I suppose."

I gave Lydia a warning nudge. It seemed wiser not to mention the limeburner's hut. Besides, we were not sure that she had been there. Father hurried out into the yard and we followed. It was still not quite dark. There was light enough to see two people going up the hill, their heads bowed against the rain.

"Hey, Graw!" father called. "Graw!"

The wind carried his voice away. Graw did not turn. As they reached the last cottage his cloak blew up like a puff of smoke; then he disappeared over the brow of the hill and Mrs. Graw laboured after him.

"I should have done more for him. The man's a genius, I tell you. It would have been a privilege to help him instead of turning the two of them away like tinkers. You should never have let him go on such a night." The angry contempt with which he turned on Lydia would have been unthinkable a week ago. "But how could you be expected to appreciate the qualities of such a man?"

It may have been the last straw: the final prick that confirmed her intention; but I believe her mind was already made up.

"I did it for the best," she said in a heart-broken way when father had gone indoors and we stood dejectedly in the porch. "You know that, Isobel." Drops of rain slid from the clematis leaves on to her hair. "If he's a genius he must have seen me as I really am. Am I like that? I didn't know. I'm not fit . . ." She put her hands on my shoulders and looked at me, really looked with a concentrated attention as if she were memorising my features. "Dearest, dearest Isobel."

The stinging rain, the fierce air, the tossing trees, the anger and despair were all at once too much for me. I could do nothing but yawn and long for the day to be over. If only I could have found words to comfort her or been wise enough to tell her how slight a thing in our lives the whole affair of Graw really was: how little the manner of his coming and going mattered to us, safe and settled and united as we were by ties of affection that nothing could break. If only I could have told her what I now believe, that her love for father would in time have been returned; that there was hope.

The words had not come when I went wearily to bed but all night long, awake and asleep, I thought and dreamed of Lydia: talking and singing: laughing and crying: appearing in the brightness of firelight: half hidden in shadow. Once long ago she had fished me out of the stream gasping my last, had shaken me back to life and dosed me with rum. Tossing on my pillow, I experienced again the visionary backward glance granted to those who are drowning and every memory centred upon Lydia as if I had

never lived for a second without her; as if I had needed her to
show me how to breathe.

Her voice sounded all night in my ears. "I'll look after you,
Isobel," she seemed to say again as she had said in the first deso-
late days after mother's death.

"It's for you, Isobel." I saw again the crimson velvet bonnet
she had made me years ago from a remnant of the drawing room
curtains: a spectacular creation edged with swansdown sewn on
in huge stitches. I felt again the ecstatic joy of putting it on. In a
passion of gratitude I had knitted her a shawl, a very small one,
being then at an age (seven I think) when passions rapidly cool.
Prue cast on the loops for me but she was too busy to supervise
my reckless plunge into the hazardous seas of plain and purl. The
disastrous result must have strained Lydia's devotion to the limit,
but she wore it gallantly two or three times and would never part
with it.

I fell asleep and dreamed of the snow lady we made, the very
day I first wore the bonnet.

"Why should it always be a man?" Lydia demanded, as she
scooped up handfuls of snow in long, graceful swoops. In my
dream the lady grew tall, shimmering and smiling with her red
mouth of holly berries: then melted in a hopeless yielding to a
thaw crueller than any frost until there was nothing left of her at
all.

The sense of loss remained when I woke. Then came relief in
the thought that Graw was gone. We had Lydia to thank for that
as for so much else. Father must soon see that she had done the
right thing. She had risen to the occasion again.

And for the last time. For it was not only Graw who had gone.
Addy came running upstairs to tell me—the anguish of it grips
me still—that Lydia had gone too.

6

She left a bleakness in the house: a silence. Still unbelieving, I found that Addy had rearranged the breakfast table and put the coffee pot at my right hand. To my left, at the foot of the table, plate and cutlery had been removed; the cloth was bare; the chair empty.

Despite the appalling gloom of the meal we sat over it longer than usual, from inability on my part at least to face the problems looming in the kitchen. It was Sunday. No mention was made of going to church. The guilt of not going deepened the pall already hanging over the day.

"She didn't say anything," father asked for the third time, "about going away?"

I shook my head. It was as clear to me as daylight that she had meant to go but she had said nothing. She had cast herself into the unknown without a word. The mystery of it frightened me: the impossibility of picturing Lydia anywhere else but in her chair at the foot of the table where she so patently was not.

"She must have left a message," father said. "Have you looked everywhere?" I nodded as if deprived of any power to communicate save by these forlorn movements of the head. I had not then found the note in my workbasket: "I'll always love you, Isobel," scribbled on the back of a mercer's bill for black tape; and I never did tell father about it.

"If she wanted to pay Mrs. Welbecome a visit, why ever didn't she say so? It would have been perfectly reasonable. Instead of going off in this peculiar way."

"Yes, that's it," I said, with such relief that it was almost joy. "She has gone to Ash House. She often talked of going."

The alternatives had been so vague and frightful that Lydia's departure to Aunt Welbecome's seemed quite normal, or would have seemed so but for its silent speed. Addy had seen her go to the attic early on Saturday morning (only yesterday) and was

sure now that she had been fetching a valise. That was all she had
taken. Her wardrobe was still full of clothes. Lydia would never
go away for good or even for long without taking her dresses. I
sat up, feeling better.

"Where else could she go?" It was reassuring to hear the dis-
passionate note in father's voice. "As to why she should leave in
such an inconsiderate way I cannot imagine. But it will do you no
harm to be separated for a while."

"Her feelings were hurt," I said boldly. "Lydia sent Mr. Graw
away because she thought he would stay on and abuse your kindness and you reproached her for it. You don't understand, father,
how much we disliked having him here and how we hated the
portrait."

It was a blunder to mention it.

"Where is it by the way? I saw that he had taken the easel,
naturally. Could he have taken the portrait too? He's a peculiar
fellow in some ways."

I pondered. This was no time to draw father's attention to any
of Lydia's misdemeanors.

"It's the sort of thing he would do," I said falsely.

"These artists cannot be judged by conventional standards."
Father was thinking no doubt of Chelsea. "It was foolish to fuss
about his habits. One has only to look at his sketches of Emberside to forgive him anything."

"I shall never forgive him," I declared, without defining to
myself the exact nature of his offence but with an emphasis and a
toss of the head I knew to be Lydia's.

Breakfast dragged to an end at last. I went out of doors. The
summer storm had blown itself out, leaving the lane strewn with
broken twigs, the air moist and cool. It was after all such a little
thing, I thought, responding to the vast curve of sky and the long
sweep of hills. She had gone off in a huff, that was all. We would
talk it over when she came back. Father had joined me at the
gate. From time to time he looked up the lane. Was he too expecting to see her come walking home, a trifle dishevelled, pouting
and smiling, glad to be back from wherever she had been?

"Perhaps I should have broached the subject of a housekeeper
more tactfully. It may have seemed to Lydia that I was taking
away her authority."

"She felt that you had turned against her and the way she did
things."

"That's absurd. I've always been very fond of Lydia. Haven't I treated her well?" He asked it anxiously, not in any spirit of injured merit.

"Until Mr. Graw came. He spoilt everything. And Lydia seemed to realise all at once that this was not her own home. She very much wants a home, I believe."

"But this is her home until she marries and that was why I wanted to have things on a proper footing so that nothing should stand in the way of her marrying well."

"Oh father, she didn't think of it like that."

It was not for me to tell him what Lydia had really wanted.

"I'll write to her," he said, "and to Mrs. Welbecome. We could ask the old lady to come for a visit. In fact to have her here might tide us over our difficulties for a time. Why didn't I think of it before? Better still, I'll go and see them and talk things over. Tomorrow."

While he consulted a Bradshaw, I went to the kitchen to give Addy her instructions for the day.

"There's more than one pair of hands can manage," she snapped. "I don't know, I'm sure."

It was my turn to rise to the occasion but Lydia's soaring spirit was not one of the attributes she had passed on to me. Apathetically I put on her sleeves and shelled a basin of peas. They were young and sweet but I was too depressed to eat more than two or three. Afterwards I found the beds still unmade, the plants unwatered, the breakfast china unwashed. Lydia had always washed the Derby cups and plates herself, first spreading a towel on the parlour table and fetching a bowl of water from the kitchen.

I was engaged in this ritual when father came to tell me that there was no direct connection by rail to Martlebury until Tuesday.

"That may be just as well. I shall have time to write and prepare Mrs. Welbecome for my visit. Can you find me her address?"

Lydia's writing desk stood on her chest of drawers with her letter case and bible. Together with the unopened tin of nut toffee I had bought her in Netherlaw and the sprig of mint in a green glass vase to discourage flies, they made it clear beyond all doubt that she had gone for only a little while. The impression was cheering. I sang a phrase or two from 'While in a shady grove', heroically resisted the nut toffee and scrupulously refrained from reading anything but the senders' addresses as I turned over her letters.

There were very few: two or three from Charlie: several from a school friend in Martlebury, Minnie Nash, and a wedding card. It would be pleasant for Lydia to meet Minnie again and talk over their schooldays in Aunt Welbecome's stately rooms amid the Sheraton and Chippendale furniture with the Lorne portraits looking down from the wall and the fabulous bird cage gleaming on the marquetry table. But only for a short time, for a very short time. I was all at once miserably aware of the unslept-in bed, and more gradually of the absence of any letter to Lydia from her aunt.

I lifted down the desk. The key was in the lock. The letter I sought might be in the inner cavity; but one glance at the sheet of notepaper lying white and candid on the red velvet made me close up the desk with a snap, resolved to meddle no further. There were only two words on the paper: Eugene, Eugene; as if Lydia had begun to write a note, then given up the attempt; or indulged in the stolen pleasure of simply writing his name.

"Ash House, Martlebury, should be sufficient direction," father said, unconscious as ever of the emotional tides beating beyond the study door and he would have written the letter there and then had not Addy come, panic-stricken, to tell us that a carriage had drawn up at the gate. Visitors at such a time were so shocking an affliction that fate seemed to have singled us out for chastisement and humiliation, for after Graw's inroads upon it, the larder was as nearly empty as is possible in a respectable household.

Fortunately the hired carriage set down no more than a single visitor, a bachelor friend of father's, Mr. Egbertson. He was visiting the neighbourhood after an absence of years and had taken the liberty of calling. His stay would be brief. No more than cake and wine was required. He would drive on to Oversay Hall to spend the day with Edwin Kirkdale, but he was happy to accept father's invitation to come to us for dinner and stay the night.

Addy and I sprang into action. A ham was boiled, a pair of ducklings sacrificed. I sped across the fields to Mrs. Wayland for advice and came back with a leg of lamb and a jug of white potato soup.

"Robert could have brought them," his mother said, "but he isn't back. For some reason he went back to Netherlaw on Friday. There was something he wanted to do there on Saturday evening, he said. He was in one of his silent moods and I didn't fuss. How long is Lydia to be away? So unfortunate, a visitor just at this time. But the holiday will do her good."

In looking out linen, concocting a custard pudding and decorating it with cherries and angelica, I had no time to think of Robert or even Lydia, except to wish fervently that she was there to deal with the emergency.

Apart from our ordeal in the kitchen, Mr. Egbertson's visit was uneventful but its effect was to be far-reaching. Not until long after did I realise how significantly his chance arrival had changed our lives: mine, father's and Lydia's. Oh, Lydia's most of all.

He had just left after luncheon on Monday when a package was delivered by hand: the photographs. Mr. Handiside's assistant had broken his journey by train to Bainsacre to bring them 'as Miss Penrose was so anxious to have them.'

My hand shook as I unwrapped the package from dread lest Mr. Handiside might have produced from under his black cloth yet another pair of strangers. One glance reassured me, though father was not spared the broken column and the flower pot. The two poses were much the same. In each, Lydia and I stood side by side, bolt upright as if held by invisible wires: staring ferociously out at the world: resolutely unsmiling: fearful, I remember, of bursting into hysterical giggles. There was nothing sensitive or delicate or artistic about Mr. Handiside's work. We looked so very like two people having a photograph taken and making no bones about it that I sighed with relief.

"The little goose," father said, looking over my shoulder. "We must have her back."

I slipped my arm through his.

"She is my dearest friend and truly, father, you couldn't have found anyone better to bring me up. Mother loved her too."

"I was wrong to criticise her." Father looked with amusement at Lydia's baleful glare. "It's just that she lacks restraint sometimes. Lydia is . . . not quite a lady, that's all."

"How can you say that, father, when she is so very particular about her gloves?" I have altered my definition of a lady since then and I have reason to think that father altered his too. "We have never done anything you might not like. Only one thing," I said, determined to wipe away all trace of deception from our

lives. "That was when we went to a Revival Meeting last year.
Lydia thought it best not to mention it, knowing how you feel
about Dissenters. But there was nothing you could have disap-
proved of. It was in a marquee over at Bainsacre . . ."

We had worn plain bonnets and neat dark shawls to conform
as closely as possible to the fashion of Dissent as Lydia imagined
it to be: and had resolved to take no part in the service, only to
creep in at the back to see what went on and to find out if possible
what it was that made Prue Bailey so good. But the pallid light
under the canvas roof, the strange dim green of the grass, the
rows of benches packed with tensely listening believers, all went
to our heads like wine (though this cannot have been intended)
and when the harmonium lumbered into the strains of 'Come,
sinners, to the gospel feast', sung to the tune of Fulda, no voices
were more fervently raised than ours, Lydia's as usual just a little
higher than the note, like the trill of a wayward lark.

Afterwards the clergyman who took the service spoke with
such sincerity in his deep, rich voice, of the infinite mercy of the
Lord towards sinners, that Lydia and I were spellbound. I had
not been aware of my spiritual danger but he made me feel safe.
Lydia told me that she felt purified and uplifted. We took a solemn vow to go to the next meeting at Bainsacre in two years'
time.

"I should like to speak to him," Lydia said. We had not caught
his name. "He's a good man."

But there were too many others of the same mind. A crowd
gathered round him in the field and we had to leave before our
turn came. But I carried away with me an impression of weary
souls revived by the promise of new life. The same vitalising
promise was breathed from green banks decked with primroses. I
felt it in the cool air, its sharp edge softened by the first breath of
spring. A blackbird after weeks of experiment, had found a brand
new song, confident and sweet, with the same note of salvation in
it so that spirit and sense were both uplifted and I seemed to float
dizzily into the violet sky.

We hurried home, gradually thinking less of our redeemed
state and more of the hot bread-and-butter pudding which Lydia
declared would be just the thing to round off the evening . . .

"But we didn't testify, father, I assure you. Lydia didn't think
you would like it."

Father roared with laughter. The happiness of that cool April evening at Bainsacre came surging back and warmed me to the tips of my fingers. Father cared for Lydia. I could tell. He would bring her back. We would be all the happier for having known what it meant to do without her. The blissful thought made me reckless.

"It was because she loves you, father, that Lydia went away. She loves you and thinks you don't love her. She didn't want to go."

I saw the astonishment in his eyes: the new tenderness in his face as he looked again at the photograph.

Then to my surprise Robert came in and stood just inside the door. He seemed to have lost his usual easy confidence; and he was behaving oddly, if not playing truant, by coming home on a Monday. I said so.

"It doesn't matter if they sack me for it," he said. "I wanted to find out what was going on here."

His pause, his whole manner, frightened me.

"Mother made me come to tell you in case you haven't heard. I went to Netherlaw station on Saturday night to see Charlie for the last time. That was why I stayed in Netherlaw."

"Was he in good spirits?" father asked.

"I didn't speak to him. He didn't see me. Lydia came running over the bridge."

"Then she must have caught the eleven forty-five to Martlebury. It stands in the bay."

Robert shook his head.

"He took her valise. They got into the Liverpool train. She's gone to Canada with Charlie."

7

Sheer sorrow, painful and prolonged, made me indifferent to other discomforts. I could bear father's angry reproach as he turned on me, knowing I had led him to betray a tenderness he now regretted.

"Don't speak of her," he said. "Don't ever speak of her again. She has disgraced herself. I always knew there was a—laxness in her. She has stuffed your mind with ideas that have no business to be there. We are better without her."

His mouth and eyes were hard: his voice was strident: he was quite shaken out of his unworldly mildness. I had never seen him in such a passion. He was beside himself, ashamed of his anger and more angry for being ashamed.

"It isn't what she wanted," I wailed. "She never wanted to marry Charlie."

"She'll have to marry him now."

He walked out of the room with quick, uncertain steps as if the rage had penetrated right down to his feet, and shut himself in the study. Had it not been for Robert, I would have sunk to the floor and let the misery overwhelm me. Not that he could offer any consolation, only the comfort of being there to talk to and of feeling, I soon discovered, a regret similar to mine.

"I'm sorry she's done it, for her sake, but it's Charlie I'm thinking of. He'll never come back. There's nothing to bring him back now that Lydia's with him."

As we talked about them, uncomfortably, my view of elopements was painfully revised. I had thought of a runaway marriage as the triumph of love over parental tyranny. In this case there were no parents, no tyranny and on Lydia's part, no love.

"Perhaps she'll change her mind about marrying him before it's too late."

Lydia often changed her mind.

"Ladies can't go off with men without marrying them," Robert was not the first to decree; and I knew that even if in father's eyes Lydia was not quite a lady, she would in this case, however tardily, behave like one.

They would be married at sea, we thought: a chilly, unstable ceremony with Lydia in travelling dress and a sea captain masquerading as a clergyman. I thought of the rose petals she had renounced, the lockets of hair, the Brussels lace and tulle; of the bridesmaid I would never be; and shed bitter tears.

I put the photographs in the frames she had bought, shrouded one in a silk scarf and laid it to rest in the depths of a drawer; and hung the other one as she had suggested on the wall opposite my bed where night and morning I could refer to it. For a while each sight of it renewed my grief. But it was difficult to impose the likeness of the old Lydia upon the very different creature her flight had turned her into. After a while, the young woman beside the broken column took on an air of unreality. It was not by looking at her that I could best remember Lydia.

In the confusion of Mr. Egbertson's visit father had not written to Mrs. Welbecome. The letter would have been kind and conciliatory but now he felt it his duty to acquaint her stiffly with the facts and assure her that the elopement had been quite unnecessary: there had been nothing to prevent a conventional marriage but Lydia's own regrettable lack of principle. He had always felt that she lacked proper seriousness. For Isobel's sake he could not be sorry that she had gone. I read the letter and knew it to be cruelly unjust but my resentment towards father was stronger than my instinct to defend Lydia. I sulked and said nothing. It didn't matter now, Mrs. Welbecome preserved the silence she had not broken, judging by Lydia's letter case, for years.

Mr. Egbertson's visit had another outcome. It clinched father's intention to take on more servants. His comfort had been threatened by the atmosphere of ill-concealed frenzy which even he could not ignore. A week or two later Ruby arrived to take over the heavier work from Addy. Mrs. Petway came in daily to help with the cooking. With Will Petway as groom and handyman, we were sufficiently well looked after for me to have more leisure than I had hoped for. Addy and I adapted ourselves to our new responsibilities at about the same rate. She became as faithful a servant as I have ever been blessed with.

By 'leisure' I mean freedom from household tasks. The old days of dreaming in the garden under my canopy of halcyon blue were over. In revenge, I have sometimes thought, for Lydia's misdeeds, father took my education in hand more resolutely than ever before. My geography, history and arithmetic were thoroughly overhauled and on the flimsy grounding in Latin he had managed to impart to me over the years, he now proposed to erect a sturdier knowledge of the classics.

If he had realised how shaky the foundation was, he might have been discouraged; but for a time his enthusiasm got the better of his judgment and at best his judgment was faulty. I must not be hard on father. He had inherited a fortune of exactly the size to limit his development. He was too well off to need a profession: not rich enough to travel and sharpen his mind by contact with educated equals. It made him idle, content enough but sometimes troubled by a sense of wasted opportunity. He was always more interested in schemes that could never be fulfilled than in those he could with moderate effort have carried out successfully.

He now began to speak openly of 'the son I never had' and to inflict on me the education my unborn brother was lucky enough to escape. The hours we spent in the study must have been as irritating to father as they were stupefying to me, but at least he felt that his wits were being sharpened. Mine, on the other hand, seemed to fall further and further into disarray.

"You'll have to tell him," Robert said when he had rapidly finished an exercise I had puzzled over for hours. "It isn't the least bit of use my doing them for you. He's sure to find out some day that you don't do them yourself."

"I know. But it makes him happier to think that I'm improving. It's uncomfortable to deceive him but it's just as uncomfortable in another way to try to do the exercise myself. I'm uncomfortable all the time now."

Robert had not been at home when I called to beg his help.

"He'll be at Hackets," Mrs. Wayland said. "He's always there," and it was there, after a short walk through the fields, that I found him.

The house took its name from the family who had lived there until its last member died and the property passed to Mrs. Wayland. It stood due east of Emberside at the same level below the ridge and close to the water line where springs broke from the limestone. The place had looked sadly neglected when I had last seen it some months before but I had no sooner opened the gate than I felt a change. Sheep had been put to graze in front of the house. Their constant cropping had reduced the turf to something like a lawn. A few new tiles redder than the old ones showed where the roof had been recently patched. The sound of hammering drew me to the kitchen end of the house where Robert was fixing boards across the doorway. The oak door lay on its back among the nettles, waiting to be repaired.

"I'm doing this to keep the sheep out," he explained. "It's a shame to let the place go to rack and ruin. It's been a fine house. Charlie said so. He always liked it."

"No one could live in it."

"Not yet."

I sat down on a stone quern and watched him. Mrs. Wayland had often said that the expense of repairing Hackets would be beyond her purse. Robert was apparently attempting the restoration singlehanded. It was, after all, his property or would be some day. Through the kitchen door I could see a rusted fireplace and an ancient stone sink fouled by birds. The whole place was so dank and ominously suggestive of bats, the task so hopeless, that I looked at Robert with new interest and was aware of something more in his manner than satisfaction in wielding a hammer. A spirit of dedication?

"You're doing it in memory of Charlie," I said respectfully.

"He isn't dead." Robert came and sat beside me. "But in a way you're right. At first I planned to improve things here in case he ever came back. I'm pretty certain now that he never will. But I've got into the habit of patching up here and there. When I have money I shall spend it on the house."

He took from his bulging pocket an old brass door knob and shaft and tried to fit them together. He had grown so much during the summer that his wrists stuck out a good two inches from his shirt cuffs and his jacket was far too tight across the shoulders; but these inconveniences did not rob him of the confident ease he seemed to have been born with. It rarely deserted him.

"No matter what he does," Lydia said once as she briskly mixed a dose of salt and water when Robert, whey-faced from eating green apples, lacked spirit to go home, "he always looks refined."

His deportment must have been severely tested on that occasion. I reminded him of it and he laughed.

"Why couldn't they have settled here?" he said.

I sighed, remembering the old days; then got out of my satchel an exercise book and Solomon's Latin Primer and handed Robert a pencil.

"You know how it will be, Isobel. When you've worked your way through old Solomon, your father will put you on to Caesar. The longer we go on like this, the more hot water you'll be in. When I leave school, I may not be able to help you."

There were difficulties enough as it was. Skill and forethought were needed to ensure that each Sunday evening he left me with a supply of work ready to copy out in my own hand. Moreover he was determined to leave school at Christmas and find some occupation, despite his mother's insistence that he should cram for Oxford.

"Why should a man spend his life in a study," he demanded, "when he could be out of doors doing some good to the land? These studious fellows miss half that's going on. I don't mean to be rude about your father, Isobel."

But I could only agree mournfully. Anyone but father would surely have discovered the iniquitous deception I was practising on him. Even he might find out at any moment. My days, especially if Robert deserted me, were numbered.

For an hour or two I yielded to the spell of the September afternoon, pretending it would last for ever. Robert walked homeward with me as far as the quarry, one of our childhood haunts where I had loved to play. It was natural, I suppose, to feel an affinity for the place. It was the source of our family prosperity, or one of the sources. Nature had provided my great-grandfather, Samuel Penrose, with a number of assets within a few miles of Emberside, which he had bought for an old song in 1770: limestone to quarry; coal in the hills above to fuel the kilns; a steady demand for mortar, for lime to feed the thin, acid soil of intake fields, and for crushed stone to make and mend roads. He had made the most of his opportunities. By the time our family industry was threatened by the big rival company of Lessings at Netherlaw, my grandfather was rich enough to retire at fifty and enjoy a leisured country life.

The quarry had been scooped out at the base of the long hillside. Close to the upper limit of the excavations a green promontory reached out, a favourite viewpoint overlooking the great semicircle of ravaged stone and its grass-grown floor sixty feet below.

"Be careful," Robert said as I sat down by the mountain ash that leaned perilously over the edge. "You're not safe there. There's been another landslide since that storm in June."

He pointed to a new gash in the rock face and a huddle of stones among the seeding willowherb at its base. I shuffled back a few inches but only to please him. There was not the slightest danger. I had sat there many a time.

When he had gone, I lay face down and looked over into the quiet amphitheatre enclosed in its walls of layered stone, in colour paler than honey, deeper than milk. Far below and to the right through a screen of birch leaves one caught a glimpse of the brick-arched kilns, mysterious tunnels built into the escarpment, and beyond them the limeburner's hut. A robin perched on a bough above me. Its plaintive song in that deserted place awoke in me a mournful sense of loss and change.

Not so long ago Lydia would have been with me, and if Lydia, Charles, and if Charles, Robert. Here we had picnicked and played hide-and-seek and afterwards gone home in the twilight to the warm house. I closed my eyes, straining memory to the utmost in an effort to bring back one of those lost companionable evenings. But the ebbing tide of time refused to flow. Blurred by distance, our remembered shapes seemed as insubstantial as the figures in one of Charlie's shadow shows. In Lydia's solo at the piano and Robert's dignified rendering of 'How Sleep the Brave', I heard an elegiac note, wistful as the robin's.

Even the robin left me. No one came here now. Bramble and thorn and guelder rose had overgrown the path which twisted, steep as a spiral stair, to the quarry floor. A stone slipped and went hurtling down the precipice in a deliberate, suicidal way as if it wanted to fall. I peered over and was suddenly terrified by the perpendicular drop. Jumping up, I felt the turf move under my feet. Robert had been right as usual.

It was no fun to be there on my own, or in the pasture or by the river. I went home because there was nowhere else to go. Could even Emberside—coming out of the shade I saw it in sunshine—could even Emberside be changed?

Only to become lovelier still. Every inch of it, stone, tile and wood, bore evidence of the centuries it had stood there, serene and lasting as its fields and trees. Each year had brought a richer mellowing. If age had given it beauty, then time could only add to it. I saw no flaw in such reasoning any more than in the

cloudless blue of late summer behind our chimneys; or the pale
amber of the south wall above the pear tree and its ripening fruit;
or the last profusion of michaelmas daisies and roses under the
window.

In the field beyond the house the wheat had ripened and been
harvested. I remembered how Charlie had walked away through
its green waves and a sudden baseless conviction came to me that
we would hear from them soon: Lydia would write for my birthday in October, my sixteenth.

But no letter came. Summer faded into autumn and autumn
into winter. With only Sambo for a companion the days seemed
long: and he was growing eccentric in his old age. One night in
the following spring he wakened me with such a burst of whimpering and short barks that I went to the landing window and
looked down into the yard. It was a night of extraordinary
beauty, the sky brilliantly studded with stars. The coach house
steps, the water butt and the kennel were clearly visible and
Sambo straining at his chain, his nose and paws evidently pushed
between the gate bars though the gate itself was just out of sight.
At first I thought he must have smelt or seen a fox; but the
staccato barks were joyful rather than aggressive as if his dreams
had been pleasantly disturbed.

I pushed open the casement and discovered the cause of his
excitement: the faint sounds of someone lingering at the gate: the
movement of feet and, I thought, a voice. A stout padlock secured us from intruders at night and I was not in the least nervous. Besides, I recollected almost at once that it was April 8th,
the day of the Revival Meeting which had been held again at
Bainsacre after an interval of two years. In the morning a few
decently dressed folk had passed our gate carrying hymn books,
bibles and provisions wrapped in coloured handkerchiefs. Some
good soul returning home late from the Meeting must have spoken to Sam, who being himself of a nonconformist temperament,
had responded with suitable enthusiasm.

In view of all that had happened, I had absolved myself from
the vow Lydia and I had taken. In any case it would have been
uncomfortable to go alone. But the memory of our uplifting experience at the last Meeting was still vivid. I could imagine some
devout believer walking home, strengthened in faith by that divine pattern of stars.

Again I heard or thought I heard a voice. Sambo's whimpering had become quite ecstatic as if he had relapsed into a second puppyhood. The light footsteps went quickly up the hill and I soon ceased to hear them.

Though we knew nothing of it at Emberside until afterwards, the Revival had turned out to be one of unusual fervour. It must have been through Mrs. Petway, I think, that the details filtered through to us though she had not been there herself. The same visiting minister who had so impressed us two years ago had preached on the parable of the Good Samaritan and many conversions were made. When the Meeting ended there was a spontaneous outburst of singing outside the marquee and people went away through the woods and along the field paths still singing:

> Long my imprisoned spirit lay
> Fast bound in sin and nature's night;
> Thine eye diffused a quickening ray,
> I woke. The dungeon flamed with light;
> My chains fell off, my heart was free,
> I rose, went forth and followed Thee.

The occasion was talked of for years.

"This religious excitement is all very well," was father's rather sour comment, "if it doesn't unsettle people and make them forget their station." He may have been thinking of Prue who had always irritated him. But I thought how Lydia and I would have thrilled to the quickening ray and the falling off of chains and I quite wished that I had gone.

Another summer passed and another birthday, bringing no word from Lydia. Nothing was said about the older person who was to have taken her place. Occasionally there was talk of my going away to a finishing school. Soon I would be too old.

"There's something erratic about you, Isobel," father said. "At times your work is surprisingly good; but sometimes I wonder if you have the smallest understanding of what I say."

His sense of duty had sustained him for longer than might have been expected. Somehow we had advanced, if our lurching progress could be so described, through Caesar's Gallic Wars. Robert had done his best to help but he had found a position with a well established firm of land-agents and valuers, Adam and Jayson, with the promise of a partnership later on. His work took him farther afield than Netherlaw and though he often came home, his visits were short.

He never knew—I never told him—how much those visits meant to me. I used to look forward to them for weeks; then in no time at all they were over, he had gone and I was alone again, scarcely knowing what it was that I missed; taking it for granted that he would come back.

As Lydia had foreseen, I did have to let out the bodice of my lilac dress, which I wore for a while longer before giving it, I remember now, to Addy for her young sister. How clearly those scraps of material brought back the vanished scene! As I said, I found them only the other day in the third drawer down where they had lain undisturbed for years; faded, useless, unwanted as the memories they revived. I shall never use them. Barège, with its mixture of silk and woollen threads, is a little too loose in the weave for quilting.

But it was surprisingly difficult to drop them into the wastepaper basket; foolish to fish them out again the very next moment and carefully smooth away the creases as if the touch of my fingers could restore the girl I used to be when I wore the dress. Sentiment, I believe, has been too strong an influence in my life; and it was sheer sentiment that made me fold the pieces and put them back in the drawer. But time takes so much away. One cleaves instinctively to the little it leaves behind.

A few grey rosemary leaves clung to my skirt. I picked them off one by one and held them in my palm, remembering, with painful tenderness, those far-off days at Emberside: the lonely hours when I sat by the fire, companionless, too young to be already looking to the past to supply my happiest thoughts.

I used to wish as I sat stitching through the dull, silent evenings, that some unexpected event would rescue us from our solitude; and when father stoically suggested that we should proceed from Caesar to Cicero, I wished even more fervently that he would find some other interest.

Both wishes, as it happened, were granted and many a time I was to long for the uneventful days I had wished away.

8

For once Sambo refused pointblank to come for a walk. I had unhooked the chain from his collar and taken it for granted that he would follow when I set off for Limmergill. At the field gate I discovered my error. He was sitting in the lane, gazing intently up the hill. When I called, he agitated his tail without actually wagging it and did not budge.

I soon found that he had more sense than his mistress. The path was muddy, the grass soaking wet. The November day with a suggestion of mist was not inviting. I gave up my walk. But when I tried to coax Sambo back to his kennel, he whined apologetically and stayed where he was, his muzzle turned towards Saxon's Gate, his nostrils quivering. Then to my consternation he pointed his nose at the cold sky and howled, a long melancholy lament that chilled my blood.

Whatever unseen cause had stirred him to this doleful behaviour, Sambo seemed so dispirited that I thought he would lie down under the bare trees and die. He offered no resistance when I dragged him back to the kennel and chained him up. Reluctant to face another dull evening in the drawing room, I loitered out of doors, watching the cloud thicken over the hills and the meeting point of road and sky draw nearer.

So that this time I saw them coming. At first only one figure materialised from the mist halfway down the hill. Recognition was instant even before the second dark shape came trudging after. There was no time for surprise. I had always known they would come back. I could have run into the house and bolted all the doors as in a dream one might; but the inescapable reality of their return kept me standing hopelessly at the gate, wondering what fresh disaster they would bring this time.

They walked slowly as if the bundles they carried had grown heavier in the eighteen months since they had left; and when they came close enough I saw that Graw was altered. He was so thin that his clothes hung on him as on a scarecrow; and they were not the same clothes. He wore a narrow brimmed hat and a shabby ulster too short for him. Even with the easel and portfolio he looked less like an artist than a pedlar down on his luck.

"Miss Penrose." He raised his hat. The day was cold but his brow was beaded with perspiration. "I trust you are well. And Mr. Penrose?" The conventional greeting was in fact a question. He asked it anxiously and at once went on: "We have been in some trouble, my wife and I. We are greatly in need—of rest and shelter."

At first I saw him through a haze of panic and distaste but his voice was, as always, sufficiently reassuring to revive in me some notion of decorum. I must have murmured a greeting, however grudging. As he leaned heavily against the wall, I involuntarily pushed open the gate and then regretted even so slight a gesture of hospitality. Once, he might have stalked inside with the confidence of an invited guest. He stayed where he was. With a gasp I could not restrain, I saw that his face was pitted with small scars of fading red. His eyelids were crusted and sore-looking.

"We have been ill, of a fever."

"Both of you?"

She had caught up with him at last and silently laid down her bundle. I had never seen her at close quarters and couldn't really see her now. She wore her bonnet pushed back but her head was tightly swathed in a knitted shawl and she kept it bowed, so that only a thin triangle of face was visible in a diminishing perspective. Yet, from no more than that first imperfect view of her, I felt something unexpected in her appearance: unexpected (this is the curious part) not in the sense of being unusual but familiar. I must be mistaken. There could be nothing familiar in the outlandish collection of garments she was wearing, from the ancient green paletot which had obviously been made years ago for a much bigger woman, to her worn-down Balmoral boots.

"Have you come far?"

Graw hesitated.

"From the other side of Martlebury."

I guessed then, from having read of the epidemic in the newspaper, what the fever had been, though I had not seen its ravages before. Instinctively I drew back, then felt ashamed. It was out of the question to leave them there, much less to turn them away.

"I'll tell father."

I burst into the study with the news.

"They've come back. The Graws."

Father had been sitting with his feet on the fender with his eyes closed: but he jumped up at once and hurried out as if he was pleased at the prospect of a change of any kind.

"Well, Graw." He held out his hand. "So you're back. Good God, man!" as Graw turned his scarred face—"You've had smallpox." He looked sharply at the silent Mrs. Graw.

"My wife. Betsy." Graw blurted out the introduction baldly without a trace of his former grand manner and went on breathlessly as if every word cost him an effort: "We fell ill six weeks ago and by a miracle have both survived, as you see. But we are not quite able, not just yet . . ." Into the depths of his brown eyes came a look of consternation that was absolutely genuine. " . . . to go back to our old—er—nomadic way of life."

Father may have seen the haunted look and heard the note of whimsicality Graw tried rather desperately to sound; but in any event he would have done exactly what he did then because he was incapable of doing anything else.

"Isobel, tell one of the maids to light a fire in the coach house and prepare some food. You can stay there, Graw, until you and your good lady recruit your health. Of course I must ask you to keep away from us all for a while."

The maids brought chairs for them and they waited in the wood-shed while the coachman's rooms were got ready. I remember how they sat like a pair of glazed Staffordshire figures, not speaking but expressing in every line and feature a weary gratitude for the blessing of being no longer in motion. Fires were lit in both rooms and a few comforts added to the simple furnishings: a warming pan, two armchairs, hot water, food and mulled wine. Father came out again to give his approval. Graw wrung his hand and stumbled up the steps after his wife. What was it about her that stirred a memory, an echo of former times long ago, long before she had come the first time?

"What a tragedy!" Father was deeply moved. "I'm glad they chose to come here. One has a duty to such people and especially to an artist of Graw's calibre. Do you remember how he seemed to love this place? And here he has come like a wounded bird for refuge." Having struck this poetic vein father retired to the study and during the next few days composed a sonnet entitled: 'The

Broken Wing'. As a young man he had toyed with the idea of
becoming a poet.

"I only hope," Addy said, "that they'll soon get their strength
back. With winter coming on . . ."

She had no need to say more. We understood each other. The
advantage of restoring the Graws to marching order was clear to
us both. The difficulty was to hasten them back to health without
making them so comfortable that they would never leave.

For a few days we scarcely saw them. Food was left on the
steps in the dishes they put out for it. Ruby and Addy and Will
Petway picked up snippets of information. Graw had been given
a commission to paint a series of parish churches. The fever had
come upon them at a village about ten miles south of Martlebury.
They had been found literally by the wayside, by a minister's
wife: a selfless creature she must have been, who tended them in
an empty cottage outside the village, when even the local surgeon
made excuses not to go near them. She had fed and clothed them
and given them a small sum of money to set them on their way.
As father said, with such an example before us we should exert
ourselves a little for the Graws.

Some of these details must have been wrung from the usually
silent Betsy, and in answer to questions. She volunteered no information. Graw had not exaggerated her shyness—if shyness it
was that kept her so mysteriously remote. For a few days in
December the weather turned bright and crisp. The sunshine
tempted Graw into the stable yard and then the garden but Betsy
never appeared except to put out dishes and collect food. I wondered if she had suffered even more grievously from the fever
than her husband had done. Once I caught a glimpse of her face
from the dairy. Though still swathed in the brown shawl, it
seemed unscarred. Again a fleeting memory of some kind
brought me almost to the point of recognition. Something about
her was familiar. While I pondered, she vanished.

As time went by I accepted their presence with a sort of fatal-
ism and even sometimes yielded to the illusion that they had
always been there. One morning before breakfast I went into the
study to do the dusting. No one else was allowed to touch father's
papers. Addy was on her knees laying the fire.

"It's like old times," she said grimly—and sniffed, not only in
dudgeon but because the room reeked of tobacco smoke. There

were brandy glasses and a half empty bottle on the table. "He's got his foot in the door again."

I could not speak, being all at once overcome by a more heart-felt longing for Lydia than I had experienced for a long time.

If only she had been there to toss her pink-ribboned head, open the window with a flourish and flounce out of the room to wash the glasses with her own hands as she used to do! The memory made me thoughtful. By this time I had exchanged a few words with Graw and had listened while he strolled in the garden talking to father; but I had never once heard him mention Lydia.

How had he proposed to deal with her when he came back to Emberside, like a wounded bird? I found myself eyeing the brandy bottle with cynical mistrust, for all father's poetic senti-ments. Had he been relieved to find her gone, or too contemptu-ous, or sick, to care? I was old enough, now that the heat and flame of it had died, to realise that the battle between them had probably been less momentous to Graw than it had been to Lydia —and so to me. All the same they had been enemies. Surely he would never forget how she had burned his picture. His expres-sion as he watched had been murderous. The thought was un-pleasant. Deeply as I was now missing her all over again, I was glad that Lydia had slipped out of his clutches, though only just. They had left Emberside within an hour or two of each other and had gone, very likely, in the same direction. If Robert had not seen her himself, safe in Charlie's arms, I could have imagined, with a shudder, that she and the Graws might have met again out there in the dark as she dragged her valise through the rain-soaked fields . . .

Graw must, however, have mentioned her to father.

"I've paid Graw for the watercolours," he said. "He tried to refuse the money but naturally I insisted. You obviously didn't know, but he told me about the portrait. Lydia took it upon herself, if you please, to burn it, before the man's eyes. It was an extraordinarily insensitive thing to do but like her, I'm afraid. I must say Graw shows very little resentment. He wouldn't have told me if I hadn't asked straight out what happened to it."

"He must have been surprised to hear that Lydia has left us." I spoke awkwardly. He had forbidden me to speak her name and so far I had obeyed, though from reasons more complicated than mere obedience.

"Er—as a matter of fact, I can't say that he was. He knew. I concluded that you or one of the maids had told him."

"Well," Addy said when I approached her on the subject, "I never mentioned Miss Lorne to him but he mentioned her to me. 'So Miss Lorne has left,' he says. 'Miss Lorne has gone to Canada', I told him. 'She's lucky to have gone so far away, as things have turned out', I says, and give him a look. 'Oh, to Canada,' he says in his mocking way. The smallpox hasn't improved his looks but he hasn't changed much in other ways. He'll be his old self again soon, you'll see, miss."

Though she was shrewd enough in most matters, Addy's prediction was a little wide of the mark. Graw did regain his swagger in spite of the bedraggled state of his secondhand clothes, which had been begged for him by the minister's wife who had befriended him. The too short ulster and narrow brimmed hat sat so awkwardly upon him that father declared it was for his own sake that he sent Graw to Netherlaw to buy himself more suitable clothes. Then new cloak and slouch hat restored his dignity.

"We must encourage him to take up painting again," father said. "Naturally he will feel a loss of power after all he's been through but the sooner he goes back to his easel the better, considering his age."

What his age was I never knew. He must have been in middle life and probably looked older than his years, especially since his illness. In response to father's encouragement he began to make sketches and one fine winter morning set up his easel by the wicket in the west wall of the garden. I came quietly down the path and was startled to find him there, sitting with his head in his hands. Presently, with a deliberate effort he took out a handkerchief, carefully wiped his eyes and looked steadily at the west gable. Sambo's growl disturbed him. He got up, and stood in the sun with his head stiffly poised like the reptile Lydia had declared him to be, but an older, wearier reptile.

"Pray go on, Mr. Graw." My one thought was to escape. I glanced at the blank paper. "You were just beginning. I won't interrupt."

"I have had some difficulty." He wiped his eyes again and looked at the house through half-closed lids. "The light . . ."

His obvious discouragement, the absence of any wish to impress, were disarming.

"The light is very bright this morning," I agreed. Indeed the sun glittered on the grass where a touch of rime still lingered, and struck crystalline sparks from the stones of the wall. "Quite bright enough for a sunshade, if it were not winter."

"You find it so?" He turned to me with eager relief, still screwing up his eyes as if to focus them. "I must wait. And yet, if I could have caught the old place in this mood, what a picture it would have made!"

He must have seen it with his inward eye, the winter beauty of Emberside heightened to a perfection I could not even imagine without his help. At the very moment when he must have realised that his powers were failing, I felt in him the pure aspiration of his calling, as if I shared with him a glimpse of the ineffable, all that is left to an artist when skill of hand or eye deserts him.

He sat down, pulled his hat over his brow and began to work quickly with an air of confidence.

"You shouldn't sit here in the cold, Mr. Graw. You have been very ill."

He half rose to acknowledge my departure without looking away from the easel but a few minutes later from my window I saw him throw down the pencil and bury his face in his hands again. It occurred to me to rummage out the old green umbrella from the cupboard under the stairs. He accepted it gratefully but had no opportunity of using it. Next day the weather changed. Snow and rain kept us mainly indoors and my encounters with Graw were not of a kind to encourage the sympathy I had briefly felt for him.

Inevitably, father and he spent the stormbound days together. At first Graw's visits were limited. He dined with us two or three times a week and left when he had taken a glass of port. I grudgingly admitted that the company was good for father. When he joined me in the drawing room he was lively and talkative. The talk was often about Graw: his views on Reform: the clever suggestion he had made for solving the Irish question: his interpretation of Rossetti's St. George and the Princess; but there father had been able to set him right. They shared an admiration for Disraeli though naturally Graw could not feel for the man as did father, who was also a widower. Storms had delayed the newspapers and we had just heard the news of Lady Beaconsfield's death on December 15th.

Gradually Graw's visits became more frequent. He dined with us every evening and stayed later. The range of his advice narrowed from the Houses of Parliament to our own house, from the national purse to father's.

"Graw thinks I'm losing an opportunity by keeping so much money in the Funds. In my position he would be more inclined to speculate. He knows a surprising amount about the Anglo-French Marezzo Marble Company, I find."

I began to dread seeing in father's eyes a certain look of excitement, stimulated not only by Graw but by the brandy they drank together in the evenings. Alone in my small circle of lamplight by the drawing room fire, I used to hear them talking and laughing too loudly in the study. Once, from the stairs, I watched them come out. Graw was flushed and confident. Father stumbled over the doormat and laughed rather foolishly, waving his candlestick and dropping grease on the hall chest.

"Graw has made a most interesting suggestion," he told me the next morning. "He thinks the time may be ripe for opening up the limestone trade again. He really has a very good grasp of the various processes. It hadn't occurred to me that there might still be coal to be got out of Limmergill Fell."

I wondered anxiously what knowledge Graw could have of our local resources. He must be less well informed even than father who, so far as I knew, had never taken the smallest interest in either coal or limestone. My uneasiness drove me to the heroic step of reminding father that my lessons had been neglected for a few days.

"No matter," he said expansively. "A short rest will do you good. We have kept too closely to our studies, you and I. There's more in life than books. Ah, here comes Graw."

They retired to the study and though it was only eleven o'clock, father rang for brandy and later for a tray of luncheon. I saw him no more that day.

Next morning he came down late and complained that the fire smoked and the room was cold.

"Don't, I beg of you, worry me about your lessons, Isobel," he said irritably though I had not spoken. "You can surely find other things to do."

Snow had fallen again in the night. It clung to the window panes, darkening the house and limiting the view of garden and leaden sky. I was sick to death of sewing. By no amount of ingenuity could another stitch be added to the embroidered flower garden which had occupied my spare time for more than a year.

Without help I could not stretch and frame it. Mrs. Wayland would have lent a hand if it had been possible to walk to Limmergill House and we could have gossiped a little in her comfortable parlour. To talk to anyone at all had become a craving.

"I've made up my mind," father said, looking with distaste at a boiled egg, "to employ Graw as my agent. He'll never be able to support himself as an artist. We can't let him go back to the hand-to-mouth style of life he's been leading. I can manage to pay him a modest salary. It will be worth a good deal to me to be free of worry about practical matters."

"What will he do, father?"

"Oh, er, see to the rents and that sort of thing. There are two or three fields to be re-let for grazing, or I might sell. Ready cash can be put to work and bring in more than a bit of pasture, as Graw says."

As father's agent, Graw would be here for ever: for the rest of my life. Every morning I would hear him come through the kitchen as at that very moment he came. Each day I would feel his presence everywhere in the house, even in rooms he had never entered. A longing for release drove me to put on a hooded cloak and pattens and open the garden door. The air was bitterly cold but fresh and clean. I walked over the untrodden snow to the archway leading to the stable yard.

A movement between the coachman's yellow curtains reminded me that I was not the only one who lacked a companion. Betsy Graw had remained so completely withdrawn that she might have ceased to exist. All at once I was consumed with curiosity to find out what she did all day: how she felt and thought. I went up the steps and knocked on her door.

9

My tap produced no answer. If anything the silence was more intense as if small movements had suddenly ceased.

"Mrs. Graw?"

I pressed the latch and stepped into the living room. She was sitting by the fire, staring at me. Her eyes were very light and wide. A tiny flicker of my old superstitious dread of the woman revived; but I was more sensible now. Besides, in so far as her enormous eyes expressed anything at all, they were startled. Could she possibly be afraid of me?

"I called to ask how you are, Mrs. Graw. Have you quite recovered from your illness?"

She nodded without taking her eyes from me.

"No, please. Do sit still." But she had not intended to rise, only with a trance-like movement of her arm to set down the iron spoon she was holding. "I just wondered . . ."

Why had I come? I looked round in some embarrassment. The room was clean. A plate stood on the shelf above the oven. It was there that she had laid the spoon after stirring the pot that simmered on the bar. I could not identify its contents from their smell, a heady, aromatic perfume which had nothing to do with food. "Are you quite comfortable here in this cold weather?"

Her wide-eyed, feline gaze had not altered. She seemed a creature of slow responses. "The woman's an imbecile," I thought, and had turned to go when she astonished me by saying in a low, ardent voice:

"Sometimes I seem as if I'm in heaven, Miss Penrose."

"Oh, I'm so glad. Then you must be feeling better."

I sat down in Graw's chair, prepared to talk but alas, the outburst had apparently exhausted her powers of conversation. Talking may be unnecessary in heaven for all I know. A chat with Mrs. Graw was plainly out of the question. Nothing I said drew from her more than a nod or a muttered yes or no, until worn out by the fruitless effort, I got up. She opened the door, the one positive act I had seen her engage in, and suddenly spoke again. Her voice was husky, from disuse perhaps.

"Simeon says it's best not to talk."

"Oh, I see."

Since her statement did not fit into any conversational groove, I was at a loss and answered lightly as if she had spoken about the weather. But afterwards I was to give a good deal of thought to the question of why it was better not to talk and about what, in particular.

Mrs. Graw's deep breathing suggested that she was labouring to bring forth more information in defiance of Simeon. At last it came.

"Only don't give him money, Miss Penrose. Don't ever give him money."

"Your husband? Why not?"

She was in deadly earnest. Her great eyes—they were too colourless to be called blue, too yellow to be called grey, too translucent to be hazel—whatever their shade, they blazed so that the upper part of her face was all light. I thought she trembled. But she produced no reason for this extraordinary request, or warning. Whether or not she watched me as I went back to the house, when I turned to look back, the panes between the yellow curtains were blank and lifeless.

She was in heaven in old Grimshaw's dreary quarters with a draught whistling under the door and steel engravings of long dead pugilists on the walls because previously (the conclusion was obvious) she had been in hell. Awestruck, I contemplated the horrors, so far as I could imagine them, of her wandering life: the possible disadvantages, to use no harsher term, of being married to Graw; the uncertainty of her future; and I felt ashamed of ever having been discontented. As an act of atonement I sent across some of mother's warm nightdresses and two petticoats. At the same time I was conscious of difficulties ahead. Was it right—would it be possible—to turn a woman out of heaven?

"She's always dosing herself with herbs," Addy remarked when she had delivered the underwear; and added mysteriously, "Well, I can't say I blame her. However would she manage? It's bad enough with just the two of them."

Betsy had some skill, we discovered, in the use of herbal reme-

dies. As spring drew on she took to wandering along the lanes
with a basket I had given her. Once or twice we almost met but if
possible she would sidle away under cover of the hedgerow as if
in dread of having to talk.

Thanks to her concoctions of speedwell and eyebright or to
liberal doses of Lamplough's Pyretic Saline supplied by father,
Graw's skin and eyes improved. At least the soreness and inflam-
mation left them but it was evident that his sight was deteriorat-
ing, whether as a result of his illness or from some other cause.
He did try to paint but seemed unable to recapture the delicacy of
his earlier work. The few pictures he showed us had a fierce
boldness of line and colour that somehow gave an impression of
despair. As his health improved without restoring his skill, he
grew more reckless in speech and manner. His behaviour to father verged on impudence. He came to the table when he pleased,
ordered second helpings and helped himself freely from the de-
canter. It was not unusual to find him lounging in the parlour in
the middle of the day.

One morning—it was early in May—for the first time for
months I took my needlework to the summer-house. Under its
fluted white arch I stopped, sickened by the smell of pipe smoke
and signs of spittle on the tiled floor.

"I can't bear it," I thought, too deeply revolted for tears. "It's
beyond bearing."

I put on an apron, fetched a bucket of water and with my own
inexpert hands scrubbed the seat, walls and floor until they smelt
austerely of carbolic; but all my pleasure in the place was gone. I
never sat there again. The incident simplified and coarsened my
attitude to Graw. It became one of sheer physical revulsion.

It was wrong, inhuman even, to feel disgust instead of compassion for the man. I have to remind myself that I was young and
lonely. For most of the time there were only the maids to talk to
and I could not discuss with them what they must long since
have seen for themselves: the change in father. His fine features
and fair complexion thickened and grew florid. His once thoughtful blue eyes were either empty of expression or unnaturally
elated. He neglected his beard. When I pointed out stains on his
velvet jacket, he answered irritably. His temper had never been so
uncertain. The books littering his table lay unopened. He could
settle to nothing until he heard Graw's arrival.

"Is that Graw? Come in, come in," he would call, as if the day had only taken on a purpose.

By this time he had begun to pay Graw a salary. I first heard of it when he mentioned that Graw preferred to be paid monthly rather than quarterly. It was too late then to pass on Mrs. Graw's warning. Besides, she was not a person whose advice would influence father. But slow-witted as she was, she had spoken from experience. With money in his pocket, Graw had more freedom. He used it to make daily visits to the Cross Keys and went several times a week to Netherlaw where, Addy thought, he patronised billiard rooms and gaming tables.

"It's absurd," Robert said bluntly when at last the paths were dry again and I could visit at Limmergill House. "Your father has no need of an agent. And why pick on a travelling artist who knows nothing of business? If he did, he wouldn't be the penniless pauper he is."

"You mustn't worry Isobel." Mrs. Wayland patted my hand. "We're only too glad to see her. You must come more often, dear. Are you eating well? I believe you're thinner."

Robert brought me a glass of negus and sat down beside me.

"The last thing I want to do is to worry Isobel. But it would have been a pleasure to me to help Mr. Penrose in any of his affairs connected with the land and tenants, as an act of friendship. As for the idea of quarrying again, it's quite out of the question. Mr. Penrose could never compete with Lessing. I hope" —he disregarded his mother's warning frown as if he felt the subject too important to neglect—"I hope Graw doesn't handle your father's money."

I was almost sure that he did, having seen him fill in a banker's order in payment of an account; and I had an uncomfortable feeling that father had transferred money from the Funds to the Anglo-French Marezzo Marble Company. It seemed disloyal to mention these errors of judgment. I said nothing. In spite of my worries, it was pleasant to be with the Waylands, to feel summer coming on and persuade myself that things would improve.

"I wonder"—a deliberation in Mrs. Wayland's manner and her glance at Robert made me wonder if they had been talking about me—"if your father would consider letting you go away to school. He talked of it at one time."

"But I'm much to old."

"Seventeen!" Mrs. Wayland laughed. "I hadn't thought of you

in a classroom with a slate. My friend Mrs. Haley is quite intimate with Mrs. Hurst, the Principal of Beech Grove House in
Martlebury. She takes three or four young ladies as parlour
boarders, as well as her younger pupils. They have the advantage
of a little society and music and French lessons from visiting
masters."

"It would be pleasant for you to be with other girls, Isobel,"
Robert said as he walked home with me. "Mother will mention it
to Mr. Penrose if you don't care to."

When I made no response, he tactfully turned to other topics.
It was no lack of enthusiasm that kept me silent. To escape to
Beech Grove House would be delightful, a happy solution to all
my problems, save one, father. Whereas he might be safely left to
his own devices, could he be safely left to Graw's?

We went home by way of Hackets. In June it had a more genial
look. We rescued a venturesome lamb from the stream which
murmured between sprouting ferns at the east end of the garden.
The lilac bloom was over but a newly planted rose had already
climbed to the stone mullions of the front windows. I recognised
it as the very rose that grew so profusely at Emberside, covering
the house front with its pink blooms.

"They've thrown away the finest house in Limmergill." Robert
assumed that I would know who 'they' were. "And for what? A
log cabin. All very well in its way . . ."

I tried once more to visualise Lydia's new way of life, drawing
upon recollections of mocassins and beads seen at a Church ba-
zaar and pictures of sledges drawn by fierce dogs between mighty
trees in a cool forbidding land. The random images gave way to a
vision bright in all its details of Lydia making the snow lady and
laying her own pink cheek against the lady's white one: both of
them beautiful: the one radiant with life: the other cold with the
pallor of death. The visionary moment passed. I was finding it
increasingly difficult to hold on to Lydia. Was it time to let her
go?

"You're shivering."

"It was father I thought she would have married."

"She would have looked after him, I suppose," Robert said
briefly. He declined to come in. Hearing voices in the study, I did
not urge it. The atmosphere of the house was no longer inviting;
but I was sad to see him go and felt the contrast between his

courteous and gentle manner and the growing raffishness of the
two men with whom I spent my days.

The drawing room with its velvet chairs and footstools sociably
arranged was no place for a girl doomed to sit alone. In the
parlour one was not safe from Graw. I went up to my room and
knelt on the bed, to look over the brass rails at Lydia on the wall;
unsmiling, resolute, positive. She had done the wrong things, especially the one big thing of going away without a word, but she
had never been passive. If she had stayed she would have looked
after father. By a natural sequence of ideas I moved on to the full
realisation that father, like a child or a simpleton, needed looking
after: thence to sad acceptance of the fact that he was a failure.
An outburst of laughter from the study filled me with angry
contempt for both men. They were alike, two failures, neither of
them able to see himself as good for nothing.

The study door opened and closed. Graw must be leaving. I
waited for him to go, my head bowed on the bedrail, and was
roused with a great start to find him at my own open door.

"His lordship"—he jerked his head towards the study. His
pitted skin had a purplish tinge. He laughed—"is not quite
able . . ." He lurched into the room. "No matter. I'll come and
talk to you, Isobel, my dear."

The familiarity was new. It warned me that another protective
barrier had gone. I was embarrassed and slid to my feet on the
other side of the bed. He came nearer and stroked my hair.

"Pretty," he said.

There was something wolfish about his long teeth as Addy
would have agreed.

"If you touch me again, Mr Graw," I began formally,
"I'll . . ."

The threat was never uttered. What could I threaten him with?
The bedroom fire irons were flimsy affairs. Father was useless. I
felt the impossibility of calling the servants. But it was for none of
these reasons that my voice trailed into silence.

Graw had forgotten me. He had turned his head and found
himself looking into Lydia's eyes. The effect was extraordinary.
He became absorbed in her as he had been that night in the hot
bright kitchen when they had glared at each other with such
single-minded fury that not only I but the whole world had become invisible.

He drew himself slowly upright from the bedrail where he had

been leaning, swallowed some obstruction in his throat and became—astonishingly—sober. Certainly the impudent high spirits
left him as the mottled purple faded from his face. Pale and quiet,
he looked at her, half closing his eyes to see better; and he seemed
in some unaccountable way to shrink so that his physical being
ceased altogether to disgust me: ceased to matter at all except as a
vehicle for the emotion that gave a drooping, defeated look to his
whole person. I had never seen remorse and did not think of the
word but I could not fail to recognise distress.

"Miss Penrose." There was no denying his sincerity. "Forgive
me. I have drunk too much and offended you. I have a great deal
to regret." He looked again at our two faces on the wall and said
almost with a groan, "So much that I would undo . . ."

For the life of me I could not have accounted for his change of
mood. Was he regretting his malicious portrait of Lydia and the
poisonous seed of scandal he had sown? It was high time he did
regret it, I thought, but with only a faint revival of the magnifi-
cently revengeful spirit I had enjoyed at the callow age of fifteen.
The quarrel had been regrettable but it could have been no more
than an incident in Graw's adventurous life; and after all Lydia
had retaliated with some success. I saw it as yet another proof of
her remarkable vitality, that he could still be affected by so brief a
relationship, which had ended on the night they had both left
Emberside two years ago.

With the memory came something of the old feeling of catastrophe as if I stood again under the threshing trees in the stinging
rain and felt again the same sense of fatality, the conviction that
one of them, or both, would come to grief.

"If I drink more than I should, it is because my sight . . . I
cannot see as well as I could and yet"—his smile was apologetic
—"some things I see more clearly."

Was he actually confiding in me? An unfamiliar impulse to
rescue him made me blurt out:

"You have great skill, Mr Graw. Father thinks you a genius.
Would it not be better to use your time well and paint something
beautiful and true? A picture which would be your very best.
Before," I hesitated and went on with a brutality I writhed over
afterwards, "while you can still paint."

What could he say in answer to such a piece of arrogance? His
grave nod of assent as he left me was more than I deserved. From
my window I watched him go down the garden path, bump into

the wall as if he had misjudged its position, then stride over it and make his way through the white daisies and red sorrel towards the quarry.

He walked quickly as if he wanted to shake off the shadow behind him, the blackest thing in all the sunlit scene.

10

"You haven't seen Graw, I suppose?" Father was in
the hall frowning over a letter when I came down.
"He didn't put in an appearance at all yesterday."

"He went off early the day before yesterday, father, to Martlebury. Will Petway was at the station with his milk cans and
heard him ask for a ticket."

"Why on earth should he go to Martlebury? I can't understand
this letter from Bathursts. A curt note demanding immediate
payment for the rail fencing they delivered in March. We settled
the account, I'm sure."

I followed him into the little room Graw used as an office and
watched him turn over the confused heap of papers on the table.
His worried manner gave me courage to say:

"Are you sure, father, that Mr Graw is absolutely reliable?
With regard to money, I mean."

"You don't imagine that I would have employed him if I had
not been sure?" He spoke testily but was reasonable enough to
add, "So far as one can be sure. At any rate I'll look into this. I'll
write to Bathursts myself. They've no need to take this high and
mighty tone. I've done business with them for years."

He scowled at the disorderly mass of papers. I wondered if he
felt as I did that Graw could never have been in his element in
this improvised office. He cared nothing for father's affairs or
business of any kind. The Anglo-French Marezzo Marble Company meant no more to him than the rail fencing. Now that I
know more of the world, I have no doubt that in time he would
have ruined us not so much from dishonesty as from a cynical
contempt for possessions, other people's, that is: he had none of
his own. He cared for nothing but his painting.

All the same he had spent sufficient time in this room to make
it his domain and I felt uncomfortable in it. He was presumably
miles away, pursuing some unimaginable business of his own; and

yet his personality was so strong that even the absence of it was a positive experience. He might have been there, leaning on the door jamb and watching us sardonically from under his weary eyelids.

Since the incident in my bedroom three days ago I had done my best to avoid Graw; and I had no intention of allowing thoughts of him to spoil so fine a day. It would be hot again. The garden shimmered under a heavy dew. Robert was at home and would certainly spend the morning at Hackets. Soon after breakfast I set off to find him, going by way of the quarry, where the heat, the stillness and the honey-sweet fragrance of elder blossom tempted me to linger. I lay face down on my green headland and looked over into a warm wilderness of flowers and butterflies until the dazzle of light on pale rock made me turn my eyes to the restful green of fields on the far side of the lane. From this high point I could see the grey walls of Hackets between the trees and occasional movements. I had guessed correctly. Robert was working in the garden.

I picked my way down the steep path, passed the kilns and came within a few yards of the limeburner's hut, where an unexpected sight made me stop. Graw had evidently come back. He had wasted no time at the house if he had been there at all. He had set up his easel on the patch of grass in front of the hut. A pile of wood and stones supported the green umbrella I had thoughtfully provided for him. There was no escaping the man. He had taken over the parlour, the summer-house and now the quarry.

There was no sign of him. The door of the hut was ajar. From the threshold I saw that Graw had used it as a makeshift studio. At least there were a drawing board, paints and a few rags and bottles; and on the stone bench in the recess by the fireplace, a portfolio. I wondered if the place served as a retreat, from the silent Betsy for example. She could scarcely be an enlivening companion. Then I remembered that he had left her alone here the first time he came to Emberside and I hardened my heart; though she might well have preferred to stay here alone. A woman who could find heaven in the coach house was modest in her aspirations. This place was at least dry, and quiet enough even for a nature as retiring as hers.

It seemed an impertinence to turn over the contents of the portfolio. More than that. Here, as in the office, I could have persuaded myself that he had died and I was looking at his effects. There were three or four scenes of places unknown to me, delicately drawn and full of light, and several sketches of churches. Some of the pictures were no more than half finished, others the despairing over-coloured daubs I have mentioned. Together they recorded the history of his fading sight and failing powers. More than ever I regretted my presumption in taking it upon myself to advise him and yet I half believed that he might have taken my advice. He would waste no more time. Whatever he tried to do now must be worth the effort it cost him. What subject would he choose for his swan-song? What, in all his turbulent life, had left the most lasting impression? I went and looked at the picture on the easel.

It was a pastel sketch of Lydia. After the first pang of recognition my flesh grew cold. The colours were pale. Her face had a ghostly refinement. She seemed to lean forward with a look of deep compassion and concern. Her sparkle was all gone like her curls and ribbons. Her hair was plainly dressed. In his anxiety to show those aspects of her nature he had neglected or distorted in the first picture, he had even given her a cap and turned her into an older, quieter woman. I knelt down and gazed at her with the sad feeling that the high bloom of her youth and vitality had declined and she had begun to melt like the snow lady long ago. With this same hopeless sense of loss I had picked up the holly berries, once her lips, already dark and shrivelled. "They're all that's left," I had cried, mourning the vanished radiance of the lady herself.

I scrambled to my feet. He was there, quite near in the shade of the young birch trees, smoking his pipe. My eyes travelled unwillingly up its long stem to his face: to the full lips: the dull, sorelooking eyes under their heavy lids. Through the birch leaves a softened light touched his cheeks but could not heal their deep white scars or smooth the heavy lines that dragged down the corners of his mouth. More than ever he seemed larger than life: more powerful than the trees and rocks with their inoffensive air of quietly waiting. He was there, physically, as forcefully and unexpectedly as when his long shadow on the floor had first announced his arrival at Emberside. At the same time I felt instinctively that in some way he was absent: withdrawn into a private element where he suffered alone; suffered, moreover, an affliction deeper than regret.

Was it self-torture? I ought to know, having experienced it to some extent myself. Again and again I have relived that encounter and always with the miserable conviction of having let slip a moment that should have been grasped and put to better use. But at least when I said, "You've been away," I knew that it was more than literally true.

"I had business, near Martlebury, concerning . . ."

I thought he wanted to say more, though his business near Martlebury could scarcely be of a kind to interest me. He murmured something about having to make enquiries and seemed on the point of telling me their nature.

"I have been wanting to talk to you, Miss Isobel . . ."

I had had enough of his confidences. In my concern over the picture I paid too little heed to him. Afterwards I remembered that as I turned to it again he came nearer and glanced at me anxiously as if hoping that I would like it.

"It isn't finished of course," he began. "I couldn't . . ."

"It isn't Lydia," I burst out. "You've changed her again. Why can't you make a picture of her as she really is?"

"Do you mean—as she was when you last saw her? Or as she . . . may have . . . People change."

He spoke with deep seriousness and looked perturbed as if wrestling with a problem that troubled him.

"You never knew her. You don't know how I miss her, how I long for her to come back. It was your fault that she went away. Nothing has been the same since you first came here. We were so happy." I broke into a passion of tears for the bright days that were gone. "We could have gone on being happy if you had never come. Oh, I can see that you've tried to make amends." In fact I had no idea of the intense and painful effort he had expended on the sketch and can still only guess at it. "But it's no use now. It's too late. Too late."

"Yes. It's too late." The bleakness of despair in his voice made my own distress seem no more than a childish tantrum. "You are unhappy and I'm sorry. I don't know what to do or say. If I've harmed you in any way—or her"—he looked at the picture and drew a deep sighing breath—"I'm sorry. So bitterly sorry that . . . You cannot know the wretchedness of a life such as mine: the worthlessness of it: the waste. There was only my work, and now—I'm not fit to live, I tell you."

His voice broke and he turned his head away. His distress was

embarrassing and painful and, above all, private. I left him and
went quickly away between the birches, but the memory of his
face made me hesitate to leave him altogether alone. I paused
where the path curved and looked back. Through my tears I saw
him take the long pipe from his mouth, look at it with a touch of
hesitation and deliberately throw it away. Then he walked off
past the kilns, across the level grass and up the steep path: and I
was glad that he had gone. But when I had mopped my eyes with
a handkerchief, I saw him still climbing. Something about his
manner of walking frightened me. More than once he stumbled
over tree roots and slithered over stones; and he let the brambles
rip his clothes as if he no longer needed them, until at last he
came to the top.

He seemed taller than ever with the sky behind him as he stood
on the green headland far above.

"Mr Graw," I called and again more loudly, "be careful. You'll
fall."

He took hold of a bough of the mountain ash as if to balance
himself, then let it go, raised his arms and took a long stride out
into space.

I watched him fall like a great spider from the air. The terror
was so overwhelming that it was as if I fell too. In that cataclys-
mic fall all my notions of security came crashing down in a convulsion of nature as though earth and sky had changed places
and nothing was where it had been.

It seemed a long time before he reached the bottom and even
when he came at last to rest, stones came hurtling after him as if
they wanted to treat him as unmercifully as I had done.

Grave-faced and silent on the easel, Lydia watched him die.

11

"There's nothing we can do for him," Robert said.

We stood hand in hand, waist-deep in cow-parsley.

With my fingers tightly interlocked in his, I felt no surprise that he was there when I needed him; never questioned my right to count on him, or gave thought to the relief of having him at my side, but stood as near to him as I could get, clutching his firm hand, relying on him to take charge of the catastrophe and bring some element of seemliness into its unbearable reality. I had tried to scream for help but found it impossible to break the awful silence and ran panic-stricken towards Hackets, in search of help. In fact Robert had heard me call out to Graw and met me as I stumbled over the footbridge. He put his arms round me and listened and called me Belle as he used to do when we were little; and told me that it couldn't possibly have been my fault, until I was calm enough to go back to the quarry and show him the place.

We looked down at the twisted remains of Simeon Graw. His battered head had come to rest by one of the fallen boulders that lay about like misshapen tombstones. The butterflies had come back. There were flowers everywhere.

"He must have died at once," Robert said.

"That's what he wanted." I still dared not speak above a whisper.

"People will think," Robert went on slowly, "that he missed his footing and fell."

"You mean I needn't tell that he meant to do it?"

"It's a crime, suicide."

"I drove him to it, by what I said."

"No one can do that. It will seem like an accident. There would be no disgrace in an accident."

It had not seemed to me disgraceful but terrible and brave.

"I can't help thinking it was all because of Lydia." I stammered out the story of the pastel sketch and told him how strangely remorseful Graw had been.

"You think too much of Lydia. You must forget her, Belle. She has gone her own way. Graw was right. If you were to see her again—and I'm afraid it isn't likely—she wouldn't be the person you remember. No. The man's sight was failing. That was enough to make him lose heart."

All the same he let go my hand and made his way over the stones to where the easel stood. He looked steadily at the second picture as he had once looked at the first: at Lydia's sad face. And yet the expression was not quite one of sadness but rather of intense concern, as if she had been visited by an experience so compelling that it had altered her for ever and she had accepted the change, unwillingly perhaps.

"I wonder why he drew her like that? Why should he see her in that way?" As usual Robert went to the heart of the matter. "It's unlike her . . . but true."

We left them there together and Robert took me to Limmergill House where I stayed with Mrs Wayland until the next day. Meanwhile he rode off to fetch the surgeon, policeman and curate. It was Robert who broke the news to father and Mrs Graw. It was to his discretion that Simeon Graw owed his respectable funeral a few days later and his burial in hallowed ground.

Mrs Wayland begged me to stay longer. When I insisted on going home the next morning, she came with me. Since Robert was dealing with the practical problems arising from Graw's death, father was free to talk of its less unpleasant aspects: Graw's genius, his suffering, his friendship. It would be fitting, he thought, to compile a little volume on 'The Art of Portraiture' and dedicate it to Graw as a memorial. Mrs Wayland, who had never met Graw, listened patiently. I guessed that she was waiting for an opportunity to make a suggestion she had already discussed with me.

For my part I had begun to feel the first stirring of gratitude that we were at last free of the Graws, though the tragedy would never cease to haunt me; and to look forward to a new and less anxious way of life.

We were interrupted by Robert.

"I beg your pardon, sir, but I must ask you. What is to be done with Mrs Graw?"

"Done with her?" Father looked bewildered.

Robert himself had spent some time with her the day before. When he broke the news to her, she had not seen her husband for three days. She had been comforted with a glass of wine; the servants had been asked to be kind to her; Addy had sat with her in the evening. When she left the coach house, Mrs Graw must have followed her to the foot of the steps, where she had evidently been sitting all night. Robert had just found her there, numb with cold. She had refused absolutely to set foot in the coachman's rooms. He had coaxed her into the kitchen where she was recovering by the fire.

She was still shivering when we all trooped round the oak screen. Addy had put a quilt over her knees. She was wearing neither the green paletot nor the knitted shawl. I had never seen her bareheaded. Except to express his sympathy the day before, father had scarcely seen her at all, Mrs Wayland never. Under our united gaze she sank back in the chair, her peculiar eyes lighter than ever under the mass of black hair. The feeling of familiarity had quite gone. Whatever else she might be, Betsy Graw was totally unfamiliar: a creature whom it was impossible to know as one could know other people. The very rocking chair in which she sat seemed taken aback. The homely kitchen was not her place any more than it was the place for winds and waves and clouds, all of which came to mind in her presence. Not that there was anything gipsy-like in her complexion and features. Besides, a gipsy would have been recognisable as being like other gipsies. Mrs Graw was like no one I had ever seen.

"I understand, Mrs Graw"—father was at a loss—"that you don't wish to stay in the coach house any longer."

"He's there," she said baldly. "Simeon. He's still in there."

"But I gave instructions that the—er—body should be laid in the office."

Father turned to Addy who tapped her forehead significantly.

"I don't mean his corpse," Mrs Graw said.

The statement was unanswerable. It jolted us out of any of the conventional attitudes we might have thought suitable to the occasion. In spite of her shrinking manner, Mrs Graw was not impressed by us so much as by her delusion. In that she was inflexible. I think we all felt the uselessness of argument. Indeed I was not at all sure that it was a delusion.

"Have you any relatives," Mrs Wayland asked, "whom you

could go to in your"—she paused and added with less than her usual assurance—"sorrow?"

Betsy's eyes were wary.

"There was only Simeon."

Mrs Wayland shook her head grimly.

"She'll have no money, I suppose," she whispered.

"Well," father said loudly as if to persuade himself that a solution could be found, "this is no time to worry Mrs Graw. There must be a room she could have for the time being, until . . ."

"There's the other maid's room, sir," Addy volunteered reluctantly.

"That's it. Put Mrs Graw in there and—er—do what you can."

"Eugene," Mrs Wayland began when we had returned to the drawing room, "I really must warn you not to keep that woman here. She'll never make a good servant. She has a weird look. One can see that at a glance. And she'll upset the maids if she sits about in the kitchen. As soon as she has recovered a little, she must be sent on her way."

"Certainly," father said. "I have no intention of letting her stay."

"Isobel has had quite enough to put up with. In fact it was chiefly to talk about Isobel that I came."

Robert and I took the hint and withdrew. Mrs Wayland's suggestion that I should go to Mrs Hurst's establishment in Martlebury had been thoroughly thrashed out between us the previous evening. If only father would agree!

No persuasion was needed. He was eager for me to go, not because he wanted to part with me but because he was full of self-reproach and anxious to make some act of atonement.

"I've behaved disgracefully," he said. "I cannot forgive myself. Had your dear mother been alive . . . But there is no excuse. The fault has been mine. I've neglected you and my work and failed poor Graw. I had no idea his sight was so bad as to put him in danger. No, he was not to blame for my folly. It's time to make amends."

Mrs Hurst replied within a few days. Miss Penrose would be welcome as a parlour boarder. The summer recess presented no difficulty. Miss Penrose would have the company of several young ladies whose fathers were engaged in Her Majesty's service in India . . .

"They'll teach you a few airs and graces and leave your mind untouched," father predicted. "But Mrs Hurst will take you into society, such society as there is in Martlebury."

In his enthusiasm he arranged for me to stay a whole year and gave me fifty pounds to equip myself with clothes. We had a dressmaker from Netherlaw to stay for two weeks. So many fittings were needed that I spent much of the time in my room wearing a peignoir and knitting a purse of claret and blue silk with steel beads. When free, I made trips into Netherlaw with Mrs Wayland to buy shoes (fawn kid with Louis heels and moiré rosettes), gloves and a parasol. In these activities, frivolous as they were, I took refuge from the terrible memories of Graw's death. They helped me through the days; but at night there was nothing to protect me from the nightmares from which I woke sweating with fear.

Skirts, petticoats, mantles and jackets overflowed from my room to Lydia's where they were laid on the bed ready to be packed. It was usually Addy who dealt with the growing problem of where to put them but one morning, having spent an absorbed half-hour in trying on my first evening dress, I took it along to Lydia's room and found Betsy Graw there.

For some reason—surprise, no doubt, at seeing her in a new setting—I paused on the landing. She had been sent up with a pile of newly laundered linen and did not see me. She stood on the sheepskin rug by the bed, looking round her with a blankness of expression that may have been wonder. By this time the bed was laden with cambric and lawn, poplin and velvet, satin and gauze. Lydia's cupboard stood open, her abandoned dresses pushed to one side to make room for mine. With its muslin bows on the toilet table and curtains, its silk damask chaise-longue and the fernery in the window, it was a pretty room, naturally, having been Lydia's.

Betsy's wandering gaze became fixed. She had discovered herself in the looking-glass: a strange, pale-eyed woman with loosely dressed black hair, wearing a limp stuff gown, the skirt gathered at the waist with a bumpy fullness which must once have been supported by a crinoline. The plain neck of unrelieved black could not have been less flattering to her colourless skin. I wondered if she would be tempted to take some of the finery from the bed and hold it against her in front of the glass as almost any woman would have done.

She was no longer looking at her reflection but down at the sheepskin rug. Slowly, with no fear of being surprised in the act, she took off her heel-less shoes, then her stockings, and stood on the white fleece. She had strong, shapely feet and she moved them so as to feel the silky strands between her toes with a look of slow growing ecstasy. It made me uncomfortable. Just for a second the childish terror she had inspired in me when I had watched her creeping along the hedgerow, trembled into new life.

"Good morning, Mrs Graw," I said briskly.

She did not start or feel obliged to explain.

"Good morning, Miss Penrose."

She picked up her shoes and stockings and went out of the room, her strong bare feet incongruously turning the patterned carpet into a wild sea shore. Her dress was stained and patched with white where other stains had been scrubbed out.

I had partly overcome my reluctance to touch Lydia's possessions but even now, looking at her dresses one by one, I had to tell myself to be sensible, to care as little for them as she had cared when she left them without a pang. Yet if I were to give one of them to Betsy, Addy and Ruby would certainly leave in a huff. I quailed at the thought. It seemed wiser to give a dress to Addy and suggest that she might charitably part with her second best.

The stratagem proved successful. Addy was delighted with the grey twill, which the dressmaker's assistant altered for her, and patronisingly passed on her own green merino, which needed only a darn or two to make it more than good enough for Mrs Graw's best.

Not that Betsy was voluble in her thanks. Her curious circumstances had developed in her, I suppose, an intense inward life not easily revealed in words. That it might be revealed in other ways did not then occur to me. It was on my last day, the day after Addy had given her the dress, that I made my round of farewells and learned that Mrs Graw had gone back to the coach house for the first time since her husband's death.

"I have come to say goodbye, Mrs Graw."

After a pause, she called to me to come in. She was in the inner room. A wooden bath tub stood unemptied before the living room fire. The whole place smelt of soap and damp hair. In a moment she came in, wearing her green dress. Her newly washed hair hung in dense tresses to her waist. She showed no shyness in appearing thus transformed: nor did she ask me to sit down or express any sense of my thoughtfulness, as I saw it, in seeking her out to say goodbye.

I, on the other hand, felt no resentment. Envy would have been a more suitable response to her peculiar independence of spirit. Having endured every conceivable humiliation, having escaped the iron grip of Graw, she had, I believe, no fear. Nothing could ever be worse than what she had already suffered. She had become unassailable, without regard or respect for any living person (except one, as I presently discovered). Even her dread of Simeon's disembodied spirit had evidently left her.

"Goodbye, Miss Penrose," she said huskily, emerging from her private dream.

"I don't suppose we shall meet again."

She did not reply. A certain way she had of tilting her head gave the impression that she was attuned to unseen forces, from whom she heard hints and warnings, instructions even, I nervously felt, denied to the rest of us. I groped awkwardly for the latch and saw a pile of her own discarded clothes on the floor by the window.

"You won't need them now." I smiled kindly, as I imagined.

She came and snatched them up with fierce tenderness. Her eyes had taken on a greenish tint from the dress. They were incandescent: not warm like candles, nor sparkling like stars, but like the pallid petals of an exotic flower. The poetic fancies they roused surprised me as much as what she said.

"I'll never part with them, never, so long as I live. Mrs Thane gave me these things."

She laid the hideous brown shawl against her cheek caressingly.

"Mrs Thane? Was she the minister's wife who looked after you?"

"She's a saint. I tell you she's a saint, Miss Penrose." I was growing used to Betsy's celestial metaphors. In this case I believed her. "No ordinary woman would have cared for us as she did. Two outcasts like us. Day after day . . . She had no fear. Do you know what makes a woman put her life in danger like that?" Words flowed from her more freely than ever before. "It's love, Miss Penrose. A loving heart."

She stopped suddenly and glanced over her shoulder. Did she see Simeon there, lounging in the doorway, urging her not to talk?

"She must be a very good woman."

I left Betsy clutching the pitiful garments as if they were holy relics sanctified by the touch of Mrs Thane. As I turned for a last look (after all I would never seen her again and I did not expect to meet anyone quite like her at Beech Grove House or anywhere else in the wide world, for that matter), she smiled, for what reason or with what motive I could not be sure; but her teeth were splendid, so strong, white and perfect that their effect was startling, like a message from another woman encased in the form of Betsy Graw and able, on occasion, to get out.

Father had intended to go with me to Martlebury but his plans were changed by a letter from his lawyer, who proposed a professional visit to Emberside on the very day I was to leave. The business arose from enquiries into the fate of the five hundred pounds Graw was to have invested in the Anglo-French Marezzo Marble Company. Father was suffering so painfully from what he now saw as unpardonable folly that he could scarcely speak of it. I dare say we should have been thankful that the losses were no worse, as they might well have been.

If Robert had been at home he would have taken me to Mrs Hurst's. As it happened, Adams and Jayson had sent him to London for six months to a firm of dealers in antique furniture and works of art so that he could learn the value of such things. His interest was in land and farming but as a partner he would need to know every branch of his firm's business. He had left two weeks ago with as good a grace as he could muster.

After much discussion it was settled that Addy would come with me as far as Netherlaw. From there I would travel alone in the care of the guard. In the excitement of arraying myself in my braided jacket and sailor hat with blue feathers and strings, I said goodbye to father with scarcely a pang.

Only when he had handed me into the carriage and looked up wistfully, did I see the parting from his point of view.

"You'll be lonely."

"Nonsense. A year will soon pass. I shall have my work, and your letters. If you're homesick, I'll come and see you. Goodbye, darling."

"I could come home at Christmas."

"Why, that will be the very time when you'll want to stay. There'll be parties and dancing. It's time you enjoyed a little gaiety."

I got down again and hugged him, persuading myself that it was all for the best. I would come home finished, elegant, composed, and take up my position as the lady of the house. We would entertain. People would angle for invitations. Emberside would be as it had been in mother's time.

Tree shadows dimmed the front of the house. From an upstairs window Ruby was peeping out. Behind her in still deeper shadow hovered a pale face which must have been Betsy Graw's . . .

Addy left me in a first-class compartment, with a tea basket to refresh me during the ten minutes' wait at Hagthorpe Junction, a footwarmer though the weather was mild, and a new-found confidence in being well able to manage my own affairs now that I was alone for the first time.

The line from Netherlaw to Hagthorpe took me through a pastoral landscape of farms and corpses and quiet country stations with flowerpots and polished brass lamps, milk cans and crates of pigeons; until gently sloping fields yielded to wilder country. Railway cuttings grew deeper and rocky embankments higher, shutting out the view. My thoughts turned inward. As I submitted to the racket and rhythm of the train, there came over me a sensation of being poised between the old life and the new: released like one of the crated pigeons to search the air for a direction.

The new life at Mrs Hurst's existed only in the form of a few ill-defined pictures of ladies dressed with quiet opulence and conversing in well-modulated voices. About what? Baffled, my mind slid back to the life I had left, already distant and shrouded in a sadness I had no wish to dwell on.

Dreamily suspended between past and future, I forgot the immediate present until the train rushed into a tunnel and after a minute of pitch darkness hurled me into the sunlight of Hagthorpe Junction, where it stopped. I looked out of my window full in the face of a man waiting on the platform, recognised him with astonished delight, flung open the door and stepped down into the arms of Charlie Stack.

He was heavier, swarthier, dressed in a plaid reefer and wide hat. The blue eyes under their curling lashes were harder, I saw at once, forgetting that I too had changed. He stood back respectfully and took off his hat.

"Little Isobel. Miss Penrose, perhaps I should say. I can hardly

believe it. You've turned into a beautiful young lady in the height
of fashion."

"Oh Charlie!" Already the spontaneous joy of seeing him was
fading—in a cloud of complications. From all the questions demanding an answer I disentangled the simplest. "Why did you
never write?"

He looked unhappy. I noticed the expression but gave no heed
to it as I glanced eagerly up and down the platform; at the bench
where two or three ladies were sitting.

"You know me," he began. "I did try . . ."

The half-dozen words were enough to alarm me.

"But why didn't she . . . ?" All the bewilderment and grief of
the past years revived. Like a hurt child I cried out in lamenta-
tion, "How could she leave me like that?"

"She?"

"Lydia. Where is she?"

I looked again at the seated ladies, at the lace-curtained window of the dining room, then at Charlie. The colour had left his
face.

"Lydia?" He gripped my arm. "What do you mean? I haven't
seen Lydia since I left Netherlaw two years ago."

12

I remember the small commotion. The guard came up and one of the lady passengers.

"A touch of faintness," Charlie explained, pale-lipped. "The young lady's father is a friend of mine. This was an unexpected meeting and I've given her bad news, I'm afraid."

Even in my agitation I was struck by the fact that he saw the news as bad, though I was still far from realising that it was as startling to him as it was to me. I could only feel as I had felt when Lydia first went away; as if the earth had opened and swallowed her up once more. It took me some time to grasp that the reverse had happened. In a few words Charlie had swept away the ocean, the one insurmountable barrier between Lydia and me: the one physical barrier, at any rate. I forgot that there could be other kinds.

A glass of soda water appeared. I was helped into my compartment. Charlie joined me. We sat with the door open, talking as he and Lydia must have talked on the night when she met him at Netherlaw station almost by accident, having not so much forgotten that he would be there as failed to think of him at all. If only Robert had stayed to see her get out of the Liverpool train ten minutes later and go to her own, the eleven forty-five to Martlebury!

"She never meant to come with me," Charlie said. To Lydia it had been a welcome coincidence that he had been there to listen as she poured out the story of her hurt feelings and impulsive flight. "She was homesick for Emberside already. You know Lydia. Some fuss about an artist who'd turned up like the devil in a black cloak and a puff of wind. He had insulted her. I gathered there had been a quarrel. Mr Penrose was angry with her."

"I've learned my lesson," Lydia had wept. "He doesn't care for me and never will."

"But she hadn't learned," Charlie said. "You never do. There's only one way to stop hoping . . ."

He had managed to calm her down a little. It seemed a good idea for her to go to her aunt's for a while, until she felt better.

"He may think more of me," Lydia had said, "When he has to do without me for a time. But I've been too high-handed. For that I'm sorry. Only it's too late now to make amends."

All the same she had intended to write to father that very night (though there was not much of it left). Charlie had suspected that she would be back at Emberside in a few days.

We leaned forward, facing each other; facing too the problems that rose thick and fast. The minutes sped by. Charlie looked at his watch. He was travelling across country after visiting his Grandmother Lucerne. The old lady was dying and had asked for him. That was the only reason he had come back.

"Lydia has been there all the time," I said, hardly listening. "At Ash House."

"It beats me to understand why you've never heard from her."

"I believe it must have been father's letter. He wrote to Mrs Welbecome when he thought Lydia had—eloped."

I told him about it, feeling sure that Lydia must have seen or heard its contents. Father had been cruel and unjust in accusing her of lack of principle. For Isobel's sake, he had written, it was as well that she had gone away.

"He had no right." Charlie had every reason to be angry. He had shown none of the excitement which had begun to stir in me: after the fear the first throb of joyful relief.

"I shall see her again. Oh Charlie, I shall see Lydia." He looked glummer than ever. "Won't you . . . ?"

"I never shall." He stepped out on to the platform. "There's only one way to stop hoping, Isobel, and that's to marry another. I've a wife back there in Canada. We were married six months ago. What could you expect," he burst out bitterly, "when I left Lydia crying her eyes out for another man? She can mean nothing to me now."

I didn't believe him. I knew that his future lay elsewhere. He had not intended to visit Limmergill, had not even asked about Robert or Hackets. At the very mention of the wife in Canada the old days of birch-bark boats and picnics in the quarry, shadow shows and polkas at Emberside, went tumbling irrecoverably into the depths of time past. But I didn't believe that he would forget them any more than I would—or Lydia.

His train came in on the opposite side of the platform. He wrung my hand, jerked out a few unfinished sentences of regret and was gone. My own train had pulled out before it occurred to me that I had not asked for his address. We were unlikely to meet again. A sobering sense of the vast extent of the world and the ease with which people could be lost in it depressed me as much as the gradual acceptance that Charlie had no longer any part in my life. To the feeling of reproach, unjustified of course, that he had not kept faith, was added a deeper resentment against father and even against Robert, whose terrible blunder had given to a trifling quarrel so tragic a twist.

Mentally I banished them all and gave myself up to the unexpected and blissful prospect of seeing Lydia again, soon. With a pang I remembered her note: "I'll always love you, Isobel." It was there in my writing case in my bag on the rack, together with the photograph. Why had I made no effort to find her? Now that there was no need, it was perfectly obvious that a letter to Mrs Welbecome asking if she knew Lydia's address, would have resolved all difficulties long ago. Lydia must have thought us as ruthless and unforgiving as we had thought her.

In view of father's letter, how could she have made the first move? Dimly I understood how much courage and how deep a hurt must have kept her silent, leaving us in the mistaken belief that she had run away with Charlie. She had burned her boats, all of them, and endured the loss.

But at least she had been secure and comfortable all this time at Ash House. She would hear my knock. The maid would show me in. (Or even a butler?) I would wait in the drawing room amid all the dignity of the Sheraton and Chippendale furniture, the oil paintings, the marquetry and ormolu, above all the gilded bird cage. There would come the swish of silk.

"Isobel!"

"Lydia!"

Explanations. Instant forgiveness. The thrill of it made me dizzy with anticipation. The tea basket remained unopened. Miles of country sped by unregarded, like the dismal streets and chimneys on the outskirts of Martlebury as we approached the station. It was too long to wait until tomorrow. I must see her today.

The smell and hiss of steam, the crowds, the gloom of the
station were confusing at first but my one fixed intention
strengthened me. My head cleared. A porter identified the landau
waiting for Miss Penrose. When all my luggage save one handbag
had been piled inside and under the box, I addressed the driver.

"Pray make my apologies to Mrs Hurst. I have had unexpected
news of a relative in Martlebury whom I must see before I come
to her."

I bade the porter call me a cab, gave the address 'Ash House'
and was driven off.

13

Martlebury had doubled its population since the beginning of the century and was still growing fast.

From a string of forges along the banks of the Martle it had developed with the coming of the railway into a prosperous steel town specialising, among other things, in cutlery and silver plate. It had also developed a permanent pall of soot continually enriched by clouds of smoke pouring from open furnaces and household chimneys.

I looked at my watch, surprised to find that night had fallen. It was no more than six o'clock of a summer evening but not even the noonday sun, I was to discover, could penetrate the murky atmosphere of this, the lower end of the town. I groped in my bag for the gauze scarf I had not needed even in the train, swathed it round my hat and face as a protection against smuts and sat back, stifled; stunned by the noise of wheels and hooves and bawling street traders; and doubtful whether the driver was taking me in the right direction. Such streets as I could see through my veil and the grime-coated windows of the cab were narrow, cobbled ways between close-packed shops and houses.

Ash House had once stood in its own grounds above one of the wooded stretches of the Martle but its extensive garden had been steadily encroached upon and finally engulfed by rows of terraced dwellings thrown up to house workmen in the cutleries and forges.

A few dusty laurels and double gates of iron gave it just enough dignity to persuade me that the driver had made no mistake. In my excitement I paid him off and had run up the path and pulled the door-bell before he drove away. Only then was there time to notice the blistered paintwork of the symmetrical rows of sash windows, the peeling stucco of the pillars flanking the door and the tattered blinds. I wondered how Lydia could endure them and knew, even before the door was opened from within, that Lydia could have no connection with those blinds.

A little maid appeared, skimpily dressed in washed-out gingham and so painfully thin and frail that I marvelled at her success in having opened the heavy door. When I asked if Mrs Welbecome was at home and would receive me, her eyes widened. Without speaking, she took my card and darted away along the hall, leaving me, anxious now and apprehensive, on the step. In a minute she returned, took me along a brown-painted passage and ushered me into a room at the back. It was so dark that the woman in the chair by the fire appeared as little more than a plump black bolster with its feet on a stool and a glass of stout on a table at its side.

"Mrs Welbecome," I faltered. "I am Isobel Penrose."

The woman neither rose nor asked me to sit down.

"We buried Mrs Welbecome a year past December," she said flatly.

I did not know that this was the usual way of reporting a bereavement in Martlebury and was startled by her emphasis on the burial without reference to the death which must surely have preceded it. There was a suggestion of triumph in the remark as if to the very end Mrs Welbecome had resisted and been finally overcome.

My voice quivered with nervousness.

"It is Miss Lorne—I was hoping to see. Is she here?"

"Here? Miss Lorne?" It was clear that she was not, but the bolster was coming to life. Lydia always had a stimulating effect in any circumstances, I recollected. Nevertheless my disappointment was so intense that I felt too sick and tired to explain my errand.

"You'd better sit down." The woman's manner had changed. She seemed to be eyeing me thoughtfully. So far as I could make out, she was past middle age and of florid complexion. Her high colour must have been due to the stout rather than to any freshness in the air of Martlebury. "Are you a relative of Miss Lorne?"

I caught in her voice a note of calculation and hesitated, not quite trusting her. But the absolute necessity of finding Lydia was too much for me.

"Our mothers were cousins. She is very dear to me. I must find her. You evidently know her. Do you know where she is?"

"So she's a relation of yours."

She leaned forward to look at me more closely, then heaved herself out of her chair and lit the gas in the bracket on the wall. Never having seen gaslight in a house before, I was taken unawares and flinched under its bilious glare.

"You expected to find her here?"

Her eyes were prominent and hard as they explored my dress. Nothing about me from my watch and bracelet down to my Louis heels and moiré bows escaped them.

"I hoped to find her here."

She took up my card from the table.

"You wouldn't be one of the Penroses she used to live with?" When I assented, she went on in her coarse, domineering way, "I thought you'd cast her off. It's no use expecting anything from them, I said. You've blotted your copybook there, I thought to myself. Mrs Welbecome showed me Mr Penrose's letter," she added quickly. "She showed it to us both."

From her eagerness to explain I sensed that she was lying and had read the letter without waiting to be shown it.

"You lived with Mrs Welbecome?" I asked, loathing her.

"I was housekeeper to Mrs Welbecome for twenty-five years. Her strong right hand, she used to call me. 'My wonderful Mrs Dawlie,' she used to say. It wasn't the best of positions in her later years but I stayed with her through thick and thin. Miss Lorne hardly knew her."

If she had said no more, I would have guessed from the envious spite of those last words how she must have resented the change when Lydia came: but encouraged by occasional sips of stout, Mrs Dawlie had found her tongue. I bowed my head and listened, trying to piece together the scraps of information and overlook her pomposity and conceit. It emerged that Mrs Welbecome had been ill for years and unable to leave her room. The household had been left completely in Mrs Dawlie's hands. It was obvious that she and Lydia had quickly crossed swords. But why, if the house and its contents were hers, was Lydia not here to protect them—the thought was involuntary—from Mrs Dawlie?

"Please," I interrupted, "I beg you to tell me where Miss Lorne is. When did she leave? Where did she go?"

"As to when she left," Mrs Dawlie said contemptuously, "I can tell you, but where she is now I do not know and except to oblige you, Miss Penrose"—the stout seemed to have mellowed her attitude towards me—"I have no wish to know. She left this house two days after the funeral and has not been heard of since, not by me, that is, nor anyone known to me."

"But why, when this was her home?" An alarming thought occurred to me. "Surely—Miss Lorne did inherit her aunt's estate?"

Mrs Dawlie laughed unpleasantly and eased her stays.

"Oh yes. She came into everything there was to come into." Before I could breathe a sigh of relief she added, "Such as it was."

"You . . ."

"I mean that the estate as you call it was worth nothing. And naturally those that had money owing to them were anxious to have what was theirs by right."

I had contrived from time to time to glance round. There was certainly no sign here of the Lorne treasures but this must be the housekeeper's room: an ugly, tasteless apartment unexpectedly flimsy in its furnishings: a bamboo table and whatnot and a good deal of fretwork. By contrast Mrs Dawlie looked even more robust, and difficult to dislodge.

"Things had to be sold?"

"Everything," Mrs Dawlie told me with a certain relish. "Except what she took. Except what she snatched from those that had a better right to it."

Even Lydia, I thought, must have had difficulty in snatching anything from that strong right hand, which seemed well fitted to hold on to whatever it possessed itself of. And that, as Mrs Dawlie's next words revealed, included the house itself.

"It so happened," she informed me unctuously, "that Mrs Welbecome mortgaged this house seven years ago to a gentleman of my acquaintance. It was through me that the money was forthcoming as Mrs Welbecome understood. If it hadn't been for me, she wouldn't have had a roof over her head, for I can tell you, Miss Penrose, that not a penny of interest was ever paid. My friend's patience was past belief. 'It's only a question of time,' I used to say, 'and when that time comes, it'll make a fine apartment house.' 'That it will, Mrs Dawlie,' my friend always said, 'with you at the helm.' "

When the old lady died, the house passed to Mrs Dawlie's friend and Mrs Dawlie's long loyalty was rewarded.

"Yes, here I am in charge." She looked round the room as if

marshalling its dingy contents to support her claim. "On behalf of the owner, and a person couldn't find better lodgings for the terms we ask."

I rose.

"I'm sorry to have troubled you, Mrs Dawlie. Would you be so kind as to ask one of your maids to find me a cab? I'm already . . ."

"You're staying in Martlebury?"

"I'm on my way to Mrs Hurst's."

"Beech Grove House." She was impressed. Mrs Hurst's fees were notoriously high. Mrs Dawlie straightened her insufficiently darned lace fichu (had that too been Mrs Welbecome's?) and seemed to reach a decisive point in her calculations.

"A cab? There isn't a cab to be had without half a day's notice in this part of Martlebury." How I regretted having parted so lightly with Mrs Hurst's comfortable landau! "The nearest livery stable is a good half-hour's walk away and just at present there's only Alice. I'm afraid she can't be spared. There's the suppers to be got ready."

The dilemma was of my own creating. It served me right. If a cab could not be fetched, neither could a note be sent to Mrs Hurst. While I deliberated, Mrs Dawlie became almost good-humoured.

"The best thing would be for you to go no farther tonight. It isn't fit for a young lady to be alone in these streets. You may not realise it, Miss Penrose, but Beech Grove House is not really in Martlebury at all. It's fully a mile out on the other side. Luckily I have a room that would suit you. After something to eat and a good night's sleep, you'll feel more yourself."

Her hand was on the bell. From no wish to stay but from sheer inability to face the gloomy street outside, I wavered. Displeasing as her personality was, it suggested a ponderous kind of common sense. If she had shared a roof with Mrs Welbecome and with Lydia, however uneasily, then I could, for one night, share the same roof with her.

"My charge is three and sixpence, with breakfast. Gas will be extra."

"A pair of candles will do very well, Mrs Dawlie."

Gaslight, I had soon learned, revealed too much.

My room overlooked the laurels and the iron gates. The floor boards were uncarpeted; the ewer and basin chipped; a faded cotton quilt covered the bed. I looked out on uniform rows of slate roofs tilting downhill to the railway and river. Even with the window closed I could hear the hum and clamour of streets crammed with more people than I had ever imagined could exist: all sorts of people, some of them dangerous. The devil himself was to be met with as he walked to and fro upon the face of the earth, his black cloak upblown in a gust of wind. The thought (or memory?) brought a little chill of fear, not for myself but for Lydia.

Somewhere out there in the teeming world I must find her. Find her I would because I loved her. For all the soothing simplicity of my reasoning, I was aware of some element in Lydia's absence I had not yet been able to face. Possibilities existed which had not seemed to exist when I had thought her safe with Charlie or with her aunt in the Ash House she had glowingly described in many a cosy half-hour at bed time. Even now I could only eye those possibilities cautiously.

Shadows had gathered in the corners of the room, mercifully shrouding its details. With some reluctance my eyes came to rest on the chimney breast where light still lingered, and upon the picture hanging there: a savage black and white engraving. It depicted a stormy river strewn with white-faced bodies beneath a pall of lowering cloud. 'The Martle in flood, 1864' declared the thin-flowing script below. It roused in me a superstitious dread of Martlebury from which I have never quite escaped. It became for me a place where human souls could perish; be washed away and never seen again.

The front door quietly opened and closed. With my nose close to the panes I saw the little maid, Alice, in her bonnet and shawl, go hurrying down the cobbled street. For a second I wondered if Mrs Dawlie had spared her, after all, to fetch a cab. Then I saw that she had an envelope in her hand. A letter?

"Your supper, Miss Penrose. I've brought it with my own hands." Mrs Dawlie spread a cloth and laid out cutlery. "Alice is busy in the kitchen. I like to save her running up and down stairs when possible," she added, with the fatal impulse of a liar to say too much.

Could one believe anything she said? I felt a sudden loss of faith in the rules of decent conduct I had always taken for granted. What other lies had she told? What other outrages had she been guilty of? I imagined her opening her mistress's letters, including the one from father. She would manipulate Mrs Welbecome's affairs, sell her possessions and put the proceeds into her own pocket . . .

My supper—some slices from a hambone, strong tea and a heavy dark slab of fruit cake—was not appetising but it revived my spirits. I had just finished when the gate whined on its hinges. I darted to the window in time to see Alice panting up the short path. Almost at once Mrs Dawlie returned to take the tray. I had been obliged to light a candle and saw that she was looking affable, as if—I had certainly fallen victim to the most unpleasant kind of thought—her plans were going well.

"You'll be ready for bed now."

She turned back the quilt and drew the curtains. I followed her to the door. Never in my life had I slept in a locked room but when she had gone, I involuntarily reached out to turn the key. There was none; nor a bolt. I wondered if the other apartments were occupied and by whom. Mrs Dawlie had spoken of 'suppers'. There must be seven or eight bedrooms. Which had been Lydia's? I remembered her room at Emberside with its muslin bows and green glass vases and hoped that Addy was looking after the fernery in the window, as Lydia must sometimes have hoped until she forgot it in the need to exert all her splendid energy to combat new difficulties in less friendly scenes.

I took off my dress and got into bed. A good deal of noise still came from the swarming streets below but I had drifted to the brink of sleep when I was roused again by a sound from the hall, a sound perfectly normal at that hour: the sliding to of a heavy bolt: of two heavy bolts, followed by the rattle of a chain. The front door was being secured for the night. What could be more reassuring?

It was surprising how little solace I derived from the thought of being locked in with Mrs Dawlie and her silent invisible lodgers. There had been something almost too emphatic in that slamming home of the bolts as if it were meant to keep out not only burglars but everyone else as well. For that matter no one else in the world except Mrs Dawlie and Alice knew where I was. It was not only Lydia who had disappeared into the unknown.

This uncomfortable train of thought combined with the fruit cake and the unfamiliar bed to make me restless. My situation was sufficiently unusual to inspire wild fancies and, when from time to time I fell asleep, wilder dreams in which Mrs Dawlie played a leading role, even stouter and purpler than in the flesh, and more hostile. In one of these dreams she brandished a key in my face and refused to let me go. I awoke, struggling with the bed clothes; and as had so often happened in the past when I woke from a nightmare, I heard—or seemed to hear—Lydia's voice, cool and comforting. It came to me quite clearly though she spoke from some impenetrably deep shadowy place; and the words were recognisably hers:

"You need not put up with such conduct, Isobel. There's always something you can do."

Braving the mice, I went barefoot to the window and drew the curtains. From one of the houses no more than a hundred yards away came the sound of angry voices: unpleasing perhaps but a reminder that there were people close at hand. If Mrs Dawlie did try to keep me here—the nightmare had not quite left me—I had only to send the contents of the room crashing one by one from the window to raise the alarm. I would begin with the soap dish or perhaps the picture of the Martle in flood, its dark tide strewn with human debris. The prospect was stimulating. She needn't think—I slipped safely into bed untouched by any mouse—that she could get the better of *me*.

This energetic mood kept me awake long after the streets fell silent and after all, my misgivings were to some extent justified. A half-hearted dawn was breaking over Martlebury when there came a faint scratching at the door panel which was certainly not the act of a mouse.

"Miss." A quiet voice at the keyhole. The door softly opened. "Are you awake, miss?"

"Is it Alice?"

She came to the bed, already dressed for the day in her skimpy gingham and mob-cap but without her shoes. Her thin little face was grey with tiredness. It was difficult to guess her age. She was older than I had thought.

"She's asleep. She never wakes before seven. But when she does get up, she won't want to let you go. Not until Mr Gallonby has seen you. That's what I came to tell you."

There was a sharpness about her that I instantly respected, together with her resourcefulness in having outwitted her mistress and her spirit in having wanted to. I moved over and made her sit at the other end of the bed with her feet under the quilt.

"Why ever would he want to see me?"

"I'll tell you in a minute." Her wan face was eager. "Did you come asking for Miss Lorne?" When I nodded, she smiled with a look of secret pleasure that touched me.

"You knew her? You were here?"

"I've been waiting for someone to come asking for her. As soon as I saw you, 'This is the one,' I thought. It seemed as if I knew."

"Where is she, Alice? Please." Her smile had faded. "You don't know?"

We spoke in whispers, close in every sense: united by our concern for Lydia.

"It was like a ray of sunshine when she came here, miss. I opened the door to her myself, same as I did to you. It was about this time in the morning. She was tired to death. 'I'm Mrs Welbecome's niece,' she said."

"Was Mrs Welbecome pleased?"

"She was far gone in her mind but Miss Lorne used to sit with her and make her comfortable right up to the end."

"And then?" I believe it was delicacy that made Alice hesitate. "You don't know why she went away?"

"She had to or they'd have sucked the blood out of her veins. Like leeches. They couldn't hardly wait for the missis to die to have the bed from under her." Alice's voice was rough but she spoke with a compelling fluency . "It was enough to give you the creeps the way they hung about, waiting."

"You don't mean—bailiffs?" I blushed to utter the word.

Alice nodded solemnly.

"But most of the things had gone before the bailiffs came. One by one they went. There was hardly a day when there wasn't a cart outside and a chest of drawers or a wardrobe being bumped downstairs. I fairly cried my eyes out when Miss Lorne told me she was going just after the funeral. 'Then you'd best sneak off, and tell no one, miss,' I said, 'or they'll be after you for money wherever you go.' 'If ever any of my friends come asking for me, Alice,' she says, 'give them a message for me. Tell them they'll hear of me at Emberside, when I'm safely settled and some day, when the right time comes, I'll go back.' " Alice repeated the message carefully, especially the name. "There. I've told you." Her eyes filled with tears as if a sacred duty had been discharged, leaving an emptiness in her life.

"But where could she go? Surely you have some idea."

"I don't think she knew herself, miss. It worried me, a lady like
her going off on her own. But she had to go. Like vultures they
were, from the day she first came: and after missus died, it was
worse. As if it was their last chance. Nothing had been paid for,
not for months, years in some cases. Butcher's meat hadn't been
seen in this house since nobody knows when, except Mrs Dawlie's order. That was separate."

We had talked for some time when the sound of the first wheels
on the cobbles brought Alice to her feet.

"I came to tell you that a letter's been sent to Mr Gallonby. I
took it last night. It'll be to tell him you're here and he'll be sure
to come. He's a personal friend of Mrs Dawlie, a debt collector
and very keen. Everybody knows him round here. He'll pester
you for money, you being a relation of Miss Lorne."

"I'm not a relation of Mrs Welbecome."

"He'll pester you just the same and not only him. You'd best go
before he gets here."

The extent to which he and Mrs Dawlie had enriched themselves at Mrs Welbecome's—and Lydia's—expense I did not
know until long after; but I grieved to think that Lydia had fallen
into such a den of thieves and had been too proud to come to
father for help.

"I'll have to go now and get the kitchen fire going. She mustn't
know I've been here."

We agreed that I must be all ready to leave when my breakfast
was brought up, then push my way out on to the landing and
walk firmly out of the house.

"If he so much as sees you, he'll be after you wherever you go.
He'll likely think you'll put him on Miss Lorne's track. It might
be best for you to go out by the back door. That's what Miss
Lorne did. I can see her now, standing in the back lane with her
bag in one hand and the . . ." She stopped and closed her lips
firmly. I waited to hear what Lydia had taken in her other hand
and waited in vain. Alice groped in her pocket. "Miss Lorne gave
me this. 'I've nothing better to give you, Alice dear,' she said. But
there's nothing I'd rather have."

She held it up, a bunch of rose-coloured ribbon, the one bright
and frivolous thing in the dismal room.

"Oh Alice! How good you've been!" I got out of bed and
hugged her. I am not tall but she came no higher than my shoul-

der. "Some day when I've found her, we'll come back and see you. I promise."

She hurried off. Though it was still early, I dressed and watched in a fever of impatience as life came creeping back into the streets below. For a time all the foot passengers were work people going in one direction, downhill, except for a postman and a woman pushing a milk cart. Shortly after eight a man appeared at the very bottom, a heavily built man in a Derby hat and black frock-coat with a leather case under his arm. He came purposefully if slowly up the hill. Mr Gallonby beyond a doubt.

The door opened and Mrs Dawlie brought in my tray.

"I shall not need breakfast. Goodbye, Mrs Dawlie." I laid three and sixpence on the table and added breathlessly, having taken some pains to concoct the sentence, "My father's lawyer will communicate with you if he should think it necessary."

With this crushing statement I swept out, leaving her stricken with astonishment.

Mr Gallonby's knock thundered through the hall as I came downstairs. Alice's face appeared at the top of the basement steps. "This way," she hissed. A minute later I stood in the lane with my bag in my hand, wondering which way to go.

14

A blank wall faced me, appropriately enough, as it must have faced Lydia. Or had she some plan in mind? I was relieved to find a narrow alley to the left. It brought me to another cobbled lane leading uphill. Since no other way offered, I took it and soon came to a busier road where I stopped, uncertain as to which way to turn.

Apart from sleepy little Netherlaw I knew nothing of towns. Father had seen to it that I was more familiar with the ancient city of Rome than with nineteenth-century Martlebury. The unaccustomed smell of melting fat from a tallow merchant's and the nauseating stench from a skin-and-hide warehouse made my head swim. My best plan was to find a policeman or some respectable person who could direct me to a cab, in which I could escape into purer air. Borne along on a stream of strangers, I turned to the right, guided not so much by chance as by the impossibility of crossing the unswept road in my new shoes.

Lydia (my mind still ran on her movements) must have known the town a little by the time she left Ash House. For that matter she had known it as a girl before she ever came to Emberside, though it was obviously much changed since then. Had she too taken a cab? To what destination? Belatedly I realised that she must have been desperately short of money. If she had had a coin to spare she would have given it to Alice instead of the knot of old ribbon. A dreadful thought brought me almost to a halt. Lydia had not only suffered the ignominy of running away from bailiffs and debt collectors. She would actually have to find work: to work for a living. Our own Lydia! The shame and humiliation of it!

Whatever in the world could she *do* for a living? A sudden increase of noise and heat drew my attention to a small, grated window at knee-level, through which I looked down into a room packed with women. It was one of the many small cutleries to be found in Martlebury's older streets. The women were buffers whose job it was to burnish the plated knife handles, forks and spoons ready for packing. They looked rough and grimy in their men's caps but they were talking and laughing and seemed happy enough as they bent over the work with furious energy. Still, it was impossible to imagine Lydia in such a situation.

For that very reason, perhaps, a notice saying 'Young lady assistant required' outside a dressmaking establishment further up the hill caught my attention. Compared with the polishing, dressmaking seemed almost a pleasant way of making a living. The premises were small. The entrance was well swept; the half-glass door covered with a Nottingham lace curtain. I stopped, partly to rest my valise on the low wall, partly from despair at the thought of enquiring not only here but at every similar milliner's and dressmaker's in Martlebury, at every establishment where a refined young woman might find employment.

I had nerved myself to begin there simply because there I was, when the door opened and a fashionably dressed woman came out.

"If she feels no better by mid-day," she said to someone inside, "we must send her home. I'm afraid she isn't equal to the work."

She walked off, leaving the door ajar. Presently a young man appeared. He wore a rusty black morning coat, had a pen behind his ear, and was evidently a clerk.

"Step inside," he said, "if it's the position you've come about."

"Oh no." I picked up my valise in alarm. "I was just passing . . . and I thought . . ."

He was a quiet-spoken young man, a trifle preoccupied as if his mind was on his work. He had come out for a breath of air which he inhaled luxuriously as if it were sweeter than the air inside.

"I'm hoping to find a relative of mine," I found courage to say, "whom I have not seen for some time. She may have been obliged to find employment and I wondered if such a place as this . . ."

"There would be no place here suitable for a lady unless she was experienced in the trade or an apprentice learning the work. That would mean taking out indentures for three years."

"It would be more than a year ago when she . . ." The words 'when she was last seen' were too painful to utter. Besides—I took heart—someone must have seen her: scores of people. It was just a question of finding them.

The clerk looked interested.

"Disappeared? Was she a young lady?"

"Was?" I repeated in consternation. "Oh yes. She's young, and perfectly well, I'm sure." How could I be sure? I dismissed the harrowing picture of Lydia in a decline. "It's just that I don't know where she is."

"We have twenty young women working here. Several of them have been taken on in the last twelve months. Madam would have no objection to your stepping inside to take a look. You could always say," he added tactfully, "that you had seen the notice. You can leave your valise in the hall."

I followed him in. He pointed to the stairs and went back to his desk in a screened-off corner of the narrow hall.

In the room above, the apprentices and improvers were at work at long tables, some operating sewing machines, others stitching by hand. They scarcely spoke but worked in a controlled frenzy as if they dared not stop. Their plain dark dresses and pale intent faces in contrast to the yards of brilliant materials covering the tables, gave them the look of a small, well-disciplined army pitting its strength against hopeless odds.

I looked down the shimmering tide of velvet, silk and tulle, at the flying fingers and bent heads of brown, flaxen and black, in search of the beloved chestnut braids and curls; knew that I would look in vain; and as the forlorn hope refused to die, looked at them all again.

They were much too busy to notice me. During the few minutes I stood there not a head was raised; until a disturbance at the far end sent a ripple through the ranks. A girl had fainted. Her neighbours put down their work but not in any haste. Such incidents must have been common. A forewoman bent over the girl and presently brought her out, her face like wax, her feet trailing. Involuntarily I put out an arm. Together we supported her down the stairs and put her on the hall chair.

"It's Miss Parker again," the forewoman told the clerk, and hurried upstairs.

The clerk tucked his pen behind his ear again with a sigh of resignation and brought a glass of water.

"It'll never do," he said when the girl had taken a listless sip or two. "You'll have to go home. Madam said so, if it happened again."

"But she'll let me keep my place?" Feeble tears ran down her cheeks. " It hasn't happened so very often."

"As soon as you feel fit for it, you must go home. We've no room for invalids. They'll be at it till the small hours, as you know."

It was apparently a busy time. The fashionable ladies of Martlebury and the neighbouring gentry were replenishing their wardrobes for the coming season of country house visiting. A large order for mourning to be supplied the next day had added to the crisis. The clerk went firmly back to his work, leaving me in a dilemma. The poor girl could not be left. She could barely sit upright.

"They'll fill my place," she said hopelessly.

"You'll feel better at home." I thought of an invalid fire, calves' foot jelly and coddled eggs in my own room at Emberside and wondered why I had ever been unhappy there.

"It isn't home, just a room. If they won't keep me on here I might as well die and be done with it."

Her home was in the country, she told me, in Hartbeck, a village some miles south of Martlebury. She was lodging in Bayes Court. It would take twenty minutes to walk there. As we talked, inspiration came to me. If a cab could be found, I would take her to her room and drive on to Mrs Hurst's, where by this time I longed to be. The plan, with some modification, was carried out. An urchin hanging about outside in the hope of finding a horse to mind or a bag to carry, was sent for a cab, came back triumphantly riding behind it and was given a sixpence. Miss Parker protested at being a nuisance but was pathetically grateful to be helped in and driven to her lodging.

My horizon had widened in the short time since I left home. Bayes Court, a tiny square of two-storied houses with a central yard and tap, would once have dismayed me; but after a night at Ash House I saw its advantages. Miss Parker's room was clean and quiet. Her fire was unlit, but laid. She could make tea in her landlady's kitchen and her landlady, unlike Mrs Dawlie, was homely and kind. By this time Miss Parker had revived and would have told me her life story but for the waiting cab. Even so, her sickness and terror of being dismissed roused me to such a pitch of sympathy that I was loth to leave her.

I cast about for some encouragement. It was not easy to find. She had a look of wasting illness. Her hands were frail and bloodless, her eyes large and sunken.

"Fresh air and rest and good food are all you need to make you

as well as ever," I said heartily, naming the three things she could
not hope to have.

"The air is fresh enough in Hartbeck. They say it's too low
lying but it always suited me; and mother keeps fowls and Buttercup; that's the cow . . ."

Her father, a stone-mason, had last year suffered an accident
which left his right arm useless. There were four younger children. It had been a sacrifice to find the money for her premium at
Madam Reese's. When her apprenticeship was over, she could
help them all at home . . .

It was time to go. I left her resting in her chair with a blanket
over her knees.

"I don't know how to thank you, Miss Penrose." Her gentle,
heavily shadowed eyes filled me with pity and guilt. "You've been
a friend in need. I'll never forget you. You remind me a little of
Miss May. She once had a room here; and she'd lived in the
country too. It isn't so much your looks as your way of speaking
and doing things. I don't know what it is. Anyway, I'll never
forget you."

Nor would I forget her. In spite of my encouraging words, I
feared for her. The episode had given a new turn to my thoughts.
It brought home to me the perils of poverty, especially to a soli-
tary young woman. Miss Parker's gratitude had been touching
though it is rarely pleasing to be found to be like someone else. I
still thought of myself as unique and not at all likely to resemble
the unknown Miss May. Was that her Christian or her family
name?

An astonishing idea galvanised me into new life. I rapped on
the panel and pulled down the window.

"Stop. Drive back to Bayes Court at once."

The cabman growled something about the fare being two shillings already.

"Never mind how much it is." What a thing to say to a cabman! "Here. Take this now." I thrust the coins into his hand.
Reassured, he turned at the next opening.

Miss Parker had not stirred from her chair. She may have been
asleep when I burst into the room after a perfunctory knock.

"Miss May. What was she like? Tell me quickly. What was her
other name?"

15

I woke from a dream of the old quarry, where I played, a child again, on a summer day. The blue air quivered with butterflies. Again and again I thrust out my net to catch one as it hovered above a patchwork of scabious and poppies and flowering nettles: a pale vulnerable creature, soft as the petals it briefly touched but purposeful and self-reliant, taking its chance in a dangerous world. From flower to flower it fluttered, avoiding the place where something untouchable lay among pink willowherb at the foot of the rock face. Higher and higher it went. I ran after it up the path, my net outstretched, always just too late to reach it; with no wish to harm it, only to hold so lovely a thing and keep it for a while.

"Lydia," I called. "Wait. I'm coming. Lydia . . ."

Her stay at Bayes Court had been short. She had come in the December of 1871 and left in the early spring. Miss Parker had known her quite well: well enough to know her first name. She had not spoken about her misfortunes but she was obviously poor since she paid two and sixpence for her tiny room whereas Miss Parker paid three shillings for a larger one. Sometimes she went without coals, bought her meals at a pastry-cook's for not much more than a shilling a day and tried whenever possible to borrow a newspaper instead of buying one in order to study the advertisements. Miss Parker had spoken for her at Madam Reese's but Miss May was quite unskilled in the trade. Embroidery was not required and plain sewing was hard to come by. Miss May seemed surprised that so many women competed for slop-work. She had tried stitching collar bands but couldn't work fast enough or long enough for it to be worth while at eightpence for twelve dozen.

She had set her heart on a position as nursery governess or housekeeper in a small establishment. Unfortunately, for some reason she could not ask her former employer for a written char-

acter. The surgeon who had attended Mrs Welbecome had written a few lines, vouching for her genteel status and trustworthi-
ness.

Then suddenly she left, early in April. It happened to be one of
those times when a rush of orders at Madam's had kept them
working eighteen hours at a stretch and one night Miss Parker
had not come home at all. For one thing, her feet were so badly
swollen that she couldn't walk. In those two days, Miss May had
taken her things and left.

As to what she was like, Violet (as I now called her) was at a
loss. Lovely. A lovely lady. She had often thought how handsome
Miss May would have looked in pretty clothes but even in her
plain dress—Yes, quite plain without a bit of trimming anywhere
except for two rows of braid round the skirt—she had been, well,
full of life. No, not lively. There was a sadness about her, a sort of
homesickness; not just the worry of being poor. But when she
brightened up, she would laugh so that you couldn't help joining
in; and she would sing: something about a shady grove.

Violet couldn't believe that she had gone when she went into
Miss May's room and found it empty, the drawers and cupboards
bare. Then she had seen a card lying on the floor.

"I've kept it in case she ever came back. You must take it, Miss
Penrose, though it's worthless now. Fancy you being connected
with Miss May. I can't get over it."

She handed me the piece of pasteboard which she said was a
pawn ticket. On it were written the date, April 7th, 1872 and the
sum advanced: two pounds. "It was a lot of money," Violet said.
"But it's too late to redeem it now, whatever it was. A year and
seven days is the time they let you have."

I put the shameful thing away in my ivory cardcase with its
tiny inset picture of a Greek temple on one side and the mono-
gram L. M on the other. Lydia had given it to me on my fifteenth
birthday. It had been her mother's . . .

. . . The gong urged me, discreetly, to rise. Its sound was
dignified and restrained like everything else at Mrs Hurst's. I
dressed without haste, looking out at the garden where winter
sunlight silvered the bare trees. In that walled retreat on one of
Martlebury's well-wooded southern slopes one could forget the
squalid streets and their poverty-stricken inhabitants; that is, in
normal circumstances one could, to one's shame, have forgotten
them. Life at Mrs Hurst's offered all that I had expected. I had

arrived, breathless and much grubbier than I had ever been in my life, but sufficiently apologetic to be forgiven and condoled with for having, after all, missed seeing the relative I had felt it my duty to seek out. It had been on the whole wise to stay the night though Mrs Hurst would not have permitted it, had she known. An Apartment House! She had not heard of Ash House though the name Welbecome was familiar.

From the moment of my arrival I felt at home in the tastefully furnished rooms with their long windows and yellow-shaded gilt sconces. I soon began to enjoy the companionship of the other boarders and the continual conversation, which could be lively, Mrs Hurst decreed, without going beyond the bounds of decorum. Autumn brought a round of musical evenings and morning calls. In December came a curious letter from Addy. It seemed to have been written for no other purpose than to state in several different ways how much she hoped I would be at home for Christmas. A day or two later father wrote urging me to stay at Martlebury and enjoy the evening parties to which, as he had predicted, I had been invited. I was grateful for his unselfishness and wrote long letters describing the events, which it would certainly have been a pity to miss.

I could have been happy at Beech Grove House the whole year through and more than a year, if it had not been for my obsession: the urgent need to find Lydia. Because I kept it entirely secret, it made me absent-minded and withdrawn even when enjoying company most.

As a parlour boarder I was free to go shopping or to walk in the park so long as a chaperone came with me. It was easy enough to extend these outings to Bayes Court. Mrs Hurst was not averse to charitable visits, properly supervised, provided there were no epidemics. Miss Hinch, the elderly governess who usually came with me, liked nothing better than to sit in the landau resting her feet while I went in to talk to Violet. My gifts of wine and fruit and arrowroot and perhaps the new interest of having a visitor had done her good. She had gone back to work and I saw her less often once the dark nights set in.

We talked of nothing but Miss May; and I would return more absent-minded than ever.

Having done my hair, I spent five minutes in reading my New Testament and another five in pacing about the room with a dictionary balanced on my head. Thus fortified in body and

spirit, I went down to breakfast where there was much talk of the
At Home to be held, in accordance with Mrs Hurst's invariable
custom, in March. Early as it was, a musical programme had
already been prepared. Practising would begin that very day. Mrs
Hurst's At Homes were social events of some importance in Martlebury. To them she invited friends and acquaintances of the
pupils and such members of local society as she thought suitable,
drawing upon the families of steel manufacturers, well-to-do
clergy and certain carefully chosen members of the legal profession. Beyond these limits she was not prepared to go. Apart from
a distinguished physician or two, doctors were not acceptable:
surgeons never. But there was always a shortage of young gentlemen and I believe Mrs Hurst was almost as pleased as I was when
that very day Robert called.

I was summoned to her room to meet him for the first time
since his return from London. Mrs Hurst cut short his apologies
for having called at an inconveniently early hour (it was just after
twelve), made kind enquiries about Mrs Wayland, secured his
acceptance of her invitation to the At Home, sent me for my
cloak and muff and dispatched us into the garden, where we
walked up and down for ten minutes in full view of her window.

"It's been six whole months . . ."

"How are they all at home?"

"I haven't been there yet. I only arrived here from London
yesterday. Adam & Jayson wrote asking me to spend a day or
two in Martlebury. A dealer in Wood Street is offering some
pieces of antique furniture for sale. They want me to value
them."

"They must be pleased with you."

"I enjoyed working in London more than I expected. But I
won't bore you with that when it's the fashions you want to know
about. Don't pretend it isn't. I did try to notice what ladies were
wearing but it was too complicated. I brought you some fashion
magazines instead. As a matter of fact you look splendid in that
blue thing. Better than anyone I saw there."

For all my pleasure in seeing him, it was difficult to talk freely.
Conscious of Mrs Hurst's watchful eye, I felt as if a skewer had
been bored through my spine; but that discomfort was trivial
compared with the worrying decision I could postpone no longer.
It was not a matter of whether to tell Robert of the fateful mistake he had made two years ago so much as when and how to tell

him. He would be deeply upset and full of self-reproach. Moreover, I would have to tell him that Charles, the hero of his boyhood, had not even asked about him. With these thoughts to occupy my mind, I must have been a dull companion.

Fortunately Robert had a great deal to tell about his stay in London, where he had acquitted himself well. In fact he was in such good spirits that it seemed unkind just then to tell him the disquieting news about Lydia.

"What's the matter with you, Isobel?" He stopped. I glanced towards the window. A massive beech tree cut us off from Mrs Hurst. The skewer-like sensation eased and I stopped too. "You seem to be continually on the point of bursting into speech and then thinking better of it." He smiled down at me but when I said nothing, he grew serious. He knew me too well, I suppose, not to feel the slightly feverish quality that my outward sedateness (as I thought) concealed. The unflagging pursuit of a will o' the wisp must bring a hectic and distracted light to the eye. "There's nothing wrong, is there? There can't be or you would have told me."

He spoke from experience. We had always taken it for granted that he would share my problems and solve them; but in this case he too was involved. I could not bear to see his confidence fade or spoil his homecoming.

"I'm glad you've come back, Robert, and you must tell father how happy I am here. He knows, of course, from my letters. And if there's any interesting news you can tell me when you come to the At Home."

Interesting news occupied no place in father's letters, nor news, now that I thought of it, of any kind. The little volume on 'The Art of Portraiture' seemed to have been laid aside. Thoughtful observations, tender enquiries, comments on the books he had read were no substitute for gossip. For that matter the one interesting piece of news I had to tell had not found its way into my letters either, and for a complication of reasons. Father had treated Lydia abominably. He didn't deserve to have news of her. On the other hand I cherished the secret hope that some day, perhaps soon, we would all be reunited in the old harmony. Lydia's dream—and mine—would be fulfilled. As Mrs Penrose, she would forget the hardships Miss May had suffered. Incurable optimism blinded me to the fact that I was no nearer than ever to finding her.

"You're not listening. What is it, Belle?"

Robert tucked my arm through his but it was too late for confidences. We had lingered long enough behind the beech tree. I led him back to the house where my final handshake must have been as absent-minded as my conversation. In handing Robert his hat, I happened to glance at the newspaper on the hall table, caught sight of a closely printed page of advertisements and was visited by the brilliant idea that I could advertise for Lydia. People did; but how? Before the door had closed on Robert, I was immersed in a new and fascinating occupation.

"Nellie: (I read) I will be a true and honest friend to you, on my word. Send different address directly and make appointment. Much to say and hear."

How touching that was! And how reassuring to Nellie! It was not quite suitable for my purpose but could perhaps be adapted. I began to take a keen interest in the newspapers and was often waiting in the hall when they were delivered. It showed a commendable seriousness of mind, as Mrs Hurst observed. A knowledge of Latin, I was given to understand, though creditable, was of little use socially: in fact, a disadvantage. It would be best not to mention it except in answer to a direct question, which was not likely to arise.

By the end of the week I had taken to concocting notices based on those I had read, only to discard them as one difficulty after another presented itself.

"Would Miss Lydia May Lorne communicate . . ."

This stately beginning was soon abandoned. Lydia had concealed her name to escape a horde of bloodsucking creditors. Such an invitation would bring them about my head—and hers—in droves.

"Would L. M. L. communicate with Miss I. P. . . ."

I stared nervously at the mysterious cyphers and wondered if there was anything illegal in publishing so anonymous a message. And where was the intriguing Miss I. P. to be reached? Not at Emberside and certainly not at Beech Grove House. More earnest study led to the discovery that one could use a post office as an address.

Only my devotion to Lydia could have driven me to struggle on until a satisfactory version was at last composed.

"Would L. M. L. please write to Miss I. P. at the Post Office, Upper Edge Street, Martlebury. Miss I. P. will be delighted to meet her long-lost friend. Much to say and hear."

Reading it with some pride, I suddenly realised how compromising an interpretation it could be given. Suppose it should be thought that L. M. L. was a *man*. I hastily re-inserted 'Miss' and took the earliest opportunity of posting it to the newspaper office, having first blushingly discovered from a clerk at the counter the arrangements for collecting letters.

I can smile now at these exploits, so long as I forget the deep anxiety that inspired them and the disappointment when day after day brought no reply. The obstinate determination to find Lydia by my own efforts was exhausting to mind and spirit. The one fixed idea made me deaf to certain hints and warning signs, when they came, which in a more normal state of mind I would have heeded. Yet, after all, what could I have done to check the flow of events or change its direction?

I looked for her everywhere: in parks, shops and private houses. Because with Lydia anything was possible, I persuaded myself that she was as likely to appear at a ball or the theatre as in cap and streamers pushing a bassinette or buying parsnips at a market stall.

One day Miss Hinch and I had gone into Limerages to buy stockings. It was while the parcel was being made up that I glanced across at the ribbon counter and caught sight of a slim young woman with a flower-trimmed hat perched well forward over her brow to reveal an elaborate chignon of chestnut brown hair. She was just leaving. I darted after her with a suddenness that brought me into collision with the shop walker who had shown her out. Brushing him aside, I burst forth on to the crowded pavement. She was gone. The crowd thinned. I saw the flowered hat weaving its way to the corner where an omnibus had drawn up. Its owner mounted. The horses moved.

"Wait!" I called. "Wait!"

Heads turned, among them the head under the hat, halfway up the winding stair. The face was thin and peevish: a stranger's face. The disappointment was so cruel that I could not move but stood with my head bowed until Miss Hinch joined me, looking bewildered, with the parcel in her hand.

"I thought it was an old friend . . ."

For a while I infested the Post Office in Upper Edge Street until the embarrassment of asking for a letter and finding none made me lose heart—but not hope. Like a gambler absorbed in a game of chance, I was almost oblivious of the movements around me. Preparations for the At Home went briskly on. The house vibrated to the notes of Sonatas, Etudes and Impromptus strenuously practised. Dressmakers' boxes arrived and as the day approached, potted palms and tubs of camellias and gardenias. The floor of the long drawing room was waxed for dancing.

From a distance, through a mist, in a dream, I enjoyed the quiet buzz of excitement (nothing more hectic was conceivable at Beech Grove) as a pleasant interlude, an interruption to the one serious purpose of my life. Yet it was the At Home which unexpectedly shed a faint glimmer of light upon the darkness into which Lydia had vanished.

16

The maids were too busy to help us to dress. My particular friends Julia Arden, Florence Wilstone and I played lady's maid to each other, beginning early in the afternoon: not a minute too soon, since we had twelve petticoats amongst us and an unknown quantity of hooks, eyes, buttons and tapes. I had grown fond of Julia. Her parents were in India. Her only relative in England was a monstrous old uncle, her mother's brother, who lived at Netherlaw. It was this circumstance that had first drawn us together. He was coming that evening. Julia prepared to be bored.

"He wears steel-framed spectacles," she said, bravely determined that we should know the worst. "You must help me to entertain him. I simply can't manage the whole evening on my own."

"It's no use asking Isobel," Florence said. "She will be quite taken up with the charms of Mr Wayland."

Mrs Hurst's window, I recollected with some annoyance, was not the only one that overlooked the garden.

"Robert and I have known each other all our lives," I said coldly. "I am well used to his charms, I assure you," and I silently prayed that he would not appear in an old-fashioned dress-coat like the one Florence's brother had worn at Christmas.

I should have known better. Robert's black superfine coat with a velvet collar and silk facings right down to the button-holes was all that could be desired. I was impressed, and happy to see that the others were impressed too, by his distinguished manner, forgetting that he must have grown accustomed to such evenings while I yawned over my needlework at Emberside. Since my own programme was soon filled, he danced twice with Florence. An unfamiliar feeling, not of jealousy of course, but of surprise that Robert should find her interesting, made me almost yield to the temptation to tell him that Florence had been in the habit of saying 'O Lor!' until Mrs Hurst put a stop to it. I refrained, not so much because it was unworthy of me as because Robert would think it so.

In my admiration of Robert's social graces, I failed at first to notice the change in him. It was not until we were drinking claret cup after the quadrille that I became aware of his worried frown and a gloomy restlessness in his eyes. Moreover, he was quieter and more constrained than usual. I pointed this out to him.

"You seem to be thinking of something else all the time."

Robert roused himself.

"That's exactly what Miss Welstone said about you. Absent-minded. The young ladies think you are suffering from an unfortunate love affair."

This evidence of a lack of breeding on Florence's part did not surprise me. To my added annoyance, Robert laughed as if such a thing were impossible.

"So far as I can make out," I said, wondering if this was the moment to mention Charlie, "love affairs are usually unfortunate."

"They don't need to be. My parents were happily married and so were yours." Robert had become serious again: more than that, anxious. "You don't ever feel, Isobel, that you ought to go home?"

"But of course I shall go home. At the end of June."

"I meant"—Robert put down his glass and took a little time in buttoning his glove—"earlier than that. In fact quite soon."

His manner puzzled me. The word 'ought' implied an obligation.

"You and Mrs Wayland thought it a good thing for me to come here. Everyone did. And now you all seem to think I should go back."

"All?"

"Well, Addy wanted me to go home at Christmas. Father is quite happy for me to stay. I like it here, Robert."

Who would not have liked the palms and flowers, the elegant toilettes, the musicians tuning up on their platform, the warm light from the yellow silk shades on the gilt sconces? A fit of gloom came upon me as I pictured myself at Emberside again, alone. All the same it was time to pull myself together and gabble out the whole story of Charles and Lydia before my next partner came.

Robert was looking glummer than ever.

"I haven't told you," he began.

"There's nothing wrong at home, is there? Father isn't ill? He hasn't been . . . drinking . . . ?"

"No. Oh no. I'm quite sure he hasn't. You can be easy on that score. Your father is not an intemperate man. It was Graw's company that led him to behave like that." Robert's manner was almost too hearty. "It's difficult to talk here." He seemed to find it very difficult indeed and the topic he succeeded in broaching at last had nothing to do with Emberside. "You remember the last time I came to Martlebury, to see the dealer in Wood Street? Well . . ."

We were interrupted. Robert got up as Julia arrived to present her uncle from Netherlaw: a grey-haired man in a blue coat. Poor Julia! For her sake I exerted myself to pay him some attention and found him to be—Mr Handiside, the photographer.

"Miss Penrose. There is no need to introduce us, Julia. We are old acquaintances."

We had a great deal to talk about. Julia faded thankfully away and presently, Robert, as we discussed the births, deaths and marriages in Netherlaw. The musicians played the opening bars of a waltz. My partner hovered.

"I must let you go, unwillingly. I'm old enough to be allowed to tell you how beautiful you look. If only I could photograph you now!" He *was* a dear old gentleman. "But there's just one thing before you go. It has troubled me a little. Would you be so kind as to make my apologies to Miss Lorne when next you see her?"

"Lydia?"

"I was not able to oblige her with the photograph. She wrote to me—oh, some time ago—asking if she might have the third one. You remember I took three poses and sent the two best to Emberside. Yes, it is hot indeed." The room was all at once stifling. I had opened my fan. "But the third plate was completely spoilt. One of you had moved."

"When . . . when did you hear from Lydia, Mr Handiside? We have not seen each other for some time."

"I believe I can tell you almost exactly. I remember thinking that Miss Lorne had left it rather late. We destroy unwanted photographs every six months or so from lack of space to keep them. But soon after her letter came, I was struck down with a long spell of my old enemy asthma and I'm ashamed to say, never replied. Yes, that would be early in June. Not last year. I was remarkably free of asthma then. The June before last. Seeing you has reminded me of it. Otherwise my memory is not reliable, I'm afraid."

"Do you remember," I trembled on the brink of discovery, "the address Lydia wrote from?"

To my dismay he shook his head.

"London, perhaps?" I ventured, facing the worst.

"Has Miss Lorne gone to London? No, it was certainly not London. Somewhere nearer. I assumed that she was staying with friends. Indeed as I recall she was to be reached Care of someone or other."

"Not in Martlebury?"

"No, no!"

"But where?"

He tapped his forehead as if to awaken some response within and I waited, stiff with suspense. "I had thought before the letter came that Miss Lorne had gone to Canada. There was a rumour to the effect, you know. Yes," he rambled on, "Netherlaw is much given to rumours, and scandalmongering. One must not pay too much attention to idle gossip."

He was looking at me with an interest that was more than kindly. Was he, after all, rambling, or was there some purpose in these remarks? The eyes within the steel frames expressed an unexpected and uncalled-for degree of sympathy. "One must turn a deaf ear. You have not been home since last summer, you say?"

"Please, Mr Handiside, do please try to remember Lydia's address or even the name of the place she wrote from."

"There has been some estrangement? That would be a pity. Life is too short. We must cling to our friends, especially such a friend as Miss Lorne. It is indeed unfortunate that she is no longer with you, my dear Miss Penrose. I'll cudgel my old wits. I'll do my best. It will come to me."

"You really think so, Mr Handiside?"

"I have no doubt whatever that it will come to me."

The effort to remember must have spoilt the evening for him. He stood lost in thought. Later I saw him standing alone, biting his lip and looking distracted. Meanwhile my partner bowed and led me away. He must have been a real young man of flesh and blood. I have no recollection of him. Invisible arms supported me as we twirled between invisible palms.

A year past June. That was a long time ago. Nevertheless Lydia had written to Mr Handiside after she had left Bayes Court. This new discovery brought her nearer in time if not in space. If only Mr Handiside would cudgel his wits sufficiently, in a little while we might actually meet. A glimpse of Robert smiling rather wanly at some remark of Florence's made me decide to keep the secret to myself: to produce Lydia without warning to the amazement and delight of all, including father. Robert's hint that father needed me, if that was the right interpretation, had made me anxious. How wonderful then if I were to go home, in triumph, taking Lydia with me! She could have had only one motive in sending for the photograph: to see my face; to see us together once more. She felt no bitterness, only love.

With my mind fixed on the friend I had lost, I gave too little thought to the friend whose constancy I had always taken for granted. When Robert came to say goodbye, I did just notice how haggard and hollow-eyed he was. Afterwards I seemed to recall a note of urgency in his suggestion that we should meet again and talk; but at the time I only reminded him that I would be home at the end of June; and saw his depression as a sign that he had enjoyed the evening and was sorry to leave.

Florence had been watching our farewell with shrewd interest.

"I can't quite make you out," she said as we went up the stairs together. "You and Mr Wayland. It's odd that you should both be suffering from a secret sorrow. If it's unrequited love, it surely can't be for each other. And if it isn't that, what else can it be?"

I ignored the remark as beneath my attention. Julia had caught us up.

"It was good of you, Isobel, to take charge of poor Uncle Conrad for a while."

"He's the dearest old gentleman. I'm so very glad he came."

Julia looked surprised. She did not know how important Uncle Conrad was; how like a friendly wizard in his blue coat and steel spectacles, if only he could remember the magic word.

17

The elation did not last. Each morning I went down to breakfast confident that Julia would have had a letter from her uncle with a message for me. When no message came, my enthusiasm for Mr Handiside faded. The old simpleton—as he now seemed—had probably forgotten the whole incident.

The nature of my anxiety was changing. When did I hear the first note of warning that time was running out; that Lydia must not only be found but found *before it was too late?* Was it instinct or intuition that prompted me, or the sheer necessity of facing those grimmer possibilities that I had so far ignored?

It was certainly growing very late indeed. When I went home in a few months' time, it would be three years since Lydia left Emberside; two years since anything at all was known of her. I must have come by degrees to realise how disturbing her situation was but I felt it as a sudden shock. It was not like Lydia to continue so persistently in one state: a state of absence and silence; she who had always been as volatile and changeable as a Catherine wheel. Her changes, it is true, had been of mood. Her fidelity and love were never in doubt as her letter to Mr Handiside proved. But if she had kept any freedom of movement at all, by this time surely she would have given some sign.

"Tell them they'll hear of me at Emberside . . ." What was the message Alice had so faithfully passed on? ". . . when I'm safely settled. And some day, when the right time comes, I'll go back."

It was a promise infinitely reassuring; or so it should have been. Yet I could not resign myself to the simple necessity of waiting nor banish the suspicion that things had gone wrong; or rather, to be precise, that things were *about* to go wrong.

It was part of my single-minded concentration on Lydia to imagine that finding her would put things right; and to come time and again to the twofold barrier of her silence and my ignorance as to what to do about it. My conjectures grew wilder and more wide-ranging. It was as though, from scanning the busy streets of Martlebury, I turned to a map and ran a questing finger over other towns and countries, or twirled one of the schoolroom globes to find some new continent where she might be hiding.

But it was not in Lydia's nature to hide (except from creditors); nor could I believe that she was so very far away; or that no one at all had news of her except Julia's tiresome uncle. Here a positive rage against poor Mr Handiside shook me.

As it happened, there was one person in Martlebury whose existence I had forgotten, and whom in the normal course of Mrs Hurst's social round I was destined to meet.

It must have been soon after Easter that Mrs Hurst and I, on a round of morning calls, were ushered into the drawing room of her friend Mrs Haley. I found myself sitting next to a pleasant-looking lady, a Mrs Norwood, who took more notice of me than Mrs Hurst's acquaintances usually did. They must have grown a little weary of the ever-changing stream of well-behaved young women which flowed year after year from Beech Grove House. To my surprise she seemed to know something of my family and circumstances. When I asked her if she had lived in our part of the world she showed a touch of hesitation before answering.

"No, never. But I know of Emberside Grange from a school friend who used to live there: a relative of your mother, I believe."

"Could you possibly be Minnie Nash?"

My face must have lit up. Here was a stroke of luck. I had actually forgotten Lydia's school friend, whose married name I had not noticed when turning over her wedding card in Lydia's letter case.

"Lydia spoke of me?" She seemed uncertain as to how to continue. I too felt uncomfortable, not knowing whether or not she had heard the false rumour of Lydia's elopement. I glanced in desperation at the ornaments on Mrs Haley's thickly crowded mantel-shelves, then at Mrs Norwood who was eyeing me with curiosity but on the whole kindly. "Lydia often wrote when she first went to Emberside, and a good deal about little Isobel. Your mother was an invalid, I understand."

I told her that mother had not left her couch for years before she died.

"I last spoke to Lydia four or five years ago at a Charity Ball in Netherlaw. She was prettier than ever and much admired."

"I remember it."

Mrs Wayland had acted as chaperone. They had stayed over-night at the Buckingham Arms, but Lydia had tried on her dress the night before for my benefit. I sat by the open window and watched while the three looking-glasses gave back their varia-tions on the theme of Lydia herself, slender and shimmering from her white slippers on the sheepskin rug to the flowers in her burnished chestnut curls. The summer night smelt of roses and pomade. Moths blundered in, lured by the glow of the two lamps we had extravagantly lit so that I would not miss a single rosebud on the three-flounced tarlatan. I enjoyed the dress to the last inch of lace, as I enjoyed the ball, as I enjoyed everything, by proxy, through Lydia . . .

"Naturally as time went by we wrote less frequently; and then I married. In fact Lydia's last letter was in reply to my wedding card. From the way she wrote," Mrs Norwood was clearly fishing in the nicest possible way for information—"I wondered if she herself was thinking of marrying."

"There is no doubt," I replied with a discretion that Mrs Hurst would have approved, "that Lydia could have been comfortably married if she had chosen to be."

"That does not surprise me." Mrs Norwood spoke warmly.

Mrs Hurst caught my eye. It was time to go. I had reluctantly begun my parting speech when Mrs Norwood said, "I suppose Lydia could not, in the circumstances, have stayed on when Mrs Penrose died. You don't hear from her?" Her manner without being in the least presumptuous was faintly reproachful: she obvi-ously knew that Lydia had left Emberside. "I do wish she had come to me when her position in life changed." Yes, she was certainly reproaching, not me, but father. I grew hot and uncom-fortable. "As an old friend I should have liked to help her. I have often wondered what became of her. It was a shock to find her so changed, when I saw her last."

My heart contracted. With a tremendous effort I brought my voice under control to ask:

"You have seen her, Mrs Norwood? Recently?"

"Unfortunately not to speak to. A glimpse only. Mr Norwood and I were visiting friends near Bainsacre, the year before last. You may know it. If Lydia had still been at Emberside, we would have ventured to call while we were in the district, but our friends had heard from the Kirkdales that she had left the previous summer." Mrs Norwood paused and went on carefully. "There had been rumours, I believe. But here is the extraordinary thing." Mrs Hurst's meaning glance across the room had become a positive danger signal but I could not move. "We had made a long drive one day to see Bainsacre Abbey. As we drove back . . . It was quite distressing. I scarcely like to mention it. I actually saw Lydia. That is to say, we overtook a woman . . . I never thought . . . She was"—Mrs Norwood dropped her voice as she imparted the disturbing facts—"on foot. Walking along the lane. Alone. So poorly dressed and carrying a sort of bundle. I glanced out of the window as we came up with her and recognised Lydia. She looked—well—shabby. Fortunately she didn't see me. I'm sure of that. She never turned her head. I peeped out of the window at the back . . . There could be no mistake."

Mrs Hurst rose with awful dignity. I looked away, ignoring her commanding eye.

"You understand, Miss Penrose," Mrs Norwood was genuinely distressed, "I could not embarrass her by stopping. Had my husband and I been alone perhaps . . ."

"I do understand. Lydia would have hated it. I mean, in the circumstances. Do you remember when . . ?"

"It was in the spring, April 8th, the day after my birthday. I had taken such pleasure in this bracelet Mr Norwood had given me. You see, it is inscribed April 7th, 1872. But seeing Lydia, as she was, made me feel—ashamed. Must you go?" I could disregard Mrs Hurst no longer. "If you should hear from Lydia, would you please tell me? I should be so grateful. Fate treats some of us much better than we deserve?" Tears came to her eyes. "And some much too harshly. Even as a girl at school Lydia gave so freely. She deserves to be happy."

Mrs Hurst must have noticed my downcast look as we settled ourselves in the carriage, though she was too well-bred to pry. She could have no idea of the distress that swelled my throat and dragged at my heart.

"You're tired, my dear. The spring is a trying time. We must send you into the country for a week or two. You are used to country air. Mrs Norwood," she added casually, "is thought to be a very agreeable young woman. Her husband is one of the Sunderby Norwoods."

"Very agreeable, Mrs Hurst."

The agreeable world of Hursts and Norwoods had shrunk all at once: its occupants grown smug. Beyond its safe limits stretched a dusty lane, where a shabby woman walked alone, never turning her head when a carriage full of gentlefolk went by. It was that unturned head that disturbed me most, I think. It was so unlike Lydia, as if all her bright curiosity had been worn away. The thought drew from me a sigh so deep that it ended in a sob impossible to ignore. I groped for a handkerchief and an explanation.

"Please forgive me, Mrs Hurst. I was thinking of my dog, Sambo. He's growing old . . . such a faithful old dog."

Mrs Hurst may have been surprised; or in view of all the things a young lady might cry over, relieved. Since the absurd-sounding statement was in fact true, I had no need to feel remorseful when she patted my hand and murmured something about our dumb friends. Yet Sambo had been far from dumb on that night of April 8th, the night of the Revival Meeting when he had barked with joy as if to greet an old friend. Indeed that was exactly what he must have done.

I sat stiff-backed at Mrs Hurst's side, my gloved hand clutching the cardcase which had belonged to Lydia and my heart ached for the lost opportunity that might never come again. Under the fringe of Mrs Hurst's cape which overlapped me like the plumage of a protective hen, I dared not verify the date on the pawn ticket; but I was almost sure it was April 7th. Isolated facts began to take on a coherent shape. I understood that there had been a quality of desperation in Lydia's movements at the end of that first week in April 1872. She had left Bayes Court, pawned whatever object she still possessed for two pounds, and gone to the Meeting at Bainsacre, as she had vowed to do. Her act had all the reckless courage of a last throw. She would not seek us out; she would not come to us until she had made herself independent of father's patronage; but in her heart she must have hoped, have counted on seeing me at Bainsacre. And when I was not there, she had returned by way of Emberside, thinking perhaps that someone would see her; longing to have her pride overborne by the welcome that I at least would give her.

Regret much heavier than my tiresome tears could express weighed on my heart. Mrs Norwood's gently hinted reproaches fell far short of those I heaped upon myself. Why had I not gone to the Revival Meeting in memory of Lydia, even though I had believed her to be in Canada at the time? Why had I not rushed out, barefoot in my nightdress, when Sambo gave those joyful little barks as if his lost youth had come back to him? To have been so close—she had been at our own gate—and not to have met!

I thought of the first time we had gone to Bainsacre. We had hurried, glowing, along green ways and bridle paths, playing at godliness, with not so much as a whiff of lavender water to distinguish us from the truly pious. Afterwards, our heads still ringing with the sound of hymns, we had heard a blackbird sing in the dusk as we came up the lane between banks of primroses to the lamplit house. Lydia would carry with her the same memories as she trudged up the hill, small and lonely under the cold splendour of the stars.

This last unexpected glimpse of her, so cruelly short, brought with it a piercing clarity of illumination. With no knowledge of later events to guide me, only the insight of love, I felt that the starlit walk must have taken her away from Emberside for the last time: and much further; into a different self. It must have brought her to a crisis of will in which even Lydia's spirit might break. Did she look back from the brow of the hill at the soft darkness of the indifferent house—and turn away, her feeling of rejection finally confirmed? To what had she turned, and where?

That afternoon I took the law into my own hands and went out alone without permission. It was the beginning of a slow-growing rebellion against the refinements of Mrs Hurst's sheltered retreat. Out there in the real world amid the smells and dirt of Martlebury, or on the rough lanes, where shelter was to be found not in country houses, but in flea-infested inns and damp cottages— that was where I must now look for Lydia.

I was saved the inconvenience of taking an omnibus when Mrs Hurst's coachman overtook me and stopped. He was driving to a coach builder's to have some scratches removed from a panel. I asked him to put me down in the main shopping street. From there it was a few minutes' walk to my destination in a side street: a small shop with the glass door painted green halfway up. An announcement in the window, 'Money advanced on articles offered,' would have made its identity clear even without the three brass balls which declared it to be a pawnshop under the proprietorship of Messrs. Scotman and Levant.

Pulling down my veil, I pressed the latch and stepped into the dim interior. On my left was a counter, divided at the further end into screened booths. The shop was crammed from floor to ceiling with clothes, china, books, microscopes—all of them dusty, ticketed and sadly awaiting redemption. Instinctively I chose the privacy, such as it was, of one of the booths; but I could hear quite clearly what passed between the man in charge and his client, a woman, in the next one; nor was she completely hidden. Her dress was of cheap batiste, its two flounces edged with tawdry lace and short enough to show a good two inches above her ankles.

"It's no use bringing this." The man sounded tired but firm. "You've had money on it time and again. It's all but worn out."

The woman murmured something about the garment's being warm and having plenty of wear in it still.

"Then you'd best kept it. You need a warm cloak in your way of life."

"There's no need to taunt me. What other way of life is there for such as me? You'd rather see me starve, I dare say."

"God knows I'm not taunting you, but you've come to the wrong place. We do a good class of business here. Try one of the dolly shops in Shambles Lane. They'll give you a few coppers on this."

I caught a glimpse of her as she tottered out on the worn-down heels of her cotton shoes. The cruel daylight from the open door feel on her sunken cheeks. There was no doubt that they were rouged. I could scarcely believe my eyes. This must actually be one of the lost fallen creatures Addy had told me of.

It was my turn. Mr Scotman—or Mr Levant—faced me across the counter. He wore a pearl pin in his stock. The face above it was hard and weary. Being ignorant of the procedure, I silently produced the pawn ticket.

He looked at me sharply.

"This is no good, ma'am. You're too late. Whatever the article was, it's very likely been sold by this time. You pledged it for two pounds. What was it?"

" I don't know. It was not I who pledged it."

He flung the ticket back at me.

" This won't do. It won't do at all. Ours is a respectable firm. You can't pick up a ticket, walk in here and collect an article that was never yours in the first place. We have our license to think of."

"Oh pray don't be angry, Mr Levant . . ."

"Scotman."

"Mr Scotman. I didn't come for the . . . article, as you call it. It belonged to a dear friend whom I am trying to find." In my earnestness I put up my veil. "I hoped you might remember her. News of her, that is all I want. She left the ticket behind in her lodgings. I thought she might have come and told you and perhaps left an address . . ."

How hopeless it seemed!

He appeared to believe me. At any rate he looked again at the number and date on the ticket and explained that unredeemed goods could be sold at the end of a year and a week. Valuable property worth more than ten pounds was auctioned and the details were entered in a book.

" But this article was worth only two pounds."

Mr Scotman gave a weary smile.

"Two pounds were advanced on it," he corrected me, and took a ledger from under the counter.

I waited while he turned the pages. A cold-eyed fish stared from a glass case. A yellowing wedding dress drooped from a hook and I drooped too. The shop was airless. The sheer density of material objects—articles, that is—muffled the ticking of such clocks as still recorded the doleful minutes of their exile. The rest had lapsed into a depressed silence.

"Hah!" Mr Scotman triumphantly laid his finger on an entry. "A mechanical bird in cage, of Austrian make. Would that be it?"

It took me a second or two to recognise it from the terse description: the miraculous bird that sang more sweetly than a nightingale in its mother-of-pearl garden: the last of the Lorne treasures: all that Lydia could snatch from the vultures who had already closed in on the ormolu and marquetry, the mahogany and porcelain. It was to have been mine. How many times had she promised it to me, both of us flushed and solemn at the thought of such a sacrifice! She must have taken it surreptitiously with Alice's help when she made her escape, in one hand her valise, in the other, the bird cage; a pretty, whimsical, endearingly useless thing. When that too had gone, how drab a prospect lay before her!

"Yes, " I said. "That would be it."

"I'll write down the name of the dealer who bought it. He specialises in that kind of thing." Mr Scotman handed me the address. "You may be able to trace it but it could have been sold again by this time."

How drab a prospect! The street was quiet in the murky light of Martlebury's springtime. Only one other figure was to be seen, as motionless, as lacking in the will to move away as myself. She leaned listlessly against the wall on the opposite side: the woman who had tried to pledge the cloak. What would become of her, or any homeless woman, when all her possessions were gone? For a terrible moment I saw Lydia changed into just such a lost, sunken-cheeked outcast as the forlorn creature over the way. On impulse I crossed the road and awkwardly thrust five shillings into her hand.

"Please accept it. I'm sorry . . . about the cloak."

She looked at the money in disbelief, then at me. Her dull eyes did not brighten but suddenly she shivered from head to foot as if some fearful tension had been relaxed.

"You must have been sent." She pointed over the low wall. "If you hadn't come, that's where I would have been by tonight."

Down a steep embankment, at the very bottom of the long slope, motionless, lightless, smelling of decay, lay the black waters of a canal. One could fall, I thought, no lower than that. Once I would have been too complacent, too ignorant to believe that she would do—what she said. But she had spoken with stark directness as if she had indeed faced the choice between life and extinction. Besides, I had seen a man step out into space and fall with the suddenness of a spider but without so much as a gossamer thread to hold him. I knew the remorse of not having said the right word in time. Worse still I had said the wrong ones.

"You must never do such a thing. Never, never. Don't you see? It would be worse—afterwards. I can't explain it. But there's always something you can do to make things better. There's always hope. You're hungry and unhappy. Tomorrow you'll feel different. I hope, if I were in your place, I would be able to be brave."

"You'll never be in my place."

I don't think she said it bitterly though bitterness would have been pardonable. She even smiled, a pinched, dark-toothed smile.

How deeply the incident affected her, I cannot tell. It had a profound effect on me. It shook all my thoughts and feelings from

their set pattern into a new shape. I walked up the wide steps of
Beech Grove House and across the shining floor of the hall like a
stranger. It was not that the gilt sconces and yellow silk shades
had lost their charm but their charm had become frivolous.
There was no time for such things. People outside clamoured for
help of a kind not catered for by Mrs Hurst. There were circumstances wherein Sonatas, Impromptus and Preludes, however dil-
igently practised, were of little use.

In this mood, a letter awaiting me in my room stirred me to act
more promptly than it might once have done. It was a short note,
written in a feeble hand by Violet Parker from her home in the
country. She was ill and not likely to return to Martlebury. If
ever I was in the neighbourhood of Hartbeck she would be so
very pleased to see me. She hoped it was not presumptuous to
mention it, but she had missed my visits.

I took the letter at once to Mrs Hurst for her advice. The
village lay some ten miles south of Martlebury.

"You kindly said this morning, Mrs Hurst, that country air
would do me good. I wondered . . ."

She appeared dubious though not from lack of sympathy.

"It would be a kindness to visit the poor girl: a short visit, and
provided the illness is not catching. We must make enquiries. As
to staying in the neighbourhood, I must confess to some dislike of
Hartbeck. The situation is too low-lying to be healthy. One hears
of epidemics there. But Upper Hartbeck is higher and more open.
I believe the Haleys have an old nurse living in one of their
houses there."

It was not long before her enquiries produced the address and
the information that the former nurse had rooms to let.

" Quite close to the church, I understand. Early English, and
picturesquely situated. But it does attract artists, I'm afraid, so
naturally you must avoid it except for the services."

There was not much to choose, Mrs Hurst implied, between
artists and epidemics.

Upon one thing I was determined: to buy back the singing bird
at any cost. Lydia had meant it for me. On her mysterious journey she had left it behind and had left no other trace. It became
the one object in all the world I wanted. More than that, it became a talisman, a sign. Sober reasoning could bring no comfort.
I faced the seriousness of Lydia's plight and knew that the search
for her must be put into more competent hands than mine. For

the time being I fell back on superstition and invested the bird with prophetic powers. Finding it would be a sign that I would find Lydia. If I did not find it . . .

At the first opportunity, armed with all the money I possessed, I sought out the dealer in Wood Street. The mechanical bird, he told me, had been sold a few weeks ago to a gentleman from out of town.

The omen was sinister. For the first time I lost hope. She was gone. It was too late. Too late. The mournful syllables stirred echoes even more mournful; for I had heard them spoken with a despair far deeper than my own.

Miss Hinch and I left for Hartbeck at the end of the week.

18

From Upper Hartbeck on the hill to Hartbeck in the hollow was less than a mile. A winding lane went down between fields to a bridge over the stream. From there a straggle of cottages led to the village green. I found it a pleasant walk when on the first morning I went to visit Violet; and I had the lane to myself except for one other person: a gentleman in a black coat and clerical collar who was walking in the opposite direction. He wished me good day and passed on. I had no more than a glimpse of his bearded face but his stature and his deep voice put me in mind of the clergyman who had preached so eloquently at the Revival Meeting at Bainsacre. I was almost certain it was the same man.

The encounter and the memories it evoked, together with my anxiety on Violet's account, were so absorbing that for a while I did not notice what was to strike me more forcibly later on. Having reached the bridge, I became aware of a curious depression quite distinct from my own sober thoughts. Indeed its origin was not mental but physical. It was as though the place itself exerted an unpleasant influence. I felt it as a constriction in the head and a heaviness in the limbs quite out of keeping with the May morning. The hedge bordering the lane had been alive with birds, the sky open and clear; but here on the bridge between wooded banks rising steeply on either side, the silence was oppressive. In summer the valley must be no more than a sunless rift in the dense foliage. Even on a spring day with the buds just breaking into leaf, the light was muted. The stream scarcely moved and made no sound.

Close by the water and below the level of the lane stood a cottage, its door open. I paused and looked back, half expecting to see some one come out but the window was curtainless, the place presumably empty.

Hartbeck itself was more cheerful. I soon found the stonemason's house, a substantial dwelling overlooking the green. In more fortunate days, before Mr Parker's accident, the family must have lived in comfort. The wide rooms were well furnished with family heirlooms: a long case clock; a carved linen chest; an oak dresser well equipped with willow-ware and pewter. Mrs Parker took me upstairs, where Violet had her own sunny room. She sat by the window wrapped in shawls. I was startled by her thinness. Since we had last met she had faded to a shadow; but I had never seen her so happy. To be at home after an absence of more than two years was all she wanted.

Besides, their prospects had improved a little. Her father had regained some use of his injured arm and his elder son was now old enough to learn the trade. The two of them were busy in the yard under Violet's window, at work on a tombstone long overdue. A dismal occupation, it seemed, but to the Parkers a source of hope for a brighter future. When we had talked for a while, Violet begged me to go and speak to them.

"She's looked forward to seeing you, Miss Penrose," the stonemason told me. "It raised her spirits wonderfully when your letter came. She'll pick up now, I shouldn't wonder."

I watched as he directed his son's painstaking attempts to chip out the chosen text with hammer and chisel on a block before venturing on the tombstone itself. Fortunately it was short: AT REST. It was comforting too: and the Parkers worked together so harmoniously while the younger children played with a wooden horse and the poultry strutted in the orchard and Buttercup ruminated in the pasture, that the scene was a cheerful one for Violet to watch from her window.

"You haven't heard anything of Miss May?" she asked when I went back to say goodbye.

I told her about my visit to Mr Scotman.

"Not the bird," she cried in dismay. "She would never part with the bird."

It had stood on a table by Miss May's bed. Violet used to hear her winding it up and it would sing, better than a canary: a trilling, silvery song.

"She used to tell me about it when I was a little girl."

"It's a shame for strangers to have it," Violet said. "But where is *she?* That's what I would like to know. Where is she?"

I had taken her hand. The same thought occupied us both: the same deep concern. It was one of those times that seem significant: moments of transition from one experience to another; in this case—could it be?—from ignorance to the knowledge we so earnestly longed for. Our united will must surely force an answer from out of the unknown. But the tremulous pause yielded no information. Into the silence came only the sound of the mason's tools chipping out the words: AT REST. And this time, in spite of the children and Buttercup and the pink and white orchard blossom, it brought a melancholy reminder of the brevity of life, the endlessness of eternity.

Having promised Violet that I would come again the next day and read to her, I walked home. Again, on the bridge I felt the change of atmosphere, a departure of sound and movement. Cold air rose from the stream but without any bracing effect. It brought instead a lassitude like a loss of life, a purely physical reaction, presumably, to the enclosed nature of the place; the imprisoning effect of its trees; the threatening aspect of their massive trunks; the absence of any sign of human life.

The cottage door again—or still?—stood open. This time I noticed a light-coloured object lying on the path. A child's ball? Or a basin? There was no gate. I took a few steps through the damp grass that overgrew the path, saw that the object was a skull and fled back to the lane and up the hill as if the Furies were after me. It was only a sheep's skull, a common enough *memento mori* in those parts, and I rather enjoyed the panic: but it was not entirely simulated. The place was sinister. I carried away with me, even when safe between the hedgerows and among the chaffinches, an impression of death.

Our stay at Upper Hartbeck was an interlude; a break from our normal way of life yet not quite a holiday. Miss Hinch enjoyed it. A short ramble round the village, a peep at its ancient church and schoolroom, a purchase at the one shop, provided all the activity she required. I, on the other hand, spent most of my time at Lower Hartbeck, sometimes visiting Violet twice in a day. Ill though she was, she was such a cheerful companion that the visits were every bit as beneficial to me as to her. I began to look forward to them and soon learned to pass the cottage and cross the bridge with perfect composure though it was always cold there and the air smelt dank and unwholesome.

So far the weather had been fine but one day when we had been at Hartbeck for about a week, a heavy shower kept me at the Parkers for longer than usual. Mrs Parker insisted on giving me a

lunch of bread and cheese and milk and it was early afternoon
when I set off to walk home. I had got no further than the bridge
when it began to rain again. My instinct was to go doggedly on
and risk a wetting; but sunlight glancing on the long shafts of
rain above the stream persuaded me that the shower would soon
be over.

Still I wavered until a chilly trickle penetrated the back of my
collar and sent me darting into the cottage for shelter.

I had darted, in fact, right into the front room before I discovered to my dismay that the house was not empty. Not only were
there a bed, a chair and a table but also a person: a woman who
appeared from the inner room with a broom in her hand; or
rather in both hands like a pike. We gaped at each other.

"I beg your pardon. Please forgive me." I gasped out an explanation. "I had no idea . . . The house seemed empty."

"Come in," she said and put down the broom. "You're welcome, only you took me aback."

She was a decent old woman and when she took me into her
living room at the back, I found it no poorer or plainer than the
usual labourer's cottage. She had more self-respect than might
have been expected. The first thing she did was to take off her
pinafore and put on a clean apron. Since I was evidently to be
treated as company, I told her my name and learned that she was
Mrs Timothy.

"I must have frightened you. You're so quiet here."

"I was ready for anything, miss. Once bitten, twice shy."

"Do you mean that this wasn't the first time someone came in
without being invited, and frightened you?"

"They'd have frightened me if I'd been here although folk
don't frighten me as a rule. Only they weren't ordinary folk." She
paused, turned in her chair and looked quickly at the door between the two rooms. "I'd been sent for to my sister's t'other side
of Hartbeck. She'd had a fall and couldn't move. It was while I
was staying there . . ." She moved her chair as if to command a
better view of the door: a manoeuvre that I found unsettling; and
I too looked at the door, expectantly.

"They came here?"

She nodded, sitting on the edge of her chair and continually
clasping and unclasping her hands. At the thought of folk who
were not ordinary folk coming uninvited, my nerves vibrated in
sympathy. Where had they come from? Through the woods,

across the bridge or even—the fancy scarcely seemed too outrageous—out of the stream?

My hostess got up, filled a jug of water from a bucket, replenished the kettle and set it on the fire.

"I'll tell you something." She drew her restless chair closer to mine. Her blue eyes were round and solemn. "I've never felt the place was my own since then. It's never been the same. Them being here while I was away. And what they might have left behind them."

She could not have communicated the unpleasantness of the situation more effectively. I understood, with a positive chill of fear, how it must have felt: the occupation of her hearth and home by these mysterious people: a silent army . . . How many, I asked her.

"Just the two of them." She glanced again, sharply, at the door. "Just him and her and their things."

The simplicity of her story with its indescribable characters; the horrid fact that the house had never felt the same again as if the unwelcome pair had indeed left something behind them: a miasma; a permanent displacement of the air; a gap in time: these things roused my imagination to feverish activity.

"The door wasn't locked, you see. It won't lock but I wedge it. It's best left a little bit open because of the damp. It's damp here." It was cold too in spite of the fire, as if the stream occasionally changed its course and flowed through the house. "But they didn't have the excuse you had," Mrs Timothy went on. "There were curtains up in them days." A shadow crossed her face. She looked bewildered. "They all had to be burned and the bedding and that. Dimity and calico I'd had since I was married. Everything went."

A sudden suspicion quickened my interest, already morbidly excited.

"Was it because they were infected?"

"Smallpox. That's what they had, the two of them."

"They came here for shelter, I suppose, thinking the house was empty."

"You believe me?"

"Yes, I do. Of course."

"People don't believe me. Hardly anyone saw them. People think I made it all up, except my sister Meg. 'You're such an unlucky one, our Jenny,' she says. 'If you told me the Old Deuce

himself had come and slept in your front room, I'd believe you.'
'If the devil's a man six feet high in a black cloak, then the devil it
was,' I said to her.''

Every word of this extraordinary conversation increased my
astonishment and yet for all that, I had the continual sensation of
knowing what would come next. In framing the question, I knew
what the answer would be.

"How long were they here?"

"I was six weeks at my sister's. They came while I was away.
They were over the worst when I came back round about Mar-
tinmas. They might have died here." She stared past me into the
green twilight under the new leaves beyond the window. "I
wouldn't have known how to manage."

"It must have been a shock to find them here, even alive."

Our eyes met as we shared a vision of the unspeakable alternative. Under the frill of her mob-cap, hers had still a glassy look
like a pair of blue beads, though the shock had been administered
nearly two years ago. The fallen leaves had lain thick underfoot
when she came up the path and found her house occupied. Confronted by those terrified blue eyes, the visitors had gathered their
things together and gone. But the place had never felt the same.

The kettle came to the boil. Mindful of Mrs Hurst's warnings
about epidemics, I declined tea. One never knew . . . Others
were braver. I inserted the next question like a coin in a musical
box which played the expected tune but always with odd, unfore-
seen variations.

"Was there no one to tend them while they were ill?"

"The minister's wife from Upper Hartbeck. Mrs Joseph Thane.
She came and nursed them. More's the pity as it turned out. She
was the one that told the men to come and burn my curtains and
bedding. Sixpence an hour they get for burning folks' things.
That's what they get," she repeated, scandalised. "Mrs Thane
sent me blankets and sheets but she never sent curtains. She
wouldn't have time, I reckon." For the first time she expressed
disapproval. "I'm Church of England myself. Always have been.
You'll not take a sup of tea?"

The story seemed to have petered out. I could not go on plying
her with questions. There was no more to be learned. They—I
thought of them in the same nameless sinister way as Mrs Timothy did—must have gone straight from here to Emberside, hoping to find shelter there.

Mrs Timothy came with me to the lane. She looked very small against the huge back-drop of trees.

"The only thing is . . . I didn't like it when he came back."

"When was that?"

"Last summer."

The trees in full foliage would be more menacing than ever when he came the second time. She would see no sky at all. And how tall he would seem to her in his black cloak and slouch hat: how startling his face, ravaged by illness and despair!

"Perhaps he wanted to thank you," I said doubtfully.

"It was Mrs Thane he wanted to see, not me. I told him where to find her." Her face contorted in a nervous laugh. "I've sometimes thought . . ." I could tell that she didn't want to let me go. Her eyes met mine, seeking reassurance . . . "he might come back again. Any time."

"Don't be afraid. He won't come back." I patted her hand. The skin was thin and dry. Her lips quivered. "He'll never come back. I'm quite sure."

My skirt brushed the sheep's skull. It rattled forlornly.

"That dratted thing." she said.

"Is it . . . Do you . . . ?" What *reason* could she have for harbouring such a trophy?

"It's always been there," she said—and went back slowly to the house the Graws had used as their own.

She left me bemused and as deeply shaken by this unexpected discovery as if the Graws had once again materialised—from the trees or the river bed. There was no escaping them. It was to Hartbeck, then, that Graw had come the day before he died. I remembered that he had seemed about to tell me what business had taken him there. His manner had been sombre. I wondered if Mrs Thane had been pleased to see him. If an opportunity should arise, I would speak to her, perhaps even call. It would be a privilege to meet so excellent a woman. It occurred to me that the clergyman I had met on my first morning at Hartbeck might well be her husband, the Rev. Joseph Thane.

The Manse, I seemed to recollect, was at the far end of the village of Upper Hartbeck, but the little stone chapel stood to the left of the lane at the top of the hill, looking westward over its own small burial ground where a man was at work with scythe and shears when I passed. The chapel door was ajar. With a faint hope that Mrs Thane might be busy about some occupation there, I peeped inside, but the whitewashed room with its pine-wood pews was empty.

I came out into the sunshine and found to my delight that a rainbow had spread its arch over the whole valley. Within its frame the fields dipped and rose again to a luminous sky.

"Can you tell me where I might find Mrs Thane?"

The man did not answer. I thought he might be deaf.

"Mrs Thane?" I repeated.

He took off his cap, not out of respect for me but in instinctive reverence as he pointed to a grass-grown mound.

"That one."

"Is she . . . I didn't know that Mrs Thane had died."

The shock was as great almost as if I had known her.

"She died a year past November, of smallpox. She caught it from some vagabonds down yonder." He jerked his head contemptuously in the direction of Mrs Timothy's cottage. "There'd have been a headstone up long before this, only the mason had an accident. He hasn't worked for long enough."

He put on his cap and began to pull down clinging stems of ivy from the chapel window. In the field below, lambs leapt and staggered after the placid ewes as they browsed in grass shimmering with cowslips. The thorn-bushes had lost their earthly form and grown ethereal under a nimbus of tender green.

From hill to hill the rainbow brightened. I stood by the green mound where Mrs Thane lay at rest and watched until the miraculous colours grew dim and disappeared; and as always when a rainbow fades, I grieved for the passing for a radiant thing never to be restored.

Indeed, whether it was the artless innocence of the lambs; or the remembered scent of earlier springs; or the sensation of being shown, within the rainbow's mystic span, tokens of life and death; or—as I now believe—the upsurge of an instinct deeper than knowledge; whatever the reason, no personal sorrow could have touched my heart more keenly.

The hem of my skirt ruffled the white-faced daisies at my feet. I was actually trembling . . .

A woman so good, so compassionate and brave, would feel no bitterness when the fever came upon her, only resignation and forgiveness. Her example did me no good. I could not emulate it; I could feel nothing but hatred for the Graws and their heedless way of life: rootless people who went where they liked and left

behind them a trial of suffering and misery. They had survived
the fever. Mrs Thane had died. The injustice of it sickened me.
Even though she had been alive when they left Hartbeck and
Graw had not known of her death until his last visit to Mrs
Timothy, that didn't alter the fact, I told myself with a revival of
all the old hostility, that the Graws had brought Mrs Thane to
her grave as surely as if they had laid hands on her and killed her.

Any sympathy I had felt for Simeon Graw left me. His death
had not redeemed the sins of his life. I remembered the long
shadow he had cast on the bright kitchen when first he came to
Emberside and Lydia's instant recognition of 'Lucifer himself'.
We had both known that his coming was a disaster. Here too in
Mrs Timothy's haunted cottage and at the Manse was fresh evidence of the doom inflicted by the Graws on those they visited.
The same atmosphere of nightmare had corrupted the wholesome
air of my own home and never been dispelled.

But I was ready now and eager to go back and take my mother's place as mistress of the house. Homesickness seized me, for
the low-ceilinged rooms, the brick garden path, the wicket to the
meadow where larks sang in the breeze blowing softly down from
Limmergill Fell. The pink thorn must be coming into bloom.

Yet the memories were strangely blurred as if the tree shadows
which had half concealed the house when I last saw it, had
spread and darkened and buried it in shade. Trying to penetrate
the twilit rooms, I was baffled by some cause of uneasiness hidden
in the heart of them.

It was in this confused state of mind that I received an unexpected letter from father, redirected from Beech Grove House.
Its contents banished all other thoughts. I say 'contents'. It was
in fact his manner of writing rather than any definite statement
that sent my volatile hopes rocketing to such dizzy heights that
Miss Hinch was alarmed by my flushed checks cheeks and agitated gasps.

I was to go home, at once, to hear his news. It would be a
surprise: a wonderful surprise. He hoped it would make me as
happy, if that were possible, as it had made him. Something
about youth being recaptured . . . a change for the better. He
was also writing to Mrs Hurst.

It was all perfectly clear to me. I read between the lines. He
had found her. Lydia had come back. In an ecstasy of joy and
relief I laughed at Miss Hinch's suggestion that I should take

camomile tea and lie down. Miss Hinch! I flung her to the winds, together with Mrs Hurst and almost, to my shame, Violet. But I'm thankful to say that my better nature sent me scurrying down to Lower Hartbeck to say goodbye and promise to come again bringing a marvellous surprise.

"I believe I can guess." Violet's pale face brightened. "Oh, how I shall long to hear!"

I made all the arrangements myself: hired a fly at the inn, packed, drove to the nearest station, travelled by train to Martlebury, thence to Netherlaw, champing with impatience as I waited on platforms; rehearsing speeches and explanations; smiling to myself, pulling off my gloves and immediately putting them on again. Beneath the flurry of feeling throbbed a more steadfast happiness: a revival of all my deep love for father, Lydia, home, Emberside. Excitement had kindled all my faculties so that I seemed now to remember every stick and stone, every angle of the rambling house: where, at each hour of the day, light fell: how shadows deepened the mysterious intimacy of its nooks and corners.

It was evening when I reached Saxon's Gate station. Too impatient to wait for a conveyance, I left everything and ran through the fields. From the diagonal path between the young green corn I saw the house. A column of chimney smoke rose straight into the sky, untroubled by any breeze. I remembered how Lydia had once said that when smoke went straight up, the wind must be from the south because south was at the bottom of the page in the atlas. Father had teased her unmercifully for years after. I laughed—and came out into the lane.

Addy was at the gate. She was bursting with news. I could not read her expression, kissed her, but did not stay to talk.

They were in the drawing room. She was sitting in the Berlin-worked chair.

"Isobel, my darling." Father was nervous: more nervous than I could have imagined. "We didn't tell you before. It will be a surprise. My new wife."

At first I didn't recognise the lady in the silk dress. Her hair was dark, her skin pale. She did not move or speak. There was no need. She had only to smile, showing her perfect teeth, to make her lovely face lovelier still.

"Your stepmother," father said.

I looked into the strange light eyes of Betsy Graw.

19

No sound came from the other side of the sweetbriar
hedge: the sunnier side where my father and stepmother sat in the summer-house. The air was suitably
scented with orange blossom: the earth as lavishly spread with
pink petals as any bride could wish: the sky as unclouded as the
blue-lined canopy Robert had painted—for me.

They would be sitting hand in hand. They rarely talked; Betsy
because she had nothing to say; father possessed by a happiness
so rapt that it bereft him of words; as it also robbed him, except
where Betsy was concerned, of sight, hearing and every other
kind of response. The silence in the summer-house was not the
humdrum, companionable silence of a sedate couple no longer
young. The rustle of silk and a low exclamation reached me
through the hedge. I imagined father, as I had often seen him,
covering Betsy's hands with ardent kisses or holding her in a
close embrace; and I deliberately diverted my imagination to
other channels, or rather into a slightly different channel. There
could be no mental escape from the situation any more than there
could be a physical one. I was trapped.

The shock of my homecoming had left me stunned: fallen from
the heights of such very different expectations that I suffered a
spiritual concussion worse than an illness. My first panic-stricken
impulse to leave, to beg father to let me go back to Mrs Hurst's,
quickly died in a convulsion of shame. By this time everyone at
Beech Grove House must know of the scandal which had enliv-
ened the dinner-tables of Saxon's Gate, Limmergill and
Netherlaw for almost a year. Besides, the few encounters I had
had with father were so painful that I felt a positive dread of
asking him anything; not because he was ever unkind but because
he had forgotten me. He didn't see me. He saw nothing but
Betsy. His blindness confirmed my own feeling of having died
and been denied burial; of being obliged instead to take up the

threads of my old life as daughter of the house in hands as helpless as a skeleton's.

As to the stages whereby so rare a moth had emerged from so
drab a chrysalis, I learned of them slowly, helped by hints from
Addy and later the Waylands. Looking back to the day I had said
goodbye to Betsy, expecting never to see her again, I seemed to
detect signs of a change in her; but how could I have foreseen her
exotic blossoming from the bedraggled, petticoatless wife of a
vagabond artist into the mistress of Emberside?

"We saw it coming," Addy told me, "soon after you left." I let
her talk. It would have been unkind to repel her confidences and
hypocrisy to keep a distance between us at such a time. Adrift as
I was, I clung to her. "It was when Ruby had toothache. It's that
toothache I blame. She was beside herself with pain and we had
to let her go to Netherlaw to have the tooth pulled out. Then she
went to her mother's and what with one thing and another it was
three days before she got back."

There had seemed no harm in asking Mrs Graw to take in the
master's supper, since Addy was run off her feet.

"I just had a feeling though, when I put the tray in her hands
and saw those eyes. It hadn't struck me before how she'd improved. She'd had plenty of rest and peace of mind without *him*,
Graw, to pester her; and she'd left off taking those herbs as can
plainly be seen," Addy said grimly. "She looked as if new life had
come into her. Yes, that was when the damage was done but I
never thought it would come to this. It's easy to see why he's
married her in the end. I don't know which is worse, before or
after. We wouldn't have stayed, Ruby and me, if it hadn't been
for you, Miss Isobel, love."

Shameless! The word soon cropped up. I believe Addy would
have withdrawn it out of respect for my feeling towards father
but I was far beyond taking offence. Father had undoubtedly
been, and was still, shameless. But the word could not so readily
be applied to Betsy. Strange to say in view of the passion she
excited, she was quite without sensuality; nor could she be suspected of calculation. No scheming had been required to bring
her to the good fortune she now enjoyed. Her mode of life had
been to survive moment after moment in speechless endurance
until fate brought her to a moment of a different kind and endurance was no longer necessary. With the same passive acceptance
she had moved into her new orbit. I suppose, as she stood in the

doorway holding the tray, father simply saw that she was lovely. All unawares, he had been harbouring a woman of unique beauty. He was instantly entranced by a rapturous delight in her physical form and its proximity to his own. And that was only the beginning.

They were perfectly at ease together. Having no wishes, she never opposed him. Caring nothing for him—or anyone—she felt no anxiety to please him, nor fear of offending him. For her to be there was all he desired and she had no wish to be anywhere else. She made no demands.

Her recovery from the smallpox was complete, her health perfect. She had no need of exercise (indeed she had had enough of that to last a lifetime) to freshen her magnolia skin or to keep her figure slender. Every meal was a treat to her but she ate sparingly. Possessions did not interest her. The parasols, fans, gloves and brooches heaped on her by her doting husband she accepted with a smile, remembered to put them up or on, and withdrew into the private realm where her spirit dwelt. He had already given her all she could ever want: the absence of cold, or heat; the security of being still, of not having to move on; of hearing the beat of rain on the window and hearing it from the inside; of lying on a thick goose-feather mattress between clean linen sheets.

As I sat thinking of all this on the north side of the sweetbriar, I was still far from having fathomed my stepmother's remarkable depths; but I knew that she was invincible, as firmly entrenched as a stone.

A stiffness in my limbs reminded me that once again I was sitting on the extreme edge of the garden seat.

"Why have you taken to sitting in that uncomfortable fashion?" father had already asked when he found me similarly perched in the drawing room. I made no answer. He would not have heard. Having taken his eyes from Betsy for a moment, he had turned to her again. But I thought of Mrs Timothy who would never again sit at ease in her own chair. We were sisters in misfortune: both of us dispossessed.

They were going up the path. I stayed on for a while but it was cool out of the sun. The summer-house was now a place to be avoided, the quarry unthinkable. I went languidly indoors.

"Sit with your stepmother for a while," father said as he passed me in the hall. "I have a letter to write."

Was he so deranged as to imagine that Betsy would notice and
be offended if left alone? Some vague impression of my speechless
suffering may have inspired him with a wish to bring us together.
I drifted into the drawing room where she sat, as she did for
hours at a time, with the curtains half drawn, her hands idle.

We faced each other. What she saw I cannot tell. It was at such
times as this that I felt her hypnotic power most strongly; so that
to this day I can recall the impression she gave of existing in a
twilight of the mind, outwardly passive, yet drawing upon limit-
less resources within. That was why she had no need to speak or
act or even think. Was it idleness or an elemental wisdom as deep
as her femininity (I could never be sure) that made her wash her
hands of the whole tiresome business of housekeeping? The servants would have resented her orders if she had given any. (Addy
must often have thought bitterly of the green merino dress.) She
gave none; and the domestic routine continued smoothly on the
lines Lydia had laid down.

"I'm her stepdaughter," I thought, with a sensation of groping
in the muted crimson light to find my new identity. "Everything
that belonged to mother belongs to her."

Did that include me? In the half light the room took on a
slumberous quality. Birds were singing, ravished by the ecstasy of
Maytime, but the garden seemed miles away. Already—I had
been home for two weeks—callers had ceased. Mrs Wayland and
the Kirkdales had felt it a duty to pay their respects to the new
Mrs Penrose. They came together as if hoping to find strength in
numbers. Conscious of all the talk there must have been before
they came and the talk there would be as they went home, I saw
them, even dear Mrs Wayland, as spies reconnoitring from enemy
territory.

Fortunately the thought was bracing. It brought temporarily to
life Miss Isobel Penrose, a calmly correct young lady fresh from
the hands of Mrs Hurst, who chatted amiably about nothing in
particular and moved steadily but without haste into any awkward conversational breach. There were several. Recalling their
discomforts, I writhed all over again.

Father's pride in Betsy had led him to adopt a rather patronis-
ing attitude to 'poor Edwin Kirkdale' and his plain, staid wife.
The ladies noted this, I was well aware, with an admirable lack of
rancour; as they also noted every detail of Betsy's jewellery, her
midnight blue foulard and point lace; and the evidence of the

scandalous speed after her recent marriage with which she would be confined. And I knew, with an increase of loneliness which was all that despair had left me capable of feeling, that they would not come again.

It was father whom they would want to avoid, not Betsy. His absorption in her was insufferable, whereas her 'weirdness' as Mrs Wayland called it, while it made social intercourse difficult, might not have put an end to it. After all, the weirdness was interesting and the neighbours didn't have to live with it as I did. Moreover there was nothing coarse about Betsy. It was as the young daughter of a poverty-stricken bookseller that she had first caught Graw's roving but discriminating eye. Gentility—or the lack of it—did not enter into our present situation. The mere idea of such a distinction faded into empty pretence in the face of Betsy's utter disregard of it. She had her own distinction.

No, it was father who was quietly dropped by the few friends with whom we had been on visiting terms. I realise now that he had never been popular. What could be made of a man in his position who never rode to hounds or got up shooting parties? And this, everyone said, was the result. Eugene Penrose had lost his head over a raggle-taggle artist's widow . . .

She didn't look like that. Feeling my eyes upon her, she smiled. It was her smile one waited and watched for. In repose her face was beautiful. Indeed I rarely saw it animated and never—except once—saw that still surface ruffled by a storm. But each time she smiled, the miracle I had first seen in the coach house was repeated: the other, even lovelier woman was liberated; and as the outer woman grew more pleasing to the eye, the inner woman kept pace, even surpassing, step by step, the visible Betsy.

As if a climax had been reached, I got up and in the same will-less fashion as I had drifted in, drifted out into the hall and had got halfway up the stairs when Robert came in through the garden door. He had been waiting as usual.

"I thought you might come out for a while. Don't just shake your head. You really must have fresh air and company. Even mine."

His upturned face was thinner, I observed but with detachment. One more change for the worse made little difference now that everything had gone wrong. He took my hand and tried to draw me gently down.

"I wish you'd come, Belle. To Hackets. For a particular reason. You haven't been there for ages."

"Not now."

What did I care for his door handles and window frames or the removal of worm-eaten wainscot and broken hearth tiles?

"I thought we'd walk to Hackets," he went on briskly as if I hadn't spoken: or rather with an assumption of briskness. With the same wooden indifference it was possible to detect a bogus quality in his matter-of-factness. It didn't ring true. "And then go on home and have tea with mother."

"Not today, Robert, thank you."

"Belle." He gave up the briskness and looked miserable. "The fact is I've got to talk to you. I've been wanting to, needing to, for ages. And now more than ever. They're sending me away again for a few weeks."

"Talk! People can't talk when they feel as I do, or listen. I don't want to talk. Leave me alone. You can't help me any more. Nobody can."

I trailed up the stairs and left him, then at once felt ashamed of the shabby way I had treated him and went down again. But he had gone. Just for a moment I entertained the idea that he might not come back. That would be the end of everything, I thought, if Robert were to leave me. Without him . . . The very thought brought a sudden dizziness as if the support on which the structure of my life depended had shown an ominous crack, threatening total collapse.

Meanwhile there was only—and always—Sambo. Having refused Robert's invitation to go out, I veered like a spiritless weathercock. The house was unbearable; a walk my only salvation. I went out into the stable yard.

"Come, Sambo. Good boy."

I had forgotten how old and weary he was. He looked at me anxiously as I unhooked the chain.

"You don't want a walk, do you? Never mind. I'll stay with you."

I bent to stroke his dear old head. He shuffled forward and laid it companionably on my shoe—and never moved again.

For a long time I knelt beside him, feeling more lonely than ever before. The girlhood I had spent in his company had come to an end. I had grown older. Indeed I felt very old. After a while I fetched Will Petway and we buried him in the pasture just beyond the garden wall. I left him alone there and went back to the silent yard, where I leaned over the empty kennel and cried until I had no more tears to shed.

And yet Sambo served me faithfully to the end; for I believe it was grief for my old friend that revived my power to feel and helped to bring me back to life.

20

Faint currents began to stir the stagnant atmosphere as my stepmother and I settled down together. Somehow I took to embroidering bonnets for my future brother. There was no risk whatsoever, father was confident, of a sister. Occasionally I read aloud. Betsy seemed not to mind. Sometimes she nodded in what may have been approval and when I closed the book, smiled. Recovering a little, I grew restless. Betsy's lack of animation drove me to spurts of busyness. I would put on an apron, fetch a bowl of water and carefully wash the ornaments on the mantel-piece with a great air of efficiency. Betsy watched with the aloofness of a being newly descended from a cloud; and gradually the porcelain figures with their chaplets of roses and buckled shoes together with the bowl, the suds, the linen cloth and myself seemed to lose all meaning and purpose and become empty gestures on the brink of that mysterious pool of experience over which Betsy seemed always to be presiding.

Though she neither toiled nor span, she did, surprisingly, take on the mending which from long practice in harsher times she did well. Finding her in need of a crewel needle one day, I produced one from Lydia's work-table which had remained all this time pushed into a corner. Some reference to Lydia's method of grafting wool, I think it was, that led me on to speak of her. At once I felt more normal. My anxiety on her behalf was no less but it had become remote: a dark cloud in a sunless sky. To talk about her was like telling a story, the more so because Betsy had never seen her and knew nothing about her. I wondered whether Simeon had ever talked to his wife at all or whether his rule that it was better not to talk extended to every subject under the sun. So far as I could make out he had, for most of the time, disregarded her completely.

'When Lydia lived here' became the equivalent of 'Once upon a time'. There was so much to tell. In remembering I grew absorbed and sometimes rattled on quite happily though always about the earlier days when Lydia went warbling round the house in her poplin and pink ribbons.

"Why did she leave?"

Betsy's simple question brought me to an abrupt halt. There was no simple answer; no answer that did not involve either Graw or father. It had become surprisingly difficult to know which of them to blame. I made some vague reply about there having been various reasons.

"Where did you say she went?"

Where indeed? She had gone to Ash House, to Bayes Court, to the Revival Meeting at Bainsacre—and then vanished again: a poor vagrant woman with a bundle, submitting to the clouds of dust from carriage wheels; such a woman as Mrs Graw had been. Across the room I caught the faint sheen of my stepmother's dress: the sparkle of her rings: the graceful tilt of her head as she waited for an answer; and I marvelled that time could bring about such reversals of fortune. There could be no certainty in life, no security of expectation.

"She had a relative . . ."

Father, needless to say, was not there when I told my stepmother about Lydia; but once he did come into the room in time to hear the tail-end of some anecdote. I can think of no reason for what I did unless it was to goad him into noticing his forgotten daughter. It could only have been done on impulse. All at once the icy reserve which had kept me from telling him what I knew about Lydia, melted.

"Father, I haven't told you yet. I met Charles Stack at Hagthorpe Junction. Lydia didn't go away with him. She went to Ash House but had to leave when Mrs Welbecome died. There was no money . . ."

"Dear me! You do surprise me, Isobel. How have you found out all this? You must tell me about it."

He went to Betsy on the sofa, kissed her hand lingeringly as if they were alone in the room, adjusted her footstool and sat down beside her, encircling her with his arms.

I stammered out a few details, lamely, while he played with Betsy's bracelet.

"So she has gone to find fresh woods and pastures new, as Milton puts it."

"I hate Milton," I said with some sincerity but most of my spleen was directed towards father for his callous indifference and folly. I would tell him no more. My contempt for him made me compare even Betsy's company favourably with his and when presently she said unexpectedly, in her low, unemphatic voice: "She must have been sad to leave Emberside," my heart warmed to her. We drew closer.

But we might have gone on for a long time, I dissatisfied and restless, Betsy in her dreamlike state of empty serenity, if it had not been for an extraordinary development which brought us into sympathy with each other and supplied Betsy's life with the purpose it had so far lacked, however peculiar that purpose might be.

Our conversations were not entirely one-sided. My stepmother was a woman of few ideas. She seemed to manage very well without exercising her intellect—or so it seemed at first. In time I began to suspect that she was only outwardly inert. At any rate, she had a capacity for limpet-like fidelity, not to either of her husbands, whom in turn she tolerated and clove to from the lack of any alternative; but to the one human being who had ever cared for her and asked nothing in return: Mrs Thane; the compelling interest of her life; the lode star of her strange existence.

One afternoon in June we sat as was our habit, cut off from the summer day outside by the half drawn crimson curtains.

"This shawl belonged to my friend, Mrs Thane," Betsy told me as she took it reverently from her mending basket. "It was the last thing she gave me before we came away. The fever had left me with such pain in my ears as I could hardly bear. She had brought me some clothes begged from her friends. But she took this from her own neck."

It was the shawl Betsy had worn swathed round her head for a whole winter. She caressed it with a loving hand, examined it carefully, found a broken strand and threaded her needle in the devout manner of a priestess restoring a sacred vestment. What little light there was drew a dark glitter from the diamonds and rubies on her strong, shapely fingers as she plied her darning needle. As I think of her, I recognise a distillation of her whole personality in that contrast—between the luxurious beauty of her appearance and the humbleness of the one task she undertook. No one in her senses, no one, that is, but Betsy, would bother to darn the shabby shawl of dingy brown wool which would have disgraced a scarecrow.

I slit open a letter from Julia which had come on the afternoon post but it was too long and closely written to decipher in the dusky room. I put it in my pocket to keep as a treat to read later on and fell to watching my stepmother with a drowsy kind of fascination. I may even have nodded off. The day she took such pleasure in shutting out was warm. From the banished garden came the sound of birds and the scent of mignonette. The work table with its little drawers: the petals like butterflies on the chintz of mother's sofa: the wine-red glow of sunlight through the curtains, all wove themselves into a memory of happiness somehow connected with the brown strands of Betsy's shawl. But something was out of tune. A bafflement teased me, to which the figurine of Psyche, coldly lustrous on her pedestal, offered a clue: high up, white and shedding an unmoving radiance . . . There should have been voices: in particular one voice, clear and fresh, and instead of the drowsy warmth, a tingling cold . . .

Betsy had begun a low-pitched account of Mrs Thane's visits to the cottage. I listened with ever-growing respect for the woman who had so tragically sacrificed herself. Betsy referred to her with quiet pride as 'my friend' and that in itself was touching. So far as I know she had no other friend.

Told in my stepmother's toneless voice, the story had a biblical simplicity and beauty. It was the story of a woman Quakerishly dressed in black with a white collar and plain bonnet, carrying a basket of food: bread, milk and wine. Returning from Lower to Upper Hartbeck, she had seen a movement in the supposedly empty cottage where the Graws had taken shelter, had found them, visited them twice a day and after a while had stayed with them for fear of spreading infection to others. She had made fires and washed their clothes—and their persons. It was a cold place with stone floors and thick white mists rising from the stream.

All this time it lay on the tip of my tongue to tell her that I knew it; that I too had been there. But she talked for once so freely as if a long pent-up stream of feeling had at last begun to flow that I was obliged to let her go on. Besides, a certain embarrassment kept me from interrupting. At the cottage I had been so vehemently on Mrs Timothy's side, had seen the Graws so clearly as the harmful intruders they had in fact proved to be, that I found it difficult at first to see the episode from Betsy's point of view. And gradually, amid so many obstacles and pitfalls, another barrier loomed.

As I listened, I had been reliving my own adventure at the cottage, followed by my journey up the lane—almost a pilgrimage it seemed—to the low mound in the burial ground at the top of the hill; so that all the time I expected some reference to Mrs Thane's death as a climax to the recital. So far Betsy had not chosen to speak of it, evidently preferring to think of their friendship as unchangeable as if preserved in amber. Naturally, I had not mentioned it from a reluctance to tread on such very awkward ground. So far as I was concerned, the Graws were responsible, even if unintentionally, for the good woman's death.

"When she gave me the shawl, that was the last thing she did for me."

"How sad!" My interruption was heartfelt and surely in the circumstances, natural. Betsy's responses were always slow and never like other people's. It was not so much a flicker of surprise that crossed her face as a look of arrested attention.

"Sad?"

Could it be that she saw Mrs Thane's death as the reverse of sad? A kind of triumph? A martyrdom, as indeed it was? Certainly in Betsy's hierarchy of human beings Mrs Thane occupied a very high place. She was elevated almost to the ranks of the divine. The very first time we talked of her in the coach house Betsy had described her as a saint.

"You don't think of it as sad?" An instinctive caution kept me from speaking more directly.

Betsy shook her head. Her eyes held a soft tenderness such as father, I'm sure, had never seen.

"She's a contented person—and wasn't long married when we knew her."

If outwardly I gave no sign, inwardly I was startled, not so much by this new aspect of Mrs Thane who had clearly possessed all the virtues known to womankind, even a capacity for happiness, but because of the tense. Had I misheard? Betsy must have said 'was' not 'is'. A pleasantly reminiscent smile played about her lips as if the period of her illness in Mrs Timothy's cottage had been a holiday she loved to remember. It must have been purged of all misery by the purity and goodness of Mrs Thane. All the same, however uplifting the experience had been, however unearthly Betsy's response to it, not even she could fail to see that Mrs Thane's death, in human terms, was sad. More than that, tragic. *If she knew about it.*

In all her songs of praise, Betsy had sounded no sorrowful note. She had spoken all the time, I now realised, as if her friend the minister's wife were still alive. I cast my mind back to the interview in the coach house. Had she said 'She *is* a saint?' In any case that was no help. Saints are always dead. But then Betsy might not have used the word in its strict, canonical sense. I made a hasty review of events on the day of Simeon's death. He had certainly known. Mrs Timothy, in her eerily sidelong way, had told him 'where to find' Mrs Thane. On his return from Hartbeck, he must have gone for reasons of his own, straight to the quarry without seeing his wife and there would be no opportunity after that of telling her. Had he kept the news to himself because he was afraid of the effect it would have on Betsy—or for some other reason? His manner had been that of a man who had heard of a bereavement and been saddened by it. He too must have respected Mrs Thane and so he should. Even now the memory of the scene in the quarry horrified me. I tried to forget it.

Our conversation continued at its habitual slow pace before taking a sudden decisive turn.

"I often think of her," Betsy confided, "especially now that I'm expecting a child. I wonder if by this time she is a mother herself."

My question was answered. The problem remained. Second by second it swelled to disturbing proportions. In what words, in what manner should I deal the cruel blow? The prop and stay of Betsy's friendless existence must be removed. She was not like other people. The loss would affect her in no ordinary way. Even now, when I had come to understand her a little, I was half afraid of her. How much more would there be to fear in a Betsy crazed with grief as she would certainly be! I racked my brains for a means of leading her gently, so to speak, to the green resting place where Mrs Thane now lay.

"To wake up when the fever was on me," Betsy went on, "and find her by my side! The comfort of it! I would lie and listen while she and Simeon talked and I would think, 'I'm safe for a while so long as she's here' "

"She talked to Simeon?"

"He had the fever first, you see, and he'd taken a turn for the better before I did. Yes, he talked to her as he did to no one else."

I don't know why it was that this simple fact should interest me. Obviously they must have talked. Perhaps it was my sense of

the wide contrast between the two that caused me to find signifi-
cance in the fact that they had chatted together. As a minister's
wife, Mrs Thane must have been skilled in bridging every kind of
gap. It was her lot to harmonise discordancies.

"He made her some kind of promise. Something she asked him
to do."

To turn over a new leaf, no doubt, and mend his ways, suppos-
ing she knew about them. If so, he had not kept the promise. I
thought sternly of the brandy bottles and gaming tables and the
spiriting away of five hundred pounds.

"Some private thing between the two of them." Betsy produced this particular recollection as if it puzzled her. " 'It would
be best not to mention it,' Mrs Thane said. I wonder now what it
was. But I never interfered . . ."

She had laid down her needle and folded the shawl. Her movements were always unhurried; yet in her manner I seemed to
detect a spark of emotion; even a suppressed excitement. She
stood up.

"There is something I would like you to see. I have it upstairs."

I was touched. It would doubtless prove to be some other pitiful remnant connected with Mrs Thane; but the wanting to show
it to me was kind. Her more usual impulse was not so much to
share as to shy away.

While she was upstairs, I pondered on the wisest course of
action to take, thinking all the while of Mrs Thane. I saw her as a
nobler version of our good and pious Prue Bailey. She had been
young too, or at least newly married. She had gone about her
errands of mercy, suffered a fearful illness and come to rest on
that west-facing hill. The little burial ground had impressed me
with its pastoral beauty and peace. I saw it permanently enclosed
in its rainbow arch: the lambs always young: the hawthorn for
ever breaking into new leaf. If I could describe it to Betsy in such
a way, it might help her to accept her friend's death without too
much distress.

She was away a long time. I pushed back one of the curtains to
let in more light and opened Julia's letter again. It was crammed
with news of Beech Grove House and Martlebury, news which
would normally have interested me. Perhaps it did then. I have
forgotten every word of it except those of the postscript.

Uncle Conrad came and took me out to tea. He sends his compliments. I told him that you had gone straight home from Hartbeck and thought it would be the end of him. A heart attack or an apoplectic stroke in Pandrill's tearoom at the most fashionable hour of the day would have been just what one might expect of Uncle Conrad. Fortunately it was neither. He recovered quickly and said: "That's it. Tell Miss Penrose the place was Hartbeck." There. I've told you . . .

The old wizard had remembered the magic word: a disturbing one. Was it possible that Lydia too had been at Hartbeck? How strange—the strangeness of it brought me to my feet—that chance had led me in her footsteps; had shown me the way she took; from Ash House to Bayes Court; from there to the Meeting at Bainsacre: past our own gate in the starlit night to—of all places—Hartbeck! There was no way of knowing when she had arrived there but she had been at Hartbeck in the June of that year, 1872, when she had written to Mr Handiside. Violet, of course, would be in Martlebury at that time and would not have seen her. Where had she stayed? Was it possible that she had still been there when I was there? Suppose we had actually been at Hartbeck *at the same time*. How cruel an irony if I had come away and left her there!

Surely we would have met. Destiny would not have brought us so close together only to keep us apart. Besides . . . It must have been a deep excitement that made me feel all at once in touch with Lydia: in close physical touch. I knelt down by her own Berlin-worked chair and laid my head upon it as I used to lay it in her lap.

"Isobel," she said. I swear it. I heard her voice; and felt against my cheek a softness, warm and familiar: Betsy's shawl. Involuntarily, I sat up, fearful of being found to have made free with it and in doing so, dislodged it. I picked it up and looked at it, with wonder and doubt and growing certainty.

There can never have existed on the face of the earth a more dreadful shawl. It was small: an uneven triangle of dingy brown. There was no fringe. A crazy affair of lost stitches desperately retrieved: an erratic switching from stocking stitch to moss stitch with here and there a grateful collapse into plain knitting with never a hint of purl. Between laughter and tears I verified all its imperfections. I knew where to look for them. After all I had knitted it myself, for Lydia. No one but my seven-year-old self could have fashioned such a—I had recourse to Mr Scotman— such an article. Even at the time, I had felt it an inadequate return for the velvet bonnet Lydia had contrived for me from a remnant of the drawing room curtains the day we made the snow lady.

Here in my hand lay the explanation of the curious feeling of recognition Betsy had roused in me when she came to Emberside for the second time. In my confusion I could not at first make the necessary connection. I thought only that Lydia had been at Hartbeck where her path had crossed the path of the Graws once again. I thought of the brown shawl as having found its way into the parcel of cast-offs Mrs Thane had begged from her charitable friends; until I remembered why of all those garments Betsy loved this one best; and then—with a rush of distress and fear like the terror of falling—I understood.

"She took it from her own neck and gave it to me . . ."

Who in all the wide world would be wearing it?

Only Lydia.

21

It must have been Lydia. When Betsy took the shawl, she took it from Lydia's hands. The hands that bathed her brow and Simeon's, that smoothed their pillows and gave them food were Lydia's. I saw them in isolation from the woman herself since it was not possible then—if it ever has been—to see Lydia as Mrs Thane.

I fixed my mind on the shawl. Kneeling by Lydia's chair, I grasped it firmly, unprepared as yet to dwell on the momentous revelation it had brought. Was it possible that Lydia had cherished and kept it, had taken it with her when she left Emberside, cramming it hastily into her one valise when she was leaving so much behind?

More than ten years, it must have been, since I had laboured over it and bedewed it with exasperated tears.

"It will be warm," I remember saying doubtfully when at last it was finished.

"It's *amazing*," Lydia replied with perfect truth. "And you did it all yourself."

I took refuge in the memory, unable at first to face the truth: that I had found her at last and she was dead. It could not be. The strands of wool were frayed and thin with age but they formed so tangible a link with the past we had shared that I could not believe in any final parting. Lydia could not have taken so decisive a step. I felt in every nerve that she was alive still; and not only alive but close to me.

I could not think that she had ever worn the shawl; not until she had ransacked her wardrobe for clothes suitable to wear on her visits to the infected cottage. But to have kept it for so long out of loyal affection; then to give it away with quick, practical common sense when the need arose! The two extremes of mood were so typical of Lydia that I felt the whole room brimming again with her presence as if, more vitally than ever before, she was there.

The illusion faded. I felt instead the painful downward drag of grief. That impulsive action when she whipped off the shawl and gave it to Betsy was not her last but it was the last I knew of. Perhaps already when she went out bare-necked into the November mist, she felt the onset of fever: the burning heat to be followed not long after by the everlasting cold. I put the shawl round my own neck. Yes, it was warm—and comforting.

"Lydia," I whispered. "I didn't know. I tried to find you."

It was not then, in those first sorrowful moments, that the pieces fell inevitably into place. It was not the time, even if I had known them all, to trace Lydia's movements step by step beyond the fateful Meeting at Bainsacre. (If only I had gone!) In my remorse that she had not found me there I had never thought that she might have found something better. I had forgotten the Meeting itself: its fervour: its rapture: its setting free of imprisoned souls. When the woods and fields rang to that outburst of singing; "I woke . . . My chains fell off, my heart was free . . ." wouldn't Lydia be singing too, with all her heart—and just a little out of tune? That night had been, as I had guessed, a turning point, but I had not thought of so spectacular an upward turn.

Least of all had I thought of the Rev. Joseph Thane, whose handsome dark-bearded face and deep voice had so impressed us both.

"He's a good man." There had been a thrill of feeling in Lydia's voice. "I should like to speak to him . . ."

Lydia married! and to a clergyman! The change was only a little less difficult to accept than the other more lasting change she had undergone. But at least after all her adventures she was safe, not only before she died but now and endlessly.

Later, when it was possible to think clearly, I thought of all these things. But then, as I knelt clutching the shawl, knowing that my search was ended, I looked straight into the heart of the mystery and saw all the vivid life I had loved shrunk to the compass of a narrow grave under a fading rainbow.

My stepmother's dress rustled at my side.

"It was among Simeon's things. Mr Wayland brought them from the hut in the quarry and I put this one away in a special place." She held out a pastel drawing of a quiet-faced woman in a cap. "Simeon didn't tell me that he had started on a portrait of Mrs Thane. He never told me anything. He didn't treat me . . ." It was the nearest she ever came to complaining. For a moment I saw in her eyes the tragic memory of all her humiliations but with her lips she revealed no more, and never did. "It isn't finished but he never did anything as good. You can see from this what she was like, better than I could tell you."

I could look at it without surprise. It is not surprise one feels in stepping across a crevasse, but tremulous awe; and after the fearful stride, the view has changed. When I had seen the drawing on its easel in the quarry, I had not understood what was obvious to me now: that Graw could not have shown Lydia in such a way unless he had seen her looking like that. How could I have guessed that having parted in hatred, they would meet again? I have often thought of their unexpected reunion and wondered how he felt when, through the fantasies of delirium, he saw her face: how she felt when she looked down on Graw, her enemy, delivered by Providence into her hands.

The answer lies in the expression of deep concern he has given her. The picture is full of the gentleness and pain of compassion, not only in her face but in his tender drawing of it. I have sometimes thought it a kind of miracle that they should have left behind them this evidence of mutual forgiveness; of an equal generosity of spirit. If she risked—and gave—her life for him, he did try belatedly and at the very last despairing moment to summon up his failing powers for her sake. Unfinished, imperfect as it is, the portrait has a quality which neither of them could have achieved without the other: a life which has outlasted theirs and may outlast us all.

Meanwhile there remained—and remains—the heartache.

"There's something I must tell you." I drew my stepmother to the sofa and sat down beside her. "It's about your friend."

I told her and we wept together, in equal grief, for Lydia Thane.

22

"Not complete mourning," I said nervously. "I don't think it would be suitable and father wouldn't like it."

"Suitable?" Betsy ignored the second point of objection and fixed upon the first.

"In your case there was no relationship. Though she was your friend," I added hastily, as Betsy's luminous eyes showed signs of drowning themselves again in tears.

But there was no further outburst. I breathed again. Almost at once I had found myself in the role of comforter. My function was to brace and support; not because Betsy wanted to be comforted: the reverse was true; but because the proportions of her distress already frightened me.

"What shall we do?" she asked after a profound pause.

"I shall not wear black."

Why this decision had come to me so promptly I could not have told. Convention did not require me to put on mourning for Lydia but convention had little to do with our present style of living at Emberside. More likely I was forced into restraint by the spectacle of Betsy's total desolation. It was only in the first moments that our grief was in any sense equal. Deeply as I mourned Lydia, my sorrow was wholesome, natural and of course uncomplicated by the guilt that overwhelmed poor Betsy with the consciousness of a huge, unpayable debt.

"She should have left us to die," she wailed. "We weren't worth the sacrifice she made."

My one protest, when the time came to think things over, was against Graw.

"Why did he not tell me? What reason could there be . . . ?"

My anger penetrated the gloom into which Betsy had retired.

"I believe she asked him not to tell. I woke and heard them talking. It made no sense to me at the time." She made a painful effort to recall the incident as she would strive to recapture every detail connected with her lost friend. " 'There's no need to say that you've seen me,' she said, or something like that. 'In time perhaps . . . Promise.' And Simeon said, 'I promise.' "

For all his shortcomings he had kept his promise, but I realised that on our last meeting in the quarry he had been perplexed and troubled as to whether or not her death absolved him: whether or not to tell me that she was dead. I concluded too that Lydia had sent them to Emberside to find shelter but she herself had not felt ready to meet us again. The reluctance seemed to me perfectly justified. In other respects my devotion to Lydia had been not exactly shaken but threatened by a peculiar feeling of having been —let down. Fleeing from creditors without a penny in her purse, she had thrilled me with her gallantry. Trudging along a dusty lane, she had reduced me to tears of sympathy. If she had changed for the worse, I could have enjoyed the luxury of forgiving her, no matter what she had done; even of rescuing her from that long slope down to the waters of the canal.

But to have changed so conspicuously for the better! That was hard to bear. It was not that she had disappointed me. Far from it. I was overawed by her goodness. It separated us, as if, while we wandered in a shady grove, she had heard the gospel call. Her songs had become hymns: her flowery hats plain bonnets. In moving from the major to the minor key, she had stopped being herself. The living Lydia I had searched for was no more. She had died twice over and was irrecoverably dead. To me, that is. Betsy's viewpoint, as I might have know, was different.

Some notion of the difference drove me to take a firm line on the subject of mourning.

"It would be quite correct for us to wear mourning jewellery. Both of us. A single piece," I stipulated quickly, thinking of father's possible reaction to a Betsy solidified in jet.

After some deliberation we bought crosses which we wore round our necks on black ribbons. The effect must have been to strengthen our appearance of unity as though the drawing room had been given over to a sisterhood. Father became a layman admitted on sufferance. From that day I believe he began to retreat.

Certainly he disliked the jet crosses and the entire situation. He had been obliged to listen to the whole story and had shown a decent regret. But the effect of it all on Betsy must have warned him that his idyll was threatened. Irrationally, in his heart, he blamed Lydia. She was at the bottom of it all. Her behaviour from start to finish had been what one might have expected; and then to have got herself mixed up with Dissenters!

"I warn you, Isobel, never let me hear of your setting foot in one of their—tabernacles. Do you understand? All this weeping and wailing when your stepmother is in so precarious a state of health—it could be dangerous. I charge you," he trembled with earnestness, "to maintain a calm and reasonable atmosphere in the house, as it was before you came home."

As a matter of fact my own state of mind was both calm and reasonable—as yet. Indeed Betsy's morbidity restored my sense of proportion. I could see now that in my search for Lydia I had been trying also to bring back the past she embodied and so had stepped out of time, gone back instead of forward, neglected my friends . . .

I devoted myself to maintaining a rational atmosphere, with some success (I thought). My stepmother's desolating outbursts of weeping ceased. To be precise they were not outbursts. In everything Betsy did there was an inward tendency. The silent welling up and copious flow of her tears suggested similarly deep resources in her whole personality: depths I was beginning to discover.

I glanced across at her one afternoon in the drawing room. She sat with her head tilted as though attending. To what? Nothing actually visible in the room, at least not visible to me. Eerie possibilities hovered. It was time to resume the kind of unexciting conversation I had begun to specialise in. It served among other things to cut off Betsy's searching questions about Lydia; or Mrs Thane as she quite rightly called her: about her tastes, opinions, clothes, handwriting . . . It was too late.

"If Mrs Thane had had a son, I wonder what she would have named him."

"Lorne. She always said . . ." I stopped with the instinctive feeling that this piece of information should have been kept to myself.

"Lorne. I like that." Betsy smiled, as if an area of doubt had been clarified.

Suppressing a certain foreboding, I opened the newspaper and read aloud an account of the weekly meeting of the Committee of the Central Association of Master Builders, a column of such annihilating dullness as to put out the last flicker of excitement in the whole world.

My mind was not on it. It occurred to me that in every sense my stepmother and I were facing in opposite directions. I had been looking out between the heavy curtains at the garden with a wistful awareness that another summer was passing me by, whereas Betsy was facing into the room; facing, as it happened, Lydia's Berlin chair. Not only did she look towards it: she was looking at it in a curiously attentive way which brought to my mind a tiny incident of the day before. Father had brought a newly published book of prints to show us and in drawing Betsy's attention to a certain page, had sat down beside her on the Berlin chair. Betsy started.

"No, not there." Her involuntary protest surprised him into getting up though in his concentration on the book he did not ask the reason.

Our opposing points of view demanded equally contrasting adjustments. My instinct was to hold on to Lydia in defiance of Mrs Thane. With Betsy it was the other way round. She set herself with laborious concentration to find out all there was to be known about Lydia and seemed to be trying to enlarge her picture of Mrs Thane accordingly. But without success. Her heart was not in it. Mrs Thane could not be improved upon.

To her it had come as a bombshell that Mrs Thane had once lived here at Emberside where she, Betsy, was now installed as mistress. To have to leave such a home under any circumstances, she clearly thought of as a misfortune. In mentally transferring her here from Mrs Timothy's cold cottage, she was in no doubt that this was Mrs Thane's rightful place which she herself, all unsuspecting, had occupied. What recompense could be made for this additional wrong? I could not feel that Betsy's brooding silence arose from any serious thought she might be giving to the Central Association of Master Builders. That tilt of the head suggested that she was indeed listening but not to me: to intimations—voices—a voice I could not hear?

I had no sooner finished the last stultifying paragraph than Betsy spoke.

"She never came back."

"No. I can understand that. It was a sign, don't you think, of how much she cared and how much she regretted having left as she did. Later on, if she had been . . ." I meant to say that in

time, if she had been spared, she would probably have come to
see us but remembered that this would serve as a reminder that
death had intervened. In a hurried attempt to avoid the pitfall I
recast the sentence and made my great mistake. "She did tell
Alice, Mrs Welbecome's maid, that some day she would come
back when she was settled."

It was not just my stepmother's eyes that shone. Her whole
face became irradiated with some hopeful brightening of the
spirit.

"Settled?"

"Yes. She meant of course settled in life," I pointed out sensi-
bly. All the same I was sufficiently under the influence of Betsy's
other-worldliness to hear in the word 'settled' a disturbing echo
of the phrase—'At rest.'

"If she said that she would come back," Betsy said simply,
"then she will."

It was not unusual, Addy had told me, for women in Betsy's
condition to fall victim to odd fancies. I persuaded myself that
once her baby was born my stepmother would enter upon a new
and more normal state of mind. Preparations for her lying-in
went steadily on. A monthly nurse was engaged. Father spared
no expense in the matter of doctors' visits. His nervous excitement, now that the hope of his life seemed about to be fulfilled,
was so intense that Addy and Ruby and I were almost equally
nervous.

"It doesn't do," Addy darkly predicted, "to set your hopes too
high. It's like asking for things to go amiss. Still, she's calm
enough, I must say."

Calm, composed and filled with expectation Betsy might be but
the expectation, I suspect, had nothing to do with her baby. It
not only bore her up and raised her above the anxieties of the
time: it continued to uphold her when that time was past. She
remained expectant.

Nothing went wrong. My half-brother, a fine, lusty child, was
born in July. Betsy continued in superb health to the day of his
birth and resumed it a very short time after. She lay, her long
black hair overflowing the lace-edged pillow, with a faint smile
upcurling her lips as father, proud and tearful, stood over his
son's cradle.

"Eugene Samuel Penrose." His voice shook. "Like his father
and grandfather." And he added with as solemn a turn of phrase

as if he were quoting from the Book of Kings, "He shall be called Samuel."

So he was christened Eugene Samuel; and father called him Samuel; but Betsy called him Lorne. Since the child spent most of his time with the females of the household, we all followed suit. It was a pleasanter name to say than Samuel and seemed to fit the downy-haired little creature. Naturally father protested, both angrily and in hurt distress. Betsy smiled or nodded and took no notice. There was no open quarrel about it. None was necessary or possible. Betsy was unyielding; saw no other point of view. The absurdity of being the only person to call Lorne by his rightful name was harmful to father's dignity. It discouraged him, and diminished his pride in the child he had longed for. It was as if, having failed to put a name to him, he had lost his authority over his son from the cradle.

There is a great deal in a name. If father had ever been unjust to Lydia, he was punished for it by this curiously subtle and unexpected turn of the screw. It must have seemed sometimes as if Lorne's parentage was in doubt or that Lydia had presided at his christening like an unwelcome fairy godmother. But things could have been worse. I have no doubt that if the baby had been a girl, Betsy would have called her Lydia.

Lorne's name was not the only example of her unflagging determination to reinstate Lydia and share Emberside with her. On the day she left her room after her confinement, the nurse and the maids (and I too just in case there was anything in it) warned her that it was unlucky not to carry the baby upstairs before she went down. Indeed it was not unusual for women to mount step-ladders or climb on chairs rather than take the risk. Betsy obeyed. She was generally docile and agreeable. But first she carried Lorne along the landing to Lydia's room. I followed with the wraps and bags she would want downstairs, as far as the door. Betsy made no attempt to close it. She stood in the middle of the room by the bed with the baby in her arms and did nothing, so far as I could see, but stand there. A more intense raptness in her air of listening may have been purely my imagination. After a few minutes she came out and dutifully went halfway up the attic stairs before giving Lorne to the nurse and going down to the drawing room.

It became a ritual. There cannot have been a day when Lorne was not subjected to the influence of Lydia's possessions, to say nothing of the rest of us. Father unsuspectingly made no objection when Betsy said quietly one morning: "I have a fancy, Eugene, to hang another of Simeon's pictures but there is nowhere suitable to put it." The drawing room walls were already well supplied with pictures, including the two watercolours. "The chimney breast would be the best place if it were not for the looking-glass. Perhaps it could be taken down."

It was so rare for her to make any kind of suggestion that I think father saw this one as a sign of improvement in her nervous tone.

"By all means," he said heartily; and he offered with real enthusiasm to look through the portfolios again and select the work most suitable for framing.

When he had gone off to the coach house, Will Petway with Ruby's help took down the heavy gilt-framed mirror and by the time father returned, flushed and interested from his examination of the portfolios, the pastel portrait of Lydia was already hung in the central position above the fireplace, where he saw it for the first time.

It was a shock. He became quite agitated. He certainly did not see the picture as something to be included in his little memorial work on 'The Art of Portraiture'; but rather as a memorial of a different kind: a particularly striking example of the kind of unpleasantness he had contrived for most of his life to avoid. The sudden unearthing of an episode he had been content to bury took his breath away. No one but he could know what memories, what regrets had been unearthed with it; but if he should ever come to doubt the wisdom of his choice of a wife, here was an endless reminder of the wife he did not choose.

"No, Betsy. No. I'm sorry. You must take it down. It's not . . . I dislike having it there."

The resurrection of Lydia and her elevation to a position where she could supervise our daily comings and goings was the most positive act Betsy had undertaken since I had known her. Even she seemed to feel the need to say something. She put out her hand to father and when he took it eagerly, drew him to sit down at her side. Her smile enslaved him all over again.

"That lady"—I was struck by Betsy's choice of words—"that lady saved my life. If it had not been for her, I wouldn't be here."

From the depth of her wisdom she made no reference to the lady's identity. Instead, by reminding father of the blissful fact of her own presence, she made it difficult for him to do anything but cover her hands with grateful kisses.

"Besides, that is Simeon's best work. You've often said he was a genius. As a lover of art you encouraged him. You would not wish to hide away what many people would cherish—and pay a good deal of money for."

Having briefly made these unanswerable points and successfully spiked father's guns, she withdrew from the tiresome sphere of reasonable argument and ceased to pay him any attention.

It was extraordinary how that one change altered the room. Without the mirror it shrank in size. The four walls drew nearer. It was darker too. One no longer saw the gay little porcelain figures on the what-not reflected from the chimney breast. Moreover being unframed, the picture had a peculiar lack of definition as if it had not been deliberately hung but had emanated from the wall itself. The pallid marble of the fireplace below added to the sepulchral effect and the pastel tints of the face were so delicate as to suggest a being from some border country between life and death.

One grows used to pictures, seeing them every day. Perhaps in time I would have stopped looking at Lydia's portrait. But for various reasons that time did not come. For one thing, it really is a work of genius and so in spite of the marble below and the lack of robustness in the picture itself, it has a living quality. Graw has bestowed on it the power of all living things—to change. Variations in light affect it as well as the degree of attention given to it. In my own case I was obliged to look at it constantly, and with all my concentration, to insist, as it were, on seeing Lydia and not Mrs Thane. When I did succeed in forgetting them both and lost myself for a while in a book or in my needlework, a gradually intensifying stillness on the sofa would force me to look up and see Betsy's pure profile uplifted as she gazed at the rectangle above the mantel: and I too would look again.

Early in August we had another unexpected visit from Mr Egbertson, again on his way to Oversay Hall. This fact stung father and me (though without collusion) to give him the impression that all was well—indeed had never been happier—at Emberside. Baby was proudly displayed (and introduced as Samuel). We chatted merrily over the cake and wine. Betsy, in deep emerald silk, sat with her hands folded in her lap, listening.

Perhaps we overdid it. Mr Egbertson did not stay long and

seemed not quite at ease. When father urged him to stay, he made excuses.

"The Kirkdales are expecting me. Besides, I'm afraid my visit may have inconvenienced you. I see you have a guest staying with you."

The remark was pitched somewhere between a question and a statement.

"No, indeed. We are quite alone."

It was then, following Mr Egbertson's quick glance, that I became aware of another change in the room. From the position at the table where I had dispensed refreshments it had not been noticeable. Lydia's work table had been drawn close to the Berlin-worked chair. One of the little drawers was open. On the chair lay a half finished piece of petit-point in a tambour frame. The effect was exactly that of someone having laid aside her work and gone out for a few minutes.

Mr Egbertson had got up and was examining the portrait.

"An interesting face. An unusual expression. Unusual in its execution too."

Poor father! What could he say?

"A relative of my late wife drawn by my wife's late husband."

How very awkward it would have been for him to utter such a sentence! He said nothing of the kind but as he hustled Mr Egbertson along to the study to look at a case of fossils, I thought he looked a trifle worn.

It was the open drawer and the tambour frame that brought home to me what my stepmother was about. When the sound of Mr Egbertson's carriage wheels had died away, I stood at the front door for a while, unwilling to go back and face her. A deep stillness brooded over the trees in the valley below the house and held the clouds motionless above the brow of Limmergill Fell. Half a mile away across the fields rose the square chimneys of Hackets. If only Robert were at home! Suddenly I longed to see him and tell him everything and feel the indescribable comfort of being with him. It must have been the sultry somnolence of the day that discouraged me from crossing the lane, and running through the fields just to see if he had come back. August with us is often a month of oppressive weather. The heavy air seemed charged with expectation of a storm.

Inside the house the same atmosphere gave to all its occupants —the hall clock, the candlesticks, the Psyche on her pedestal—

the air of biding their time until some event rescued them from
their suspense. Most hushed and still of all, most patiently enduring in its attitude of waiting, was the figure of my stepmother.

"He's gone."

With a little snap I closed the drawer of the work table, opened
the lid, pushed the tambour frame inside and slammed it shut.
My heart was pounding. A score of times I had seen the work in
Lydia's hands during that composed half-hour before dinner and
during the readings from *The Lady of the Lake* afterwards. Betsy
knew of them as by now she knew everything about our life in
those early days. She had already quietly rectified one or two
changes which had crept into our routine over the years. The
prospect of a future dedicated to keeping things as they had been
in Lydia's time filled me with distaste; more than that, with the
revulsion one might feel in a charnel house or vault.

"You've been looking at Lydia's footstool cover." I spoke
loudly to show that it was a perfectly normal thing to do. "We
shall have to go through her things and decide what is to be done
with them."

It was not the most sensible suggestion to have made in the
circumstances.

"I should like to," Betsy said. "In fact I've already begun."

Her morning visits to Lydia's room had certainly grown
longer. It had been a relief to leave her alone there and close my
mind to what she was doing. But I could no longer ignore the
many small signs that my stepmother had developed a purpose: a
preoccupation settling steadily in one direction.

"She's waiting . . ." In daring to recognise the uncanny
thought, I waited too, and listened, and felt the whole house
change to an unfamiliar mood . . . "She's waiting for Lydia to
come back."

That night I could not sleep but lay listening to the distant roll
of thunder and thinking of Mrs Petway's grandmother who still
set a place at table every day for her dead son. He had fallen in
the Crimea nearly twenty years ago. Every night a candle burned
in the window to light him home. As a child I had taken it for
granted that he would come and used to hope, my head buried in
the pillow, that he would not come past our gate.

There was a good deal of interest at that time in the occult.
Ghosts were much talked of. At Beech Grove House we had gone
so far as to hold a secret séance and succeeded in making a table

move under our lightly touching fingers. It was all nonsense. Still, strange things did happen. The dead had been known to material-ise. Who? And when? I had no idea. Robert might know. If only he would come home soon! He might be able to tell me whether or not my stepmother was . . . mad.

Curiously enough, I didn't believe that she was. It was just that she was indifferent to the physical world which for most of her life had treated her harshly. To want to remain in constant touch with the one person who had loved her and roused her answering love—one could understand that. Betsy would have no time for the foolish paraphernalia of ouija boards and table rapping, nor any need of them. By nature she simply was in touch with forces I could only guess at. It seemed likely that by sheer persistence she would establish her twilight world here at Emberside as she had, in the most unlikely way, established herself.

What she wanted so very much, she would in time achieve: another glimpse of her friend. Suppose—the fearful prospect must be faced—suppose I shared that glimpse!

As I lay, hot-cheeked and wide-eyed in the darkness and thun-der growled between hills and sky, nothing seemed more likely than that ghosts might walk. But it was not so much the notion of haunted churchyards that troubled me as a more complicated distress. Betsy had outdone me in loyalty. The thing she longed for I most passionately did not want and could not face.

The next day was dull and airless. It was Saturday. Father had gone as usual to Netherlaw and in the afternoon the servants went to Limmergill Fair. I think they must have taken the nurse with them for I remember taking charge of Lorne for an hour or two.

As I crossed the landing on my way to the nursery, I heard an unexpected sound in Lydia's room: someone talking. I stopped, holding my breath. It could only be Betsy. We were alone in the house. It came again, a low murmur, confidential and intimate. I suppose it was not surprising that my own mental state was suffi-ciently abnormal for me to strain my ears, dreading to hear a reply, and to feel an enormous relief when there was none. All the same, the note of contented *communication* in Betsy's voice was enough to send me flying up to the nursery for refuge. Pres-ently I heard her go downstairs and then for a long time there was no sound at all.

The garden too was still. Not a bird note or even the moan of

doves. I sat by the cradle at the open window and watched the
summer lightning flare and shimmer in the leaden sky; and I
thought the maids would be lucky to get home without a wetting.

It was late afternoon when I picked up the sleeping baby and
crept noiselessly down to the first landing, not so much from fear
of waking him as simply from fear: the nervous expectancy a
motionless house can rouse. The bedroom doors were open, including Lydia's. I stopped on the threshold, arrested by a feeling
of life in the room. Having grown used to the shaded rooms
downstairs, I was astonished by the lightness and freshness here.
The furniture shone; the silver brushes gleamed; the muslin bows
were stiff and white as snow; the green glasses full of flowers. The
writing desk was open: a sheet of paper on the velvet: a pen: a
wiper.

Reluctantly, for I had already seen what was there, I turned
my eyes to the bed. On the sheepskin rug lay a pair of white
slippers ready to be put on; on the counterpane a dress. Betsy had
given thought to her choice. The white tarlatan was the prettiest
of all the dresses. And in the macabre circumstances it was surely
the most unsuitable. I think it was the girlish prettiness of the
unlaced bodice and empty three-flounced skirt outspread between
the bed curtains that shocked and repelled me. I felt a sick distaste that infected even the swift memory of the last time I had
seen the dress on the eve of the dance in Netherlaw, when moths
had fluttered on the rose-scented air into the lamplit room and
each looking-glass presented its own portrait of a radiant Lydia.

But it was none of these things that gave the room its strange
animation. I looked towards the window. The plants in Lydia's
fernery, watered with devoted care, stripped of any touch of
brown, had grown more lush and green than ever before. Their
fronds and leaves filled the whole window with such an exuberant
growth, such an effect of activity, that I could have imagined they
were visibly stretching forward inch by inch before my eyes and
would presently invade the other rooms. There was something
unnatural and feverish in the way they flourished as if they had
absorbed the living properties of everything around them. Coming out on to the landing, I felt the rest of the house as lifeless as a
grave.

The drawing room was in shadow but not the warm crimson
shade cast by the curtains. Instead the blinds had been drawn. In
the pallid dusk the two women were alone. That was the way I

thought of it: the one on the sofa looking up at the one on the wall whose features were indistinct. One felt only that there was someone there.

"They don't want me," I thought. "There's no place for me here. They have each other."

The idea, fantastic enough in itself, by some devious mental process helped me to face the reality I had been avoiding; and at that moment Betsy turned her head. Deprived of light, the flowers on her chintz cushions had faded into featureless grey. The rich emerald of her dress had deepened so that her pale face rose mermaid-like from mysterious, darkly luminous depths.

"I've brought the baby . . ."

She made an absent gesture towards the empty cushions at her side; absent but imperious. I laid Lorne down carefully, rescued him from suffocation by his crochet cap and stroked a wet ribbon away from his chin—as if nothing had happened. But in the delicate balance of our relationship Betsy's light movement of the hand was decisive. It expressed authority. I was in the presence of the mistress of the house. She had taken possession. The process had been gradual and effortless but now the house was hers. She would do with it as she pleased; use it for her own mysterious purposes.

She smiled her miraculous smile. Then her face closed again upon the captive woman within.

"Please . . ."

Some kind of desperate appeal trembled on my lips; some forlorn hope of reaching her. I could not dislike Betsy. She showed no hostility to me; nor affection; nor interest. She had long ago withdrawn from human reach and in the process had achieved the strength from which I could only retreat. That too was entirely her own, nourished wholly by her own lonely spirit.

But she had not only taken possession of my home and robbed me of all I had loved in it: she had taken possession of Lydia; and in such a way that I could no longer remember her with any kind of happiness. The brilliant imperfect Lydia I had known was gone. Every memory had withered and grown stale. I shrank from thinking of her; wanted only to forget her. With a deliberate effort I resolved to let her go; and was ashamed; and knew that to forget her was to forget the precious childhood she had made happy.

It seemed the cruellest loss in all my life.

I bent and kissed my brother with a sudden warmth of love for his tiny flushed features and helpless fingers. He was real and new. There would be a new generation of Penroses at Emberside even though I would have no part in it.

"Isobel?" they would say in years to come. "Now who was Isobel? Oh, yes. I had forgotten her."

With an effort they would remember me, a dependent aunt or great-aunt. It is indeed a terrible thing for a woman not to have her own home.

A whirring sound startled me. The kitchen clock struck six and the silver notes of the mantel clock followed. When the twelfth stroke died away, Betsy had not moved. On impulse I kissed her too. She glanced at me and turned away to resume the secret communication with her friend that would not fail her for the rest of her life.

At the front door I paused under the dead blossom of the clematis. An overblown rose or two smelt faintly of decay. The midsummer elms cast their heavy shade over the lane.

"You shouldn't leave the doors open." That was what Charlie had said. "Anyone walking this way might be tempted to walk right in."

I closed the door behind me even if it was too late. Across the quiet fields came the crowing of Petways' cock. Again I heard in it a note of farewell, this time for my own leavetaking.

I crossed the lane and took the green path to Limmergill, walking faster and faster until I was running. My body felt light as air with the relief of escaping: my steps turned instinctively, as they had so often done in the past, towards Hackets. There was no reason to suppose that Robert would be at home. I had not heard if he had come back; but I went blindly, knowing that I would at least feel his comforting presence there.

At Hackets too there had been changes. It was over a year since I had been there. I hardly recognised it in this well-kept, substantial yeoman's house with its trim garden and clipped yew trees bordering the flagged path. The door was unlocked; the house furnished: on the left of the hall a step down into a long low parlour with a carved over-mantel.

Intrigued, I looked for details but got no further than the small table near the door and the contraption standing on it: a curious dusty affair of wires once gilded: of mother-of-pearl flowers once lustrous: a bird cage with a bird which once sang. I felt about for the mechanism to set it singing but could find no key.

I might have known that he would be there when I wanted him. He came along the hall and into the room.

"Thank God you've come, Belle." He glanced at the bird cage. "You know what it is? How can I tell you? It's bad news, dearest, and it's all my fault."

"About Lydia? I know all about it."

It seemed perfectly natural now to speak of her; but curiously uninteresting. All my concern was for Robert. In pitying his distress, I forgot my own. Somehow I got it into my stupid head at last that he needed me. It was his turn to be comforted. As he blurted out his story without a trace of the self-confidence I had always admired, I put my arms round him and told him that nothing had been his fault. And having loved him in an absent-minded sort of way all my life, I came to my senses and loved him with all my heart.

23

It was at the dealer's in Wood Street that Robert had caught sight of the bird cage immediately after his call at Beech Grove House. It was so like the one Lydia had described that he had bought it for me; and sufficiently unusual for him to wonder if it could actually be the Lorne piece; and if so, why it had been pawned.

"I knew that if Mrs Welbecome had died, the property would have gone to Lydia and I was pretty sure that this was one thing she wouldn't have parted with. More likely she would have had it shipped to Canada or sent to you at Emberside."

From the dealer he learned that over the years other items had come to him directly from Ash House. It looked as if the property was being disposed of bit by bit.

With some idea of protecting Lydia's interests, Robert then went to Hagthorpe to find out if Charlie's grandmother had his address. There he heard the devastating news that Charlie was married in Canada to his foreman's daughter, had been in England and had never mentioned Lydia or anyone connected with his past life here.

"That," Robert said, "was when I thought of blowing my brains out."

In alarm and remorse he had gone post-haste to Ash House, confronted a stony-faced Mrs Dawlie and learned that Lydia had fled from creditors. As far as he could tell there had been no legal intervention to protect the estate, no sworn proofs of creditors' claims. The property had simply melted away. Robert had found a lawyer who agreed to act for Lydia if she could be found. A change of name, he suggested, was a customary disguise.

"Oddly enough, I never thought of her changing it in that way, by marrying. I can't understand," Robert said, "why people make so much fuss about loving a person and then go off and marry somebody else."

We agreed that true love meant staying together, always: a conclusion reached on my part at least in a state of quite dazzling happiness; and when at last the storm broke, we stood with our arms round each other, watching the lightning cleave the clouds and the rain sweep over the fells. Along the ridge to the west rose the chimneys of Emberside dwarfed by its overgrown trees but the house itself was lost in their shade, remote as the fantasies I had run away from.

"There's so much sky," I breathed, with a feeling of liberation.

"You like it here? Really, Belle?"

"What a pity—when you did it all for Charlie," I began cunningly.

"It's a long time since I gave up doing it for Charlie. Of course I didn't presume to think that you . . . but it just naturally turned into the sort of place you would like. The funny thing was, whenever there was a decision to be made I knew what your taste would be. And when things started going wrong at Emberside, I thought after all the harm I'd done, there would at least be a home for you here if ever you . . . Of course you might not have . . . As a matter of fact at that beastly At Home I really did wonder if Miss Florence What's-her-name was right about your being in love with someone else. You were so distant. That was when it dawned on me how much I had always assumed that some day we would . . . marry. I mean, you must know that I've always loved you. All my life, whatever I was doing, I've had you in mind."

Explanations were endless. Fortunately we had all the time in the world to make them; in the new world, that is, occupied only by Robert and me. We made a fire and sat on the hearth-rug going over the whole affair and happily telling each other how miserable we had been: for Robert's experience had been every bit as harrowing as mine. He had been convinced that but for his mistake my father would have sought out Lydia long ago and helped her. The scandalous goings-on at Emberside would have been avoided. He had tried to tell me . . .

But it was only recently that he had stumbled upon the truth as to Lydia's whereabouts. His enquiries at hospitals and agencies had met with no success.

"You didn't happen to think," I interrupted modestly, "of the advertisement column in a newspaper?"

"What good would that be? If Lydia had wanted to reach her

friends she knew where to find them without any silly palaver of that kind."

I held my peace.

"I tried to reason it out, where she might be and who might know. It came to me when I was lying awake one night that Graw must have known. He couldn't have made that pastel portrait of her—there wouldn't have been any reason—unless he had seen her looking like that. But where? Then I remembered his sketches of parish churches. I'd had a good look at them when I collected up his things from the quarry and recognised some of them, including the one at Hartbeck. Everybody sketches that. He'd obviously been in some of the villages south of Martlebury. If I made enquiries where he'd been, I might find some trace of Lydia. And that"—Robert's grip on my hand tightened. His eyes clouded—"is exactly what happened."

Shortly after my return to Emberside, he had been driving from Lower to Upper Hartbeck when his search came to a startling and painful end.

"Near the top of the lane there was a cart drawn up at the chapel. I had to wait. They seemed to be busy about something or other in the burial ground. It took some time. I got down to see what was going on. You can't guess, Belle. It shook me, I can tell you . . . A couple of stone-masons and two other men had just erected a tombstone. Can you imagine my feelings when I saw the inscription? 'Lydia May, beloved wife of Joseph Thane; who died November 13th, 1872, aged twenty-five years.' The names, the age . . . There could be no mistake."

Mr Parker had dealt as best he could with Robert's distressed enquiries and directed him to the Rev. Joseph Thane: a man in a thousand according to Robert: a husband such as few women could deserve: better by far he seemed to imply than the husband Lydia had first set her heart on.

'Beloved wife.' The phrase was conventional but I liked the sound of it. Was it, in this case, true? A clergyman surely, would tell the truth, especially on a tombstone.

"He really loved her, do you think?"

Robert was sure of it, judging not only by the feeling way in which Mr Thane had spoken of her illness and death a few months after their marriage but by his manner of describing their meeting at Bainsacre. After the service Lydia had waited to speak to him as she had wanted to do two years before. She had been

overwhelmed, enraptured, her eyes opened to the glory of God.
Mr Thane too had been overwhelmed and enraptured, by Lydia.
She had told him something of her circumstances. When he discovered that she was homeless and penniless, he gave her the
address of his widowed aunt who was in need of a paid companion. They were married from her home in the following July . . .

We talked on into the evening, less and less about the others
and more and more about ourselves. I had time to explore the
house; inside, with firelight warming its oak panels and doors:
outside, the life-giving air sweet with heather bloom and fresh
with rain: and the stream almost bursting its banks from storm
water as it rushed downhill through the garden. It is the most
delightful thing to have one's own stream: and white-railed footbridge; and a seat enclosed in honeysuckle and jasmine facing the
wide prospect of hills ever changing like the stream. My own
little parlour has the same outlook, as well as the most commodi-
ous arched and glass-fronted china cupboard. Hackets is out-
standingly well supplied with cupboards. In fact the whole house
is surprisingly spacious considering how compact and cosy the
rooms are. The kitchen, for instance . . .

There I go again. My enthusiasm for Hackets is inclined to run
away with me. Robert says I think of little else: nor, for that
matter, does he. In those early days its charm for me lay in its
homely atmosphere of long habitation by people I had never
known. From those I had come to know rather too well it was a
blessed relief to escape.

We lingered until the fire died down and hunger drove us
through the rain-washed twilight to Limmergill House. The field
path had become a brook cutting me off from Emberside, for
ever. Except for short spells I never lived there again but stayed
with Mrs Wayland (who received our wonderful news with astonishing calm) until the next year when Robert came of age and we
could be married.

There was no breach, no unkindness. They did not need me at
home and from a little distance they were easier to love, the
changes easier to bear. And some things do not change. A cowslip ball in the spring pasture, a snowman tall and white, could
bring to Lorne's eyes the same delight that Lydia must have seen
in mine; and Robert never forgot to bring him a gingerbread man
from Netherlaw market, until he grew too old for such things.

In time I found that the most painful of changes had not taken

place at all. It must have been a year or more after our marriage
that Robert took me with him when he drove over to an estate
seven miles away to value timber. What could be pleasanter for
me than to spend the morning with the woodman's wife, our very
own Prue Bailey, whom I hadn't seen since she left us? She was
plumper, mellower, gentler, with a two-year-old at her skirt and
an infant in her arms.

Her eyes filled with tears when she heard about Lydia.

"And she was so happy that night she came here after the
Meeting. Yes"—when I expressed surprise—"she'd come miles
out of her way. You could have knocked me down with a feather
when I opened the door. 'I've got stars in my eyes, Prue,' she said
and she had too. You remember how her eyes used to light up. 'I
wanted to see you, Prue,' she said. '*You'll* understand the wonderful thing that's happened to me.' She had cast off her chains, Miss
Isobel, and been delivered from the dungeon of this world."

Like a breath of spring it came back to me, her talent for
happiness. Lydia would never do things by halves. If there were
chains to be shed, with what wholehearted enthusiasm she would
shed them! When she broke free from the heartache and failures
of the old life, how confidently she would step into the new!

"And she'd heard of a position," Prue said, "as companion to a
lady, the minister's aunt. 'Haven't I been lucky?' she said."

And she was not after all quite indifferent to the things of this
world. The new Lydia, it seemed, was not so very different from
the old.

"I passed Emberside tonight," she told Prue. "It was too late
to call. And after all this time how could I let them see me
looking such a fright? If only I could have seen Isobel! But some
day soon . . ."

Footsore and weary as she must have been, they had talked all
night and Prue had set her on her way the next morning, brimful
of life and hope; and in her heart perhaps the secret joy of having
fallen in love again. She had been lucky indeed.

What more could a woman want—I put the question to Robert
—than to love God and be loved by her husband?

"Only a little more time," he said. "She didn't have much time,
did she?"

The way ahead had been short; but of one thing I am sure.
Whatever ghost Betsy succeeded in conjuring up at Emberside to
haunt the old rooms and frighten away the servants, it could

never be Lydia's. For her there would be no turning back in futile regret to the house she had loved and left. Whether in this world or the next, Lydia would find better things to do.

If we have in a sense resumed our old companionship, Lydia and I, there is nothing supernatural in it. It is memory that unites us. I remember her—and forget her sometimes—as one remembers and forgets a living friend.

Robert and I have grown fond of Hartbeck. We have been there several times: first to take curtains and a mantel valance to Mrs Timothy and later to attend Violet's wedding; but most often to call upon another friend. From the changeless peace of the little burial ground above the fields where sheep graze it is not far to the Manse and the quiet hospitality of its minister who loves to talk about his wife to those who knew her.

As for the bird, its ravishing song remains for me one of the unheard melodies sweeter than those we hear. Robert always talked of having a new key made and somehow never did. Moreover even Alice (What a treasure she has been! And how she has flourished in our country air!) . . . Even Alice admitted in the end that the wires and flowers were awkward to dust and the whole contrivance took up a good deal of space. Eventually we sent it to Emberside to be placed in the mausoleum which was once Lydia's room. There, tended and cleaned with religious devotion, it shines in the green light that filters through the ferns; but it no longer sings.

And if it did, the song could never be so magically sweet as when Lydia described it to me in the warm bright kitchen at Emberside long ago.

Reckless abandon. Intrigue. And spirited love. A magnificent array of tempestuous, passionate historical romances to capture your heart.

Virginia Henley
- ☐ 17161-X The Raven and the Rose $3.95
- ☐ 20144-6 The Hawk and the Dove $3.95
- ☐ 20429-1 The Falcon and the Flower $3.95

Joanne Redd
- ☐ 18982-9 To Love an Eagle $3.95
- ☐ 20114-4 Chasing a Dream $3.95
- ☐ 20224-8 Desert Bride $3.95

Lori Copeland
- ☐ 10374-6 Avenging Angel $3.95
- ☐ 20134-9 Passion's Captive $3.95
- ☐ 20325-2 Sweet Talkin' Stranger $3.95

Elaine Coffman
- ☐ 20529-8 Escape Not My Love $4.50
- ☐ 20262-0 If My Love Could Hold You $3.95
- ☐ 20198-5 My Enemy, My Love $3.95